FELL CARGO

LUKA SILVARO KNOWS how dangerous the waters of the Old World are, because he was once a pirate himself. But that's all behind him now. Long believed dead, he turns up out of the blue, reclaims his ship and his crew, and sets off on a deadly mission to hunt down the Butcher Ship, an infamous galleon that has been terrorising the coast of Tilea.

To hunt down such a powerful foe you need allies, and Luka has to rely on the roguish Guido to captain a ship at his side. But can Guido be trusted, or is his pirate blood too thick? With allies as untrustworthy as his enemies are deadly, Luka Silvaro has to pull every trick out of his sleeve to defeat his enemy in this rollicking tale of adventure on the high seas.

With pirates, vampires, zombies and sea monsters, top-selling Black Library author Dan Abnett invites you into the blood-stained waters of Fell Cargo!

· WARHAMMER FANTASY NOVELS ·

DARKBLADE: THE DAEMON'S CURSE (with Mike Lee)
DARKBLADE: BLOODSTORM (with Mike Lee)
RIDERS OF THE DEAD
HAMMERS OF ULRIC (with Nik Vincent and James Wallis)
GILEAD'S BLOOD (with Nik Vincent)

· GAUNT'S GHOSTS ·

Colonel-Commissar Gaunt and his regiment, the Tanith First-and-Only,
Struggle for survival on the battlefields of the far future.

The Founding

FIRST AND ONLY • GHOSTMAKER
NECROPOLIS

The Saint

HONOUR GUARD • THE GUNS OF TANITH
STRAIGHT SILVER • SABBAT MARTYR

The Lost

TRAITOR GENERAL • HIS LAST COMMAND

Also

DOUBLE EAGLE • THE SABBAT WORLDS CRUSADE

· EISENHORN ·

In the nightmare world of the 41st millennium, Inquisitor
Eisenhorn hunts down mankind's most dangerous enemies.

EISENHORN
(Omnibus containing XENOS, MALLEUS and HERETICUS)

· RAVENOR ·

RAVENOR • RAVENOR RETURNED

· GRAPHIC NOVELS ·

TITAN: BOOKS I - III
DARKBLADE: BOOKS I - III
INQUISITOR ASCENDANT: BOOKS I & II
LONE WOLVES

A WARHAMMER NOVEL

FELL CARGO

DAN ABNETT

For Jony Wardley and the crew of the Kymera.

A BLACK LIBRARY PUBLICATION

First published in Great Britain in 2006 by
BL Publishing,
Games Workshop Ltd.,
Willow Road, Nottingham,
NG7 2WS, UK

10 9 8 7 6 5 4 3 2 1

Cover illustration by Wayne England.
Map by Nuala Kinrade.

A CIP record for this book is available from the British Library.

ISBN 13: 978 1 84416 301 4
ISBN 10: 1 84416 301 6

Distributed in the US by Simon & Schuster
1230 Avenue of the Americas, New York, NY 10020.

Printed and bound in Great Britain by
Bookmarque, Surrey, UK.

See the Black Library on the Internet at
www.blacklibrary.com

Find out more about Games Workshop
and the world of Warhammer at
www.games-workshop.com

THIS IS A DARK age, a bloody age, an age of daemons and of sorcery. It is an age of battle and death, and of the world's ending. Amidst all of the fire, flame and fury it is a time, too, of mighty heroes, of bold deeds and great courage.

AT THE HEART of the Old World sprawls the Empire, the largest and most powerful of the human realms. Known for its engineers, sorcerers, traders and soldiers, it is a land of great mountains, mighty rivers, dark forests and vast cities. And from his throne in Altdorf reigns the Emperor Karl-Franz, sacred descendant of the founder of these lands, Sigmar, and wielder of his magical warhammer.

BUT THESE ARE far from civilised times. Across the length and breadth of the Old World, from the knightly palaces of Bretonnia to ice-bound Kislev in the far north, come rumblings of war. In the towering World's Edge Mountains, the orc tribes are gathering for another assault. Bandits and renegades harry the wild southern lands of the Border Princes. There are rumours of rat-things, the skaven, emerging from the sewers and swamps across the land. And from the northern wildernesses there is the ever-present threat of Chaos, of daemons and beastmen corrupted by the foul powers of the Dark Gods. As the time of battle draws ever nearer, the Empire needs heroes like never before.

And on the eighth day, a bark was espied
Full sheet, though the wind had no breath
A sea-devil carrack, fell cargo inside
Bound for the court of King Death.

– from a Tilean mariners' chantey

COME TWILIGHT, THEY rowed ashore and beached in a small, high-sided cove of shingle and mossy rock west of the harbour bay. He knew the way, and led his companion sure-footedly up the cove path, over the grassy headland and down towards the lantern lights of the ramshackle town.

The sky was violet and stars were scattered across it like a haul of silver doblons. Down in the bay, marker bells tinked and clunked in their moored baskets, rocked by the tide, and the great braziers on the horns of the harbour blazed into life, marking the port for latecomers and raising a defiant finger to the revenue men of Luccini across the channel.

Sea breezes nodded the hemp grass and tusket flowers covering the headland. His companion stopped and gazed down at the thousand winking lamps of the notorious town. Catches of music and song floated up in the night air.

'That's it?' asked his companion.

'Indeed it is,' he replied, his deep voice a purr of relish. He knew he'd missed it, but he hadn't realised how certain he had been that he'd never see it again.

'Ready?' he asked.

'Not even slightly,' his companion replied. 'Going in there. I mean, that place. And you without even a sword.'

'I'll have one,' he reassured his companion, 'when the time comes. Now be on your guard. Down there, that's everything you damn people are afraid of.'

IN DAYLIGHT, THE Hole-In-By-The-Hill was nothing to look at: a cave in the limestone cliff above Peg Street, its mouth extended with dank canvas awnings, filled with a litter of tables and stools. But after dark, it came to life. Barrel fires lit up, and torches and lanterns too, strung from the awning poles or hooked to the cliff face. Hogs and fowl, blistered black with honey, spit-roasted over the smoking fire pits in the cave, and firelight glowed like gold off the low-hanging canvas. The tavern filled up with hot smoke, laughter and the stench of pipes, hops, swine fat and salt sweat.

That night, a blind gurdy-man was turning out jigs and reels, aided and abetted by a drunken campanica player. The pot girls, all of them well upholstered, for that was the way Grecco liked them, planked out jars of muddy ale or basket-bottles of wine for those with deeper purses. One of the girls was dancing, twirling her tatty petticoats. Customers clapped in time and threw silver coins.

Grecco himself was in the cave, his huge bulk sooty and glistening with sweat as he worked the spits. He contentedly watched his custom grow. His red macaw bobbed and shuffled up and down the wooden rung above his head, between the hanging ladles and meat forks. It would be good eating one day, went the tavern joke. When it died, it would be ready-smoked.

At the main tables under the awning, the Lightfingers ate and drank and diced. There were forty or so of them, just the seniors and the veterans. The other hundred and twenty of them, the dog-sailors and ratings, were away down the bay for the night in the cheaper stews and inns.

Lightfingers, Grecco mused. They hadn't owned that name for long, maybe a year at most. It was none too well worn. Before that, they had been the *Reivers*, an altogether more virile name in his humble opinion. But names came and went, like reputations and fortunes, serving girls and lives. This was Sartosa, after all. Nothing lasted forever.

The master of the company was a bullish, shaven-headed man with a long chin-beard braided with beads. He set down his empty jar and beckoned to a passing pot-girl.

'More sup for all! And a favour from you too, little maid!'

The girl smiled and obligingly allowed herself to be tugged onto his knee.

'Do you know who I am?' he asked her, wiping his clattering beard with the loose cuff of his once-white shirt.

'You would be Master Guido of the Lightfingers.'

'Uh uh uh, now! Captain, it is! Captain Guido!' he cried. His men thumped the table boards, all except Tende, the big Ebonian helmsman, who simply gazed into his half-empty jar.

'Do you know why we're called the Lightfingers, my girl?' Guido asked, slapping the rump of the female on his lap.

'I cannot imagine,' she replied.

'Because we…' he dropped his voice and leaned into her face conspiratorially. She stopped breathing through her nose and smiled a fake smile. 'Because we,' Guido continued, 'can lift a king's ransom from under the noses of Luccini and Remas and every merchant prince in Tilea!'

Rowdy assent followed. Jars smacked together in toasts.

'Really?' asked the girl, in mock wonder.

'Oh yes!' Guido snarled. 'Manann smiles upon us, lass.' He buried his face in her cleavage, snuffling. She put up with it for a few moments, looking bored and occasionally saying, 'Oh, stop it… you beast' in a faintly encouraging way.

'Hey, Guido. Why don't you tell her why you're *really* called the Lightfingers?'

Guido halted his snuffling and slowly drew his face out of the girl's ample bosom.

The table had fallen silent. The whole damn inn had fallen silent. At the back of the cave, Grecco left his spits and moved out so he could see with his own eyes. He folded his grease spattered arms and shook his head in wonder.

Defying fortune, and the fate everyone insisted had befallen him, Silvaro had come back.

11

Everyone gazed at the big man standing in the shadows under the breeze tugged flap of the awning.

'Luka?' hissed Guido.

'Yes.'

'You're back?'

'Yes. I'm back.'

'But they said… you'd been executed.'

'Not effectively, it seems.'

Guido got up suddenly. His stool fell over.

Luka looked over at the girl. 'He's called "Lightfinger" because he's light on fingers. He used to be my number two, and I took a finger off him every time he played me wrong. Didn't I, Guido?'

'Yes.'

'Show her.'

Guido raised his hands. The heavy cuffs of his velvet jacket slid away, revealing hands that were just claws. Just index fingers and thumbs.

'How many times did you cross me, Guido?'

'Six times.'

'It's a bloody wonder I never killed you.'

This, thought Grecco, is going to be interesting.

'What do you want?' Guido snapped.

'My ships.'

Guido snorted. 'They're mine now. Passed on to me, as accords the code.'

'I know,' said Luka Silvaro, stepping fully into the lamplight. He was tall, and as massively built as a four-masted galleon, with a forked black goatee and a thick mane of curly, greying hair tied back in a pigtail. When last they had seen him, he had been fleshy, with an increasing thickness and a distinct paunch brought on by the good living his trade had afforded. There was not an ounce of fat on him now. He looked lean, pinched, hungry, and somehow that emphasised the scale and breadth of his naturally big frame. His eyes, however, were just as they remembered: the colour of the sea before a storm, cannonball grey.

He let his cloak drop off his shoulders to show he was unarmed. 'I hereby issue challenge, according the code, to take them back.'

All of the men jostled away from the table. Guido drew his sword. It was a hanger with a stirrup-hilt of gold, heavy, curved and double edged.

'By the code, then. See if any stand with you.'

Luka nodded. 'A blade?'

His companion, until then just a shadow in the background, pushed into the light and offered Luka his elegant smallsword.

'No,' said Luka. 'No, it can't be you. Not for the code to work. Step out.'

His companion backed into the shadows again, frowning and not a little ill at ease.

'Who'll blade him?' cried Guido. 'Anyone? Eh? Anyone?'

In an instant, a ribbing knife as long as a man's forearm landed, quivering, in the bench top beside Luka. It had been tossed by Fahd, the company's wizened cook from Araby. Almost simultaneously, a flensing dagger thumped in next to it, thrown by the giant Tende.

Guido grinned at the juddering blades. 'Choose your weapons,' he mocked.

There was a clatter. A sabre landed on the bench. It was an Estalian blade, a slender ribbon of watered steel, curved in a thirty-degree arc, with straight quillons and a wire-wrapped pommel. It was still in its enamelled silver scabbard.

The companion couldn't tell who had thrown it in, but Luka knew.

He picked it up, drew out the fine blade and tossed the scabbard aside. He made a couple of whooshing practice chops in the air and then smiled at Guido.

'Take your guard,' he commanded.

There was no ceremony. They went at each other as the press of men backed further away to be out of reach of the slashing blades. Vento, the master rigger, obligingly scraped the trestle table aside to give them space.

The swords struck and rang like bells, over and over. Guido danced back and forth with a low guard, his left arm swinging free, like a goaded bear at a stake. Luka was more upright, shoulders back, the knuckles of his left hand pressed against his hip like an illustration from a fencing manual. It looked almost comically dainty, for a man so big, but for the undeniable speed of his cuts.

The packed onlookers shouted encouragement. Amongst them, Grecco watched. He'd witnessed enough duels, many on his own premises, to have the measure of this one. There would be three deciding factors. First, if Guido's brute style could better Luka's tutored perfection. Second, if Luka had the sense – and skill – to guard his slender sabre against a direct blow from Guido's much heavier blade. Caught right, the sabre would break under the hanger's weight. Grecco had seen more than one fight end that way, and had still been sponging the blood off his flagstones the morning after.

The third thing… Well, he was waiting for that. It was against the code, but it always happened, so much so it was an expected part of a code-duel. Any moment now.

Guido stamped in and thrust with the tip of his sword. Luka deflected it away from his heart, but still it slashed a line through the wide sleeve of his shirt. He flicked up, caught his edge against the loop of Guido's stirrup-guard, and pushed him away, but Guido back-sliced and drew

blood from the knuckles of Luka's sword hand. Only his fat
gold signet ring had prevented Luka from losing a finger.

Now there's irony, Grecco thought.

Luka whipped round and the tip of his Estalian steel
sliced off several strands of Guido's bead-plaited beard.
Guido cursed, and presented with a down slice, followed by
a side cut, forcing Luka back towards the cave mouth and
the cooking fires. Some of the men were clapping rhythmi-
cally now, *slap-slap-slap*. The campanica player, oblivious in
his drunkenness, took this as a cue and started to play until
the blind gurdy-man advised him to shut up.

Guido cut Luka across his right forearm. The white linen
of his shirt began to stain dark red. Luka rallied and split the
tip of Guido's nose. A gout of blood splashed out and dribbled down his mouth and beard. Guido returned so hard
that Luka had to duck his swishing blade.

In the shadows, the anonymous companion began to
back away, wondering how far he would get if he started to
run now.

The fighters clashed blades, locked, pushed each other
away, and then clashed again. Guido kicked his former captain in the shin. Both swords swung, and both missed.

They're getting tired, Grecco thought. If I'm any judge,
that third factor will come into play just about...

Two of the company broke from the onlookers and
rushed Luka from behind. Girolo, a hairy brute in a blue
satin frock coat that he insisted on wearing even though it
was too small, and Caponsacci, the barrel-chested yardsman.

'Have a care!' roared Grecco.

Luka broke fast, spinning to deflect Caponsacci's razor-
edged tulwar, and then back-cutting to knock away Girolo's
stabbing sabre. The three swordsmen drove at Luka from the
front quarters, jabbing and slashing, forcing him back out
from under the awning, into the keg-yard. The audience
scattered to let them through.

Girolo lunged and Luka ripped him away with a hori-
zontal blow that sliced the meat of his shoulder. Girolo
wailed and fell back. Caponsacci pressed in. Luka darted
to the side, wrenched over a keg full of ale, and rolled it
hard at Caponsacci with his foot. The yardsman tried to

leap it, but it caught his shins and toppled him onto his face.

Guido was blocked by Caponsacci for a moment moved right, coming up at Girolo as he tried to recover, his beloved blue satin coat drenched red down one side.

Girolo's sabre wasn't fast enough. Luka sliced his throat and knocked him, choking and sucking for air, to the ground. The crowd gave a great roar.

'Choose your sides more wisely,' Luka panted at the dying man. Girolo gurgled, and expired so suddenly that his head hit the floor with a solid crack.

Guido and Caponsacci flew at Luka, who was bounding back under the awning on his toes. They came on like furies. Even with his speed, Luka couldn't fend off the heavy, curved hanger and the long, straight tulwar simultaneously.

He scrambled in retreat and managed to pluck the cook's long ribbing knife out of the tabletop as he passed. Then he turned, adopting the low, head-on stance of a sword-and-dagger fighter. He knocked back Guido's sword with the sabre in his right hand, deflected Caponsacci's broad-blade with the knife in his left, then scissored both blades, long and short, together to vice out Guido's rally stroke.

At the back of the rowdy audience, the anonymous companion rummaged inside his cloak and pulled out an engraved wheel-lock pistol, a quality Arabyan piece. He cocked it and raised it. A hand sheathed in soft kidskin reached in and gently took it from his hand.

'Don't,' said a voice.

The companion looked round with a start. A louche Estalian mariner in ostentatiously rich clothes stood beside him, carefully uncocking the pistol before handing it back. The man was unnecessarily handsome, his complexion dark, though not as dark as his eyes. His long, straight, black hair fell like a veil down the sides of his cheeks, framing a wolfish face.

'But–' the companion began.

'Silvaro won't thank you for it. This duel is by the code. He has to fight alone, or there'll be no honour in his victory.' The man's voice was thick with the Estalian accent.

'There'll be no victory at all!' the companion spluttered indignantly. 'That Guido calls in his cronies. It's not a fair fight!'

'No, señor,' admitted the Estalian with a grudging nod. 'But it is the code. The challenger must be alone. If any of the crew choose to side with the master, then… so it goes.'

'Madness. It's unfair!' snapped the companion.

'Ah yes, tut tut. But…' the Estalian shrugged. 'It is the way. Put your fine pistol away before someone steals it.'

There was another braying howl from the crowd. Luka had glanced Guido's weighty steel aside and now locked Caponsacci at the quillons with the ribbing knife. The thick-set yardsman tried to turn his wrist and plough the knife away, but Luka sank his sabre a hand's span deep into the mariner's chestbone. Caponsacci's eyes turned up, and he crashed to his knees.

Before Caponsacci had even toppled nose first onto the flags, Luka had twisted his sabre out and turned, blood flying from the blade-groove. His knife came up in a cross, and the flat of it stung away Guido's down slash. Then the long, watered steel blade of Luka's borrowed sabre was resting on Guido's left shoulder, the edge pressed to the side of his neck. Guido froze.

'I suggest… you yield,' wheezed Luka.

Guido's eyes flicked wildly from side to side. No one else was stepping forward to help him now. The Estalian blade bit gently into the flesh of Guido's neck.

'Now,' Luka urged.

The hanger hit the flagstones with a clatter. Luka's sword at his neck, Guido slowly sank to his knees.

'I yield,' he mumbled.

'Louder!' Luka snapped.

'I yield!'

'And?'

'I… I submit to you the ships and command that was previously yours, and lay no future claim on them. I say to the hearing of those here present that Luka Silvaro is captain and master of the Lightfingers company.'

Luka smiled. He tossed the knife aside and wiped the sweat from his forehead with his freed hand. 'And is this submission witnessed?' he asked loudly.

There followed a pandemonium of cheers, applause and thumping.

Luka acknowledged the tumult with a few smiling nods and a wave of his free hand. He took the blade off Guido's neck. A hush fell.

'My first act… is to exact penalty.'

Guido looked up and whimpered. 'Spare me…' he gasped.

'What is the penalty?' Luka called to the onlookers.

'Death!' someone shouted, and this notion was loudly cheered in some quarters.

'Please…' whined Guido, gazing up at Luka.

'Well, Guido, what do you suggest?'

Feeble, reluctant, Guido slowly raised his left hand and stuck out his index finger, one of the last four digits he possessed.

Luka smiled and nodded.

The sabre flashed and Guido screamed. His left hand lay on the flags. Blood pumped from his severed wrist.

'You bastard! Aaaah! The whole hand!'

'Consider yourself lucky,' Luka said. 'It's a bloody wonder I've never killed you.'

Grecco hurried out to staunch the stump with a table-cloth. Some of the mariners came forward and helped to carry Guido's kicking, shrieking body back into the cave so that the stump could be cauterised.

'My second act,' shouted Luka above the din, 'is to rename this company the Reivers.'

More full-throated cheers.

Better, thought Grecco, hearing this above the fizzle of burning flesh as he pressed a red-hot skillet against Guido's truncated wrist.

Guido howled, retched and passed out.

'Why didn't he kill him?' the companion asked.

The Estalian shrugged.

'I mean, he deserved it. From his lack of fingers he's been given many chances already. Why didn't he kill him?'

The Estalian smiled. 'He has to cut him some slack. He is his brother after all.'

THE SUN HAD been up for three hours, and a breathless heat lay upon the harbour side. Beyond the immense stone quay, an ancient structure built by other races long before the rise of man, the tiled roofs of Sartosa rose in banks and clusters up the hillside. Stucco plaster gleamed white in the sunlight, alongside mouldering grey stonework and antique timber frames. Sartosa's port was a patchwork city, sewn together by many different cultures at many different times. It was as if the buildings had been looted from all over the world, and piled here together to fade and rot. A plundered town. It seemed appropriate.

As it was early in the season, Luka was surprised by the number of ships careened on the long-beach spit beyond the bay. Gangs of ratings carrying pitch ladles, ramming irons and mallets were threading their way down to work at caulking the hulls. The thick stench of heating pitch filled the air, almost, but not quite, blotting out the acrid fumes of boucan curing in the smoking huts along the harbour side.

'Early to set up dry,' commented Luka. He took a swig of watered rum from the earthenware bottle he was carrying and rinsed the taste of the night's carousing from his parched mouth. He'd walked down to the dockside with his nervous and still unnamed companion, and Benuto, the boatswain.

'Many masters have had enough for the year, so tell,' Benuto said. He was an older man, from Miragliano originally, his face lined from years of sun and salt. He wore black buckle-shoes, stained calico trousers loose at the ankle and a crimson jacket so the crew could pick him out easily. Perched on his head was a black hat that had so many corners and so little shape that the companion was at a loss to tell its origins.

'With the summer pickings yet to be had?' Luka asked.

Benuto shook his head and sucked on his clay pipe. 'No pickings at all, sir, the seas are dry. You must've heard? About the Butcher Ship?'

'I've heard a thing or two,' Luka remarked carelessly, casting a look at his companion. 'Though I've not been abroad so much of late to hear the gossip. A few tales of woe. I see they're true... or at least the masters of Sartosa think they are.' Luka flexed his right arm thoughtfully, nursing the gash Guido had put there the night before.

'Oh, they're true, so tell,' said Benuto. 'Ten months now, the Butcher Ship's been out there. We all thought it fancy at first too. But the trade routes have emptied, and many of Sartosa's own have gone missing, to boot.'

'So he preys on more than merchantmen?'

'The Butcher preys on everything. Mainlander and pirate alike. He is the sea daemon himself.' Benuto spat and touched the gold ring in his ear to ward against bad fortune. 'Jacque Rawhead's boat, both of Hasty Leopald's, the *Windrush*, the *Labour of Love*, the *Espiritu Santo*, the *Princess Ella* and the *Lightning Tree*, unless old Jeremiah Tusk went south around the Horn of Araby this year like he's always been threatening.'

'So many...' breathed Luka.

'I told you,' said his companion.

Benuto glanced at the long-cloaked stranger who had been at Luka's side since his reappearance. The man looked clean and manicured, and his clothes, though plain, were finely made from quality cloth. A mainlander, if Benuto had ever smelled one, and from Luccini, by the accent.

Luka Silvaro had been captured the year before during a battle with two of that city-state's man-o-wars, and the company had thought him either rotting dead in a gibbet cage on the headland, or rotting alive in a rat-swarming ponton, one of the notorious prison hulks on the estuary. The former, most likely, for Luka Silvaro was an infamous pirate prince. But the night before, it had turned out neither was true. Luka was alive, and come back to them, with a gentleman from Luccini at his heel. There was a mystery there, Benuto thought, one he hoped his captain would not be long in unwrapping.

'We ourselves have just got back from a run, empty-handed,' Benuto told Luka. 'Guido was thinking of having us careen now too.'

Luka shook his head. 'We'll be putting to sea,' he told the bo'sun. 'I've called in the company and already told Junio to make up the stores.'

'You have the funds for that, sir?' Benuto asked.

'Indeed. I want you to get everything seashape, as fast as you can.'

'My, there's plenty o' work there,' said Benuto, his voice trailing off.

Luka looked at his companion and held up three fingers. The man reached under his cloak and carefully drew out three leather moneybags. Luka hand-weighed them and gave them to Benuto. 'Seashape, and no corners cut.'

'No, sir!' said the boatswain sharply.

They had reached the pier end and stood by the windwall, looking over at the ships of Luka's company. The *Rumour* was a twenty-gun, two hundred tonne brigantine, one hundred paces long at the keel. She had two masts, both fully square-rigged, with a fore-and-aft sail on the lower part of the mainmast. Her low, sleek hull was painted black except for a stripe of red along each flank from which the gunports stared. A fast ship, quick in the turn and sharp of tooth. A hunter's ship.

In her shadow lay her consort, a sixty-pace swift sloop called the *Safire*, a little beauty of twelve guns. Her hull, golden oak above the waist and white below, was made of butted planks so she would slip like a sword through the water. She was fore-and-aft rigged on the shorter mizzen mast, and could raise a square sail from the main if the wind was running, but her exceptionally long bowsprit, which almost doubled her overall length, could rig a great lateen sail and make her very fast indeed.

The company was already gathering around the ships, running repairs or loading victuals under the direction of Junio, the company storekeeper. Four men were parbuckling kegs of water, oil and beer up the side of the *Rumour*, using a rope over a bitt. Up on one of the yards, Luka could see Largo, the sailmaker, hard at work with his needle, fid and seam rubber. Luka's eye drifted along to the head of the *Rumour* and the figure there, painted gold, a woman with one hand cupped to her mouth and the other cupped to her ear.

It would have been a crime to careen these two so early: to beach them and heel them over and caulk the hulls, stranding them when there was so much summer and sea left in the world. They were like greyhounds or thoroughbreds that needed to be run out.

No matter the hazard.

'Who'll master the *Safire*?' asked a voice behind them. It was the lupine Estalian who the companion had encountered the night before.

'That was always Guido's ship, till you went from us, and I'll doubt you'll give him command again.'

'I don't even know if he'll be joining us, Roque,' replied Luka. 'Who did he have master the *Safire*?'

'Silke.'

'No surprise. Though I am surprised Silke didn't jump in at his crony's side last night.'

'Silke's always had an early nose for the way a tide is turning,' said Benuto.

'Well, I'll keep Silke in his place for now. Test his loyalty.' Luka looked at the Estalian. 'My thanks for your sabre, by the by.'

The Estalian nodded politely. The companion now noticed that the fine blade Luka had used in the Hole-In-By-The-Hill was hanging from the Estalian's wide leather baldric.

'Well met again, gentleman,' the Estalian said suddenly, looking over at the companion. 'We've not yet been introduced.'

The companion shuffled awkwardly. Luka glanced from one to the other and shrugged. 'Sesto, this is Roque Santiago Della Fortuna, the company's master-at-arms. Roque, I present Sesto Sciortini, a gentleman of reputation from the mainland.'

Roque made a bow, his long straight hair hanging down like a glossy black curtain. The Estalian had fine manners, finer than might have been expected from a Sartosan sail-thief.

'Della Fortuna... Roque Santiago Della Fortuna...' murmured Sesto, returning the courtesy. 'I have in mind a fellow of that name, of the Estalian nobility, who rose to fame some years past by making great voyages of discovery to Araby and the Southlands. I seem to think he disappeared on an expedition to the west. Are you by any chance... related?'

'No,' replied Roque. 'But I met him once, before he died.'

'It seems, though, a coincidence–' Sesto began.

'I will make allowances for the fact you are a stranger to the customs of Sartosa, friend Sesto,' said Roque. 'We seldom press with questions where questions are unwelcome. There's not a man among us who hasn't secrets he would not part with. That is, in fact, why many come here and make this reckless life their own. I would say to you, for instance, your name is intriguing. "Sesto"... the sixth born son, and "Sciortini"... which means a watchman or sentinel. A name right enough, and a fine one, but also a mask, I fancy. A meaning to hide behind.'

'Not at all,' said Sesto quickly.

'Then why, pray, do you wear that signet ring turned in, so that only your palm may read the emblem upon it?'

'I...'

'There's not a man among us who has not secrets he would not part with, Roque,' said Luka. 'So you said yourself.'

'My apologies,' said Roque. 'I meant no harm.'

'That's what all pirates say,' chuckled Benuto, 'afore they slit your neck.'

ABOARD THE RUMOUR, in the great cabin, Luka called up the lamp trimmer to set the lanterns, for even on a bright day, the low-beamed chamber was gloomy. Then he laid about the untidy quarters, hurling items of clothing and other oddments out through the gallery lights.

Sesto sat and watched, sipping brandy from a thick glass chaser with a squat stem. Grumbling, Luka threw out a shoe, a doublet, an empty powder horn, a tricorn hat, another shoe, a bundle of bedclothes, a mandolin...

He caught Sesto looking at him.

'Guido's stuff. Traipsed about here like he owned this cabin. My cabin! Mine!'

'I suppose he didn't think you were coming back,' said Sesto.

'*I* didn't think I was coming back. That's not the point. Ahhh. Look. My chessboard! Manann take him, he's lost half the pieces!'

'I gather Guido is your brother,' said Sesto.

Luka frowned. 'We share a mother. That's not quite the same thing.' He made to throw a grey velvet frock coat with wide button-back cuffs out of the window, then stopped himself. 'Mine,' he remarked, then sniffed it. 'He's worn this, damn him!' He raked around in the mess of clothes and pewter vessels on the floor boarding, and fished out a sash of scarlet silk, some brown moleskin breeks and a pair of black, thigh-length cavalry boots. Oblivious to Sesto's presence, Luka began to strip off and rid himself of the plain, cheaply made garments he'd been wearing since he came ashore. Sesto was intimidated by Luka's massive naked frame: the huge musculature of his arms and back, the fading cicatrices on his skin, the pallor of his flesh from too long out of the sun. Too long in the dungeons of Luccini.

Luka dressed himself in the clothing he'd selected from the floor. They were his clothes, it seemed, for they fitted well enough. He pulled on the breeks, then the boots, slouching the wide tops down around his knees, then tucked in a white linen blouse with full sleeves, tied the scarlet sash around his waist, and dragged on the grey frock coat.

'How do I look?' he asked, tightening the laces up the front of his shirt.

'The very model of a pirate lord,' said Sesto.

'The desired effect. But not pirate now, eh? Not now.'

'No, indeed. When are you going to tell them?'

'Them?'

'The company. The Reivers. Your crew, sir.'

'Soon. When we're at sea.'

'Aha,' nodded Sesto.

'I miss my gold and my stones,' said Luka, flexing his fingers and staring at them. 'Your soldiers took it all when they fettered me. Took it and sold it, I'll wager.'

'You have that ring still,' Sesto said, nodding at the thick gold band that had spared Luka his little finger in the fight the night before.

Luka looked at it as if he'd forgotten about it. 'That one. Yes, well I wouldn't let that one go. Hid it under my tongue for six weeks, then under a loose slab in my cell. Lose that and I lose myself.'

'It has meaning?' Sesto asked.

'When I embarked on my career, I took a gold ducat from the first treasure ship I captured, and had it melted down and wrought into this. This is a part of me, a part of who I am, as surely as my hand or foot. But it's been without company for too long.'

Luka strode across to the lazarette behind the screwed-down chart table. Guido had evidently secured the locker with a new padlock during his tenure as master. Luka rummaged around in the mess and found a marlinespike, which he used to pry the door open. Inside was a pile of waggoners and furled charts, tide-books, almanacs and a double-barrelled pocket pistol. Beneath them, three brass coffers. Luka dragged them out, wrenched off the clasps, and emptied the contents across the tabletop.

Precious, glinting treasures scattered out. Garnets, rubies, malachite rings and bloodstone pins, wedges of Arabyan silver, enamelled crosses, opals, pearls, emerald pins, amethyst brooches, rose-sapphire pendants, gold snuff boxes, Tilean ducats and doblons, square-cut tierces, Estalian cruzados and peso octos, Arabyan rials, Imperial crowns and aquilas, rupeys from the Ind, Bretonnian guilders, yuans from

Cathay, Kislevite roubles and all manner of gold and silver currency, including some hexagonal and crescent shaped issues that Sesto had never seen before.

Luka rattled around in the glittering spread, trying rings for size and tossing them back if they were too small or too big. He eventually decided on a fat green tourmaline for his right middle finger, a blue sapphire for his left ring finger, a round, rose-blood ruby for his left middle, and a gold Ebonian thumb ring, coiled in the shape of a snake, for his left hand. Then he slipped a chunky gold loop into his left earlobe, rubbed it and spat for fortune.

'Gold in the ear improves the eyesight,' he told Sesto.

'I've heard that superstition.'

Luka winked. 'You'll not think it a superstition when we close with the Butcher.'

'When that hour comes, will they stand?' Sesto asked.

'Who?'

'The company. The Reivers. Your crew,' Sesto said, repeating his earlier remark like a refrain. 'When the time comes.'

'For what you're offering, I damn well hope so.'

FOR TWO FURTHER days, the victualling and repair of the brig and its consort continued apace. Sesto kept himself apart from the gathering company, fearful of every single one of them. They were free men, free in the worst way, their violent, vulgar souls loyal to no state or throne or prince. Only to themselves and their own selfish lusts, and to the creed of their criminal fraternity.

Sesto lingered around the poop and the quarterdeck of the *Rumour*, watching the graft. He got to recognise their faces, some of them at least. Junio, the storekeeper, a tall man who fussed around the provisioning work, his big eyes and long nose reminding Sesto of a goat's. Casaudor, the stern, robust master mate. Tende, the massive helmsman, bigger even than Luka, his skin black as coal. Fahd, the shrivelled cook, happily clucking in Arabyan as he worked in the sweaty confines of the galley to serve up strongly spiced meals twice a day. One-legged Belissi, the ship's carpenter. Vento, the master rigger, surprisingly nimble for a heavy man, fond of a chalk-white frock coat the tails of which he had to tuck into the waist of his breeks every time he ran aloft up the ratlines. His hands, like the sailmaker Largo's, were calloused and leathery from sewing and splicing. Benuto, the boatswain, oversaw all the work, always visible with his shapeless hat and crimson coat.

One of the common ratings stuck in his memory too. He was a dirty, narrow-eyed man whose name Sesto had yet to learn, a true boucaner by the scabby leather hides he wore. Wherever Sesto went, the boucaner seemed always to be nearby, watching him.

Silke, the retained master of the *Safire*, came aboard the *Rumour* once to speak with Luka. He was a shabby man with great, broad shoulders from which his ankle-length green silk robe hung like a kite. He had seven tight pigtails poking down from the edge of the orange turban on his head.

Roque drilled the watches hard, counting time as they raised the targette shields at the blow of a whistle. At least half the ratings were trained with calivers, or had skill with a crossbow, or were teamed to man the swivel guns mounted along the rail. Every few hours, a whistle would blow and Roque would saunter along the deck as the watch drew pikes with a clatter, slammed up the targettes and iron pavises on port or starboard, and stood ready with grapnels. The calivermen and swivel-gun teams took station and fired off a crumping salute without lead.

'They're slow,' Sesto heard Luka tell Roque. 'Guido's let them get lazy.'

They didn't look lazy to Sesto. In under two minutes, the crew of the *Rumour* could armour either flank with targette boards, rattle off a salvo with caliver and swivels, fire a flurry of crossbow bolts, and make the ship bristle like a porcupine with long-hafted pikes. And that didn't take into account the individual weapons the men carried: hangers, sabres, sashes and baldrics laden with wheel and matchlock pistols, muskets, axes, rapiers and poinards, dirks and daggers, kidney knives and short, fat, single-edged swords they called cut-lesses.

Sesto tried a cut-less for size. It was weighty and crude, a little more than a heavy dagger and a little less than a small hanger, but it sang well, and it was short enough to wield without snaring the shrouds or striking the ceiling below decks.

On the second day, Sesto sneaked down onto the red-washed gundeck, and admired the brig's guns. Six cannon each side and three culverins, along with two sakers placed as stern chasers. He was impressed to find that the cannon were laid up on wheeled trucks that could be easily dragged back inboard for reloading. The warships of the Luccinian fleet still mounted their cannon on field carriages, much more cumbersome to move and draw in. No wonder, then, the Sartosan reputation for multiple broadsides. Sesto noticed the wooden pegs laid out ready to be hammered in under the back of each barrel to adjust the angle of fire, and the brass monkeys of stacked shot – solid ball, chain shot, case shot and stone-buck. Peeking into the powder magazine, through the heavy curtains of mail-link, he saw only a stack of the small kegs made for pistol and caliver powder.

'Looking for something?'

Sesto glanced round and found himself facing Sheerglas, the *Rumour's* cadaverous master gunner. At some point in his long career, Sheerglas must have been marooned in the settlements of the Southlands, for there was no other explanation Sesto could think of for the way Sheerglas's canine teeth were filed down to a point. Sheerglas never came above decks. He lurked in the ruddy twilight of the gundeck, haunting the shadows.

'I see only pistol powder,' Sesto said.

Sheerglas smiled, an unnerving sight. His sharp canines drew spots of blood from his pale lower lip. 'On the captain's orders, we use only pistol powder,' he said.

Again, Sesto was impressed. Bulk-barrelled gunpowder, especially in Sartosa, was notoriously crude, diluted with ash-mix and prone to misfire. Pistol powder, though much more expensive, was finely milled and purer. The *Rumour's* guns would fire well, and every time.

'I was merely interested,' Sesto said.

Sheerglas nodded. 'I like a man who takes an interest. You're the captain's friend and companion from the mainland, aren't you?'

'Y-yes.'

Sheerglas beckoned with the linstock in his bony hands. It was an ebony baton, the tip carved in the form of a lion's mouth to take the match. 'Come aft with me, to my quarters. We'll take a reviving drink, you and I.'

'I thank you, but no.'

'Come now,' Sheerglas whispered, more insistent.

'Let him be, Sheerglas,' snarled a voice nearby. It was the ubiquitous boucaner.

'I meant him no harm, Ymgrawl,' complained the master gunner.

'Thou never dost. But let him be.'

Sheerglas scowled and shuffled away back into the gundeck. Now Sesto felt as trapped by the boucaner as he had by the gunner. The rough-made man surprised him by standing aside to usher Sesto past and up the companionway. Sesto turned to the side so he could get by. Close to, the man gave off the gross reek of tanned hide.

'Watch thyself,' the boucaner growled.

'I will,' Sesto assured him, and hurried aloft.

IV

THE DAY SUN rose with a lively westerly, and they put to sea. There was no fanfare or salute. Sesto suddenly realised they were under way. The voyage had started with the same abrupt lack of ceremony as the code-duel between Luka and his brother.

With the *Safire* leading off, they came around the harbour head and made sail for the west, along the so-called Pirate's Channel and into the blue, sunlit dish of the Tilean Sea. With the wind running and all standing, the *Rumour* and the *Safire* made spectacular speed. Land fell away behind; a ribbon of headland dead astern, fading to a smoky line, and then nothing.

As soon as there was nothing in sight but open sea, a fair number of the crew went to the rail and cast offerings into the rolling green water. A coin for good luck, a stone for safe return, a button for rich pickings. Sesto saw some men, Fahd amongst them, wring a chicken's neck and throw the dead bird in. Sesto shuddered to think of the cruel water-gods, like the sea daemon, these otherwise godless men were attempting to appease.

Belissi, the ship's carpenter, made the strangest offering of all. With his chisel and plane, he had shaped a rude copy of his wooden leg, and made a great show of casting that into the swell, shouting out: 'Mother mine hast take my leg, now take it again and be content, and come not after the rest of me!'

Shaking his head, Sesto went up onto the poop and stood with Luka, Casaudor and Benuto, feeling the sway of the deck. Tende's fists were clamped to the king-spoke of the gold painted wheel, with a thick necked lee helmsman called Saybee at his side. Sesto leaned over the taffrail and watched the sleek *Safire* racing ahead, its huge jibs bellying out from the long bowsprit. A piece of work, that sloop, its hull artfully light enough for speed, yet strong enough not to crack under the extreme pressure of carrying more sail than was usual for a vessel of the size.

Luka had laid out a waggoner, and was tracing a course across the parchment for Casaudor's benefit. Sesto heard him explain his intention to make speed for the western islands along the coast of Estalia, perhaps tracking even as far north as the waters of Tobaro. Casaudor said nothing, but Sesto didn't like the look in the master mate's eyes.

Luka himself seemed as animated as his craft, as if the wind was filling his sails too. Already, colour had returned to his skin, a ruddy, tanned look that melted the pallor imprisonment had lent him. He was becoming his old self. In the two months he had known Captain Luka Silvaro, Sesto had begun to trust him, almost like him. But now they were at sea, Luka was changed. He was wildly free again, cut loose, and Sesto wondered how long the terms of their fragile agreement would last.

ON THE SECOND and third days, the wind declined, and they made slower going, though the weather was still fair. They'd seen nothing but open water, deep ocean birds and, once, a silver flurry of flying fish that dashed and leapt through the waves ahead of them.

Then, at noon on the third day, the man in the main's topcastle sang out. A sail.

The lookout had a view of about fifteen miles in all directions, and his arm pointed to the south-west. The sail he'd sighted was behind the horizon from the point of view of those on the deck. Luka had some sail struck on both vessels, and as they gybed and close-hauled around, he took his brass scope and went aloft himself.

By the time he returned to the deck, two tiny white dots had come into view.

'It's Ru'af,' he said to Casaudor. 'Both his galleys, if my eyes are not mistaken.'

'Then we press on,' said the master mate.

Luka shook his head. 'I'd hail the old devil and take his news. In these unhappy times it might pay to take what intelligence we can.'

'Even from Ru'af?'

'Even from him. Set us about to meet him and hoist the black.'

Casaudor began barking orders to the crew, and the top gangs ran up the yards like monkeys. Sesto saw the *Safire* had trimmed sail likewise and was now running on their port quarter.

'What are we doing?' Sesto asked Luka, drawing the captain to one side for a moment.

'The sails are those of Muhannad Ru'af. Corsair galleys. We'll find out what he knows.'

'Corsairs?'

'Aye, Sesto.'

'Who will just come alongside and talk?'

'Oh, they're rivals, and there's no love lost, but they sail by the code too. Remember the code?'

'How could I forget?'

'We're safe if we show our colours.'

Luka gestured aloft, and Sesto saw the *Rumour* was now flying a ragged black flag on which was a hand-stitched white skeleton and hourglass. The *Safire* flew a similar badge: crossed white swords on black.

Pirate marks. The flags that warned a victim ship to give over without a fight, or informed another pirate of a fellow. If a pirate displayed his black before an attack and you surrendered without a fight, he was obliged to show mercy.

In the space of about half an hour, the corsair ships hove into view. The Reivers' vessels were almost at a dead stop, turned out of the light wind. Muhannad Ru'af's craft were

galleys, and came on under power of the massive banks of
oars. Ru'af's flag ship, the *Badarra*, was a sixty-oar trireme
painted red, white and gold, much longer and narrower
than either of Luka's ships, and dominated by two mighty
lateen masts, the sails now furled. It had a raised, crenel-
lated fighting castle at the bow. Its consort, the *Tariq*, was a
forty-oar bireme, similar in aspect to the *Badarra*, but
smaller. A great structure of red-painted wood was raised
almost upright from the bowcastle.

They were closing still, closing fast, oars stroking,
approaching the *Rumour* at the port beam.

'Lower a longboat,' Luka told Benuto. 'I'll go across myself
as soon as they swing about. Get some–'

'Have a care!' Casaudor suddenly hollered. There was a
general shouting from the crew. Sesto jumped, scared, and
heard Roque blowing his whistle.

Sesto saw what Casaudor had seen. As they closed on the
Reivers' vessels, the corsair galleys had struck the black
marks they had been flying and had run up plain red flags.

The bloody flag. The jolie rouge. The sign of death without quarter.

THERE WAS A distant banging and Sesto realised the galleys
had fired their fore cannons. He heard whistling, whizzing
sounds in the air around him. A section of the quarterdeck
rail exploded in a shower of wood splinters, and two ratings
shrieked and tumbled to their knees. A main topsail shredded and hung limp. The sea around them churned with
splashes and spouts.

Another crump of fire. Flames and wood gouted from the
port bulwarks. At least one man fell into the sea. Case shot
ripped across the quarterdeck, bursting to release whipping
chains and lead balls that turned barrels, ratlines and three
men into sprays of fibres and bloody fragments.

There was a look of sheer incredulity on Luka Silvaro's
face.

The *Rumour*'s guns began to return fire. Oar staves shattered and pieces were thrown high out of the water. A pall
of smoke filled the space between the ships. Shouts and
screams cut the air.

Roque, blasting on his pipe, had succeeded in drawing
the port watch to the rail, clattering their targettes together

as they threw them up to form a barricade. Pikemen thrust their long poled weapons out from the thick shield-line. The deck shuddered violently, both with the impact of cannon-shell and the discharge of the *Rumour's* own ordnance.

Retorts of a higher pitch, like branches snapping, rolled down the port line as the calivermen began firing. Crouching down by the taffrail on the poop, Sesto saw the figures of men toppling down on the *Badarra's* deck or plunging into the frothing sea. Swivel guns on both ships began to thump. A section of Roque's shield wall went down as a ten-pound ball from a corsair saker bowled through it, spilling broken men and twisted segments of pavise before it.

The *Tariq* had powered across the bow of the *Rumour* and was coming in from the starboard side. With precious little wind, there was slim chance of out-manoeuvring it. The *Safire*, however, was pulling away from the grappling mass of ships. Sesto saw that Silke had put out four longboats, laden with men, and these crews were now all rowing fit to break, towing the sloop clear on long lines.

Was he running? Was Silke failing his test of loyalty so early?

The red-painted projection raised from the *Tariq's* bow-castle began to lower, and Sesto realised what it was. A hinged boarding ramp, known as a corvus, large enough for two men to come down it abreast, and armoured along the sides with wooden targettes painted with Arabyan motifs. The corvus had a huge spike extended from the lip of its front end.

As Sesto watched, the *Tariq* slammed in towards the *Rumour's* waist as if to ram her, oars stroking like the legs of some gigantic pool-skater. Then the cables securing the corvus were let out, and the wooden bridge came smashing down, disintegrating the toprail and slamming against the deck, the spike biting deep through the scrubbed oak boards. Ululating, corsairs began to pour across: ragged, wild haired men in florid silks and linens, brandishing wheel-locks, shamshirs and lances.

Roque and Benuto had mobbed the starboard watch and all the available top-men to repel. There was a firecracker peal of handguns blasting at short range, and a clatter of pikes and lances. Brutal hand-to-hand fighting – a tangled, blurry confusion – spilled across the *Rumour*'s waist.

Luka was at the port rail with Casaudor when the crew of the *Badarra* began to board. He had a ducksfoot pistol in his left hand and a curved Arabyan shamshir in his right, and bellowed orders at the pikemen and the targetters. Calivermen and crossbowmen were now wriggling aloft in the shrouds under the direction of Vento and the old sailmaker Largo. They began raining shot and bolts down onto the railside of the *Badarra*. Arrows and smallshot loosed back, and Sesto saw one caliverman drop like a stone from the rigging, and another, an arrow through his throat, fall and dangle, suspended by one foot, pouring blood like a strung hog.

Vento, his white coattails tucked into his breeks, straddled a yard-arm like a man on a horse and fired lethal stone balls from a heavy bullet-crossbow with double strings. Largo, higher up still, had rammed a gold Estalian comb-morion on his head for protection, and was shooting with a curved horse bow, spare arrows clutched between the fingers of his left hand so he could nock them quickly.

'We'll not overmatch them, man-for-man!' Luka yelled at Casaudor. 'Let's take it to them! I want Ru'af's heart for this infamy!'

Sesto watched in disbelief as Luka raised a boarding action to counter the *Badarra*'s assault. Outflung grapnels closed the distance, dragging galley and brigantine side by side, and boarding planks and ladders slammed out through the targette wall.

Luka led the attack. As he leapt over the boards, he fired his ducksfoot, and the five splayed barrels of the grotesque pistol roared simultaneously. Casaudor was beside him, blowing two corsairs off the plank bridge with a blast from his blunderbuss. The heavy weapon had a spring-blade under the trumpet, and Casaudor snapped it out and impaled the next corsair on it. Dying, the corsair took the blunderbuss with him as he pitched, screaming, into the sea, and Casaudor drew a cup-guard rapier instead and set in with that.

Many of the Reivers had multiple pistols strung around them on lanyards or ribbon sashes, so they could be fired and then dropped without being lost. There was no time to reload. Surging across the gap, the men fired each weapon in turn until they were spent, and then resorted to cut-less, boarding axe and sabre.

Corsairs, swinging on lines, were now swarming over the poop rail. Tende, hefting a long-handled stabbing axe of curious and no doubt Ebonion design, led a repulse with ten men, including Junio and Fahd. Backing away, numb with terror and wondering where on earth he could run to, Sesto heard the swishing of steel, the crack of breaking bone, the yelp of the dying. Blood ran across the decking, following the lines of the boards. The corsairs surged again, pushing more men through onto the poop, despite the loss of half a dozen picked from the swing-ropes by the fire of Vento's marksmen above.

Sesto found himself in a haze of smoke. He staggered around, eyes watering, and got his hand around the grip of his pistol. Junio loomed out of the smoke. The side of his head was cloven in and he looked more than ever like a goat, a sacrificial goat. He fell into Sesto's embrace, soaking the gentleman from Luccino in hot, sour blood.

With a horrified cry, Sesto fell back under the dead weight. A toothless, raving corsair with a bloody adze came charging out of the smoke, and Sesto fired his pistol from under the armpit of the dead storekeeper. The ball bounced off the side of the corsair's head and pulped his ear. As he fell, yowling, two more followed him into view, lunging at Sesto.

The first sabre slash struck Junio's back, and Sesto was forced to use the pitiful corpse in his arms as a shield. One of the corsairs stabbed with a lance, and the iron tip came spearing out of the storekeeper's gaping mouth towards Sesto's face. Sesto yelled and retreated, dropping Junio face down.

The corsairs hurled themselves after him. Sesto tried to draw his smallsword, but slipped down hard on the bloody deck.

Ymgrawl the boucaner appeared from nowhere and interposed himself between Sesto and his attackers. The boucaner's cut-less ripped the lancer across the eyes, and then he turned, breaking the other's jaw with a blow from the blade's heavy stirrup-guard. Ymgrawl grabbed hold of the dazed corsair by the hair and wrenched him head-first over the rail.

'Get thee up!' Ymgrawl yelled.

Sesto never would have believed he'd be happy to see the wretched boucaner.

'Thee maketh my job hard!' Ymgrawl snorted, bundling Sesto down the companion ladder onto the quarterdeck.

'Your job?'

'Silvaro told me to shadow thee and keep thee safe from harm,' said Ymgrawl.

LUKA HACKED AND slashed his way down the centre walk of the *Badarra* at the head of a pack of Reivers. The corsairs had thrown their full effort into the assaults, for though the rowing benches were packed with men, most were lying where they sat, helpless with fatigue. The corsairs were all thin and undernourished, and many showed signs of scurvy. The forced row to engage Luka's ships had exhausted most of them. Luka knew he was lucky. If Ru'af's crew hadn't been ailing, the sheer number of them would have overrun his tubs already.

Through the chaos and smoke, Luka saw the big, pot-bellied corsair chief up on the aft castle of the *Badarra*.

'Ru'af! Bitch-pup!' he yelled in Arabyan, using every curse Fahd had ever taught him. 'Call off your dogs and I might remember my mark was black!'

Ru'af made an obscene gesture in Luka's direction.

Luka turned away, hacking his dagger down on an oarsman who was running at Casaudor, and looked to sea.

Silke, his wits about him, had got into position at last, the rowers in the tugging longboats gasping and collapsing over their oars. The *Safire* hadn't run at all. It had been pulled clear to present beam-on to the *Tariq*.

The first broadside almost stopped the battle dead with its thunder crack. Pieces of oar, rail and bulwark from the *Tariq* flew into the air and rained down. Another broadside, and the *Tariq* ruptured, spewing smoke and flames up into the windless blue. Its foremast collapsed, and its crew, deafened and dazed, began jumping into the sea. On the waist of the *Rumour*, Roque, Benuto and a dozen other blood soaked

Reivers struggled to dislodge the spike of the corvus before the *Tariq* dragged the brigantine onto its beam end.

Then the bireme folded in the middle, timbers shearing and splintering, and the sea rushed in to consume her.

THE FIGHT WAS out of the corsairs. Luka had to issue stern orders to stop the Reivers massacring them. Their blood was up, and the corsairs had broken the sea code. Pirates did not prey on pirates.

Luka dragged Ru'af to the *Badarra's* aft castle and spoke to him there alone for long minutes. When he returned, it was clear to all that he was disappointed by the conversation. He ordered Benuto to cut the lines holding the ships together.

The *Badarra*, smoke wreathing the sea around it, drifted away astern. The *Rumour* and the *Safire* put up what sail they could to catch the meagre breeze, and slowly hauled away west.

Luka found Sesto in the great cabin, swallowing brandy.

'They attacked us because they hadn't seen a sail in three weeks. They were famished and scurvyed and low on water. It's as Benuto said. The seas are dry. Ru'af was in no doubt. The Butcher Ship has driven everyone from the sea with its bloody fury.'

'I thought we were going to die,' said Sesto.

'We were going to die,' snapped Luka. 'That's why we fought.'

He looked at Sesto grimly. 'Ru'af was in no doubt. Common word in the islands is that Henri of Breton is the Butcher. It is the *Kymera*, his great galleon that everyone fears.'

'You know him?'

'Yes. But if Henri is the Butcher, he's not the man I knew.'

Luka took a folded parchment from his coat pocket. The sealing wax bore the imprint of the Prince of Luccini.

'It's time to tell the Reivers,' Luka announced.

'HAVE EARS, YOU all!' Luka yelled from the break-rail. All across the deck, toil ceased. The last few bodies had been pitched over the side, and repairs were now underway to crew and ship alike.

'When I was took by the Luccini warships, I never thought to see light again. Nor would they have let me out, but left me to rot until they found another use for me, and freed me. An amnesty and a thousand crowns! That's what they've offered me, and every man of you too!'

That had their attention.

Luka held up the parchment. 'This is a letter of marque and reprisal, signed by the prince himself. Under its terms, we Reivers cease to be pirates and become privateers. Payment shall be the amnesty and the thousand crowns. My friend Sesto is here to witness our work. Take heed that unless we return him safe to Luccini, so he may report in our favour, we'll not see a crumb.'

All eyes turned to Sesto for a moment, and he felt very uncomfortable.

'What work must we do?' demanded Benuto.

'Why, we must rid the seas of the Butcher Ship,' said Luka Silvaro.

IT WAS, PRONOUNCED the robust master mate Casaudor, hot enough to boil a dog.

They were eight days north-west of Sartosa, on the Estalian side of the Tilean Sea, and for the last three days of the passage, the weather had become their relentless foe.

The stifling heat commenced at dawn each day, and its intensity climbed with the rising sun. The sky was utterly cloudless, and the scorching white glare of the sun drained the blue out of it like indigo dye faded out of white calico. There was barely a breath of wind enough to fill the sheets. The decks and the wood of the rails had become too hot to touch. Tende, the Ebonian helmsman, had wrapped cotton kerchiefs around his hands to prevent the spokes of the ship's wheel from burning his flesh.

Hot enough to boil a dog. An apt description for their misery. Listless men cowered on the *Rumour's* deck in what little shadow and shade the masts and canvas availed. Cheeks, forearms and shoulders showed red raw.

Sesto lurked in the shadow of the forecastle. The sea glittered and flashed too brightly to look at. He had been tempted to hide from the sun below decks, but it was airless down there, and there was the ever likely chance of straying into the path of Sheerglas, the master gunner. Sheerglas scared Sesto more than any other person aboard, with his crisp-as-parchment voice and dry, earthy smell. That, and his hideously pointed teeth. As befitted a ship of the name, rumours abounded concerning Sheerglas, and Sesto didn't like any one of them. Even in a company of brutes and murderers, Sheerglas was a very devil, and it seemed a wonder that Luka Silvaro kept him as part of the crew. But there was no gainsaying the skill of Sheerglas and his thin, pallid gun teams. He had proved that in the fight with Ru'af's galleys.

Because of the heat, the old cook Fahd had quit his galley and refused to work. His stoves had been put out and only salt fish and dry biscuits were available to the hungry. No one had an appetite anyway. Fahd sat against the base of the mizzen, working designs into a whale tooth with his pot-knife.

The constant swelter had put a pressure into the air, as if the sky was fit to burst. Only a storm would ease that pressure, and when, in each late afternoon, the grumbles of thunder came to their ears from the horizon, they prayed to a man for a break in the weather. But grumbling was all the sky did.

The nights brought no relief either. The still air remained oven-hot until after midnight, and the full moons grinned mirthlessly at the crew's discomfort. Even the starlight seemed hot enough to tan skin.

Sesto consoled himself with the slim fact that Luka's Reivers had not mutinied at once on hearing what designs he had made on their collective destiny. To take coin from Luccini and turn from pirates to privateers, that was asking a lot. Luka had warned him that many Sartosans regarded such a twist of allegiance as treason, as a slur against the red flag of King Death to which they were all pledged. Sesto supposed the Reivers had accepted it because of the promise of fortune and amnesty. Above all things, even King Death himself, the Reivers worshipped gold. In the acquisition of gold, no action was too low, too dirty, too despicable: murder, deception, fraud, betrayal. Above all else, a pirate was an amoral creature, liberated from

civilised codes of conduct. No shame or crime could sully
his soul more than it was already.

If expecting them to become privateers was asking a lot,
the daunting task that had been set for them was asking a
great deal more. The Butcher Ship was a daemon-barque, an
accursed thing. *He is the sea daemon himself*, Benuto had
said, speaking of the daemon lord of the deep that all
pirates feared. Hunting the Butcher would be a task fraught
with danger.

Of course, the Tilean Sea, that haunt of pirates, had been
full of dangers since the beginning of history. Plunderers,
throat-cutters, boucaners and hook-handed rogues, stalking
Estalian merchantmen and Tilean treasure ships, had made
that stretch of blue the most dangerous waterway in the
world, and made themselves legends to boot. Sacadra the
Jinx, Willem Longtooth, Metto Matez and his brigands, Ezra
Banehand, Bonnie Berto Redsheet... they were names and
legacies Sesto had read about as a boy in the court at Luccini. In the current time alone, there was Jacque Rawhead,
Jeremiah Tusk and Reyno Bloodlock, not to mention Luka
Silvaro and Red Henri, naturally.

The actions of the Butcher Ship outdid the work of even
the most bloody-handed pirate, and the *Rumour* was
charged to find it and send it to the bottom.

Sesto's role in the affair as insurance made him queasy to
think on. He alone could vouch for the Reivers' work and
ensure their reward. So, though every man on the ship was
concerned to safeguard his welfare, that also made him the
most vulnerable man on board.

With great unease, therefore, Sesto was snoozing in the
midday heat when Roque shook him awake. The Estalian
master-at-arms looked like a lean hunting hound, his skin
wet with perspiration.

'Come aft,' he said.

'What? What is it?'

'Come see,' Roque answered. He stood up and fanned his
face with both hands. Dark half moons of sweat stained the
armpits of his green silk blouse.

Luka was waiting on the bridge with Benuto the
boatswain, Casaudor and Vento, the chief rigger. Luka nodded to Sesto as he came up the poop stairs with Roque. He

had affected a wide-brimmed Pavonian hat to keep the blistering sun out of his cold eyes as if he was afraid the sun's heat might thaw them.

'What is it?' Sesto asked.

The bo'sun, old, craggy and dressed in his shapeless black hat and frock coat as crimson as a sunset, chuckled and pointed forward. Several leagues away to the west, a little tiara of stationary white clouds hung above the horizon.

'Land,' said Luka.

'Estalia? The coast?' Sesto wondered aloud.

Luka grinned at the mistake. 'Not yet awhile. The islands.'

A great chain of islands and atolls peppered the eastern seaboard of Estalia. In that dense, half-mapped archipelago lay the real pirate waters. Few pirates could afford an ocean-going ship. Forming the backbone of the piratical fraternity were the island-hoppers and the atoll-skulkers, who sallied out in longboats from their small, isolated communities to prey on those passing merchants foolish enough to water in the islands after the long crossings from the western ocean.

If any place might be the haunt of a Butcher Ship, it was here. Long ago, the gunships and hunters of the Luccini navy had despaired of chasing pirates through the archipelago. So many coves and inlets to hide in, so many places where a flank pursuit could turn, at the spin of a coin, into a bloody ambush. Just twenty years earlier, a flotilla of Luccini warships had harried Jeremiah Tusk into the island chain, and found themselves prey to the merciless guns of a corsair welcome.

'We'll turn to the north,' Luka said, 'and ride the current in towards Isla d'Azure.'

'Why there?' Sesto asked.

'There is a friendly town,' said Casaudor gruffly.

'One where we might water safely and hear some stories,' Luka added.

There was something about the cautious attitude of the seadogs that disquieted Sesto. There was something… many things, probably… they weren't telling him.

THEY ENTERED THE island chain in the later part of the day. The *Safire* rode in at the *Rumour*'s port quarter, attentive as any consort. The first few islands were scrubby knots of bare

rock or spits of coral rising like nipples from blooms of
sand. Larger islands, festooned with bright green trees,
appeared tantalisingly ahead. Some had wide, circular reefs
around them, or cusps of rock and sandbars that framed
deep, turquoise lagoons. The sky was feathered with scud-
ding clouds and the temperature dropped a few blessed
degrees. Hungry seabirds dipped and mobbed in the wakes
of the two ships.

The current was taut. Luka steered the helm team with a
combination of memory and an open, annotated waggoner.
The waters here were rife with submerged reefs, coral brakes,
sandbanks and rocks. Pepy, one of the younger, nimbler
crewmen went forward and called the depth with a knot-
line.

'A sail!' Sesto said suddenly.

'What?' Luka growled, looking up from his chart. Sesto's
comment won him a hard stare from Tende at the helm too.

'I saw a sail,' Sesto insisted. 'To starboard.'

'Where?'

Sesto wished he knew. He'd glimpsed a square of flapping
canvas in the skirts of the island to their right, a great mass
shrouded in greenery that rose from the sea, crowned with
a high cliff. He couldn't see the sail any more.

'Over there,' Sesto said. 'This bluff is obscuring it now. It
was in there, in the basin there.'

'A sail?'

'Yes.'

'Taking the wind?'

'Indeed yes.'

'You're mistaken,' said Roque cattily. 'That is Isla Verde,
and its cove presents promisingly, but it is shallow and
toothed with sharp coral. No ship would be in there, certainly not one at sail.'

Sesto frowned. Maybe it had been a trick of the light, or
the white flash of a passing gull.

'Let's loose a little top and come around,' Luka said.

Benuto gave him a curious look, and then moved to relay
the command to the yardsmen. Casaudor signalled the
Safire to follow them.

'You believe me?' Sesto whispered to Luka, who had come
to the rail to scan with his spyglass.

'No,' said Luka, 'but I believe we would be foolish to ignore any possibility.'

They tracked lazily around the head of the island's cove, until the lineman called a danger of grounding on the banks.

'A sail indeed,' Luka said, lowering his glass. He looked at Sesto and grinned. 'Your eyes are sharp.'

BOTH VESSELS FURLED their sheets and dropped anchor at the mouth of the secluded bay. Before them, in the crisp heat of the dying day, a cove fringed by rocky promontories was half exposed, hinting at a lagoon within. Behind that, the green scalp of the island rose like a mountain.

There was no explaining the sail.

They could see it rising proud of the cove, full-canvassed and fat with wind, like a ship running. But it was static, and deep in the lagoon, facing the inner shore of the island.

'There might be a cut into the lagoon,' Roque conjectured. 'One we don't know about.'

'We could be here all day and all night sounding to find it, so tell,' Benuto spat.

'Whatever that, why is it yarded full?' Luka asked. 'And not moving?'

Behind them, sitting back from the wheel, Tende spat against ill fortune and touched the gold ring in his ear. He murmured an Ebonian charm.

'Lower boats,' said Luka. 'I want a dozen men. You, for one, Tende.'

The massive helmsman groaned.

'I want your good luck charms where I can hear them,' Luka said.

Under Benuto's barked commands, the crew lowered two longboats from the side of the *Rumour*. The *Safire* stood to and waited. Thunder growled again, and for the first time, they saw the blink of lightning in the southern sky.

Luka passed command to Casaudor and went to the first boat, where Tende, Benuto and four other men were taking up oars. In the second boat, Roque assembled his six oars-men and fixed a swivel gun to the prow.

'Where do you think you're going?' Luka asked Sesto as he began to climb down into the first boat.

Sesto pointed to the island.

'I don't think so,' Luka said. 'You stay here on th–'

'I was the one who saw it,' Sesto said. 'I saw the sail.'

Luka Silvaro pursed his lips and then nodded. 'A fair point.' He ordered two of the men out of the boat to make room for Sesto. Sesto was wondering why two had been called out when Ymgrawl climbed down to join them.

'Thou canst row?' Ymgrawl asked.

'Of course.'

'Show it me,' he said.

Sesto took his seat and began to plane the water with his oar as Luka called the stroke.

It had been a long time since Sesto had done anything as menial as rowing, but he put his back into it, easing the oar against its thole pins. Chopping the calm water like centipedes, the two longboats cleared the *Rumour* and turned into the cove. The rocky promontories quickly hid the anchored ships from them. The last sight Sesto had of the *Rumour* was its gold figurehead, one hand cupped to her ear, the other to her mouth.

THEY ROWED INTO the cove of Isla Verde. It was a wide, shallow basin, so lousy with coral the bellies of the longboats scraped and dragged.

'Name of a god!' Luka said, staring.

The ship lay in the shallows, bow in to the beach. Under full sail, it had run into the cove, rupturing its hull on the banks and shoals before finally foundering and running aground. Sunk up to its gunports, it leaned over in the breakers. Two of its masts were down, but the mainmast still stood proud, sheets billowing, fruitlessly driving the stationary ship against the island. The hull and breastwork were marred by scorched cannon holes, and part of the starboard side was cloven in. This ship had been wounded unto death before it had run aground to its demise, pilotless.

The men in the boats gasped and uttered warding prayers. In the second boat, Roque primed the swivel, and every man made sure his weapon was to hand. Sesto was glad he had buckled on his rapier before climbing into the longboat.

'Name of a god!' Luka said again, with greater spleen.

'Do you know her?' Sesto asked, doubling back his stroke.

Luka nodded. He was standing in the bow, a primed pistol in his hand. He took off the Pavonian hat and tossed it down into the gunwales.

'It's the *Sacramento*,' he said.

VII

THE SACRAMENTO. A notorious barque, the warship of Reyno Bloodlock. *The* Reyno Bloodlock, scourge of the seas.

'Reyno, Reyno, Reyno…' Luka murmured. 'What has come to pass here?'

The ship looked dead. There was no sign of a living soul. On the shore, the tide had flushed up scattered debris from the wreck, and some of the twisted pieces looked like bodies.

They rowed in behind the stern. The window lights of the master cabins had been smashed in, and there was a cannon hole through the taffrail. Hundreds of gulls perched and cawed along the deck lines.

Under Luka's instruction, they rowed in close, covered by Roque's boat, and Luka tied them up against the mired rudder.

Holstering his pistol, he clambered, nimble as a Barbary ape, up the carved breastwork of the stern. Benuto and Tende followed their captain, and Sesto went after them. Ymgrawl tailed him dutifully.

The deck was raked at a steep angle thanks to the foundering. Beyond the shattered taffrail, the poop decking was marred by a crater, the impact of a heavy cannonball. The deckboards were splintered up, and only part of the wheel remained. And part of the helmsman too. His hands and forearms still clenched the wheelspokes, but no other bit of him had survived the blast.

Sesto gagged at the sight of it. Tende drew his blade.

'Someone might yet live,' Luka said.

They spread out to test the validity of his claim.

Sesto crept down the poop steps and went into the upper cabin. The cannonball had spent its worst here, and the fractured decks were spotted with broken glass, shards of porcelain and the burnt, dismembered fragments of a man who had been exploded by the blast. Seabirds had found their way in and were hopping through the shadows, pecking at the scraps of cooked human meat with their long, scarlet bills.

Sesto was damned if he was going to throw up in the presence of these men. He took out his rapier and poked with the blade to scare the birds away. They rose in a flurry, banging their wings and cawing as they escaped through the window lights. What they left behind was a torso, picked half-clean and caked in burned meat.

Sesto vomited.

'Am thee arright?' Ymgrawl asked.

'Yes, I'm… yes,' Sesto said, spitting acid phlegm from his mouth.

'Tis a rude way of death,' Ymgrawl admitted, jabbing at the torso with his cut-less.

Sesto ignored him and went through the partition door into the stepway that descended to the second deck.

The second deck was half submerged. Halfway down the stairs, Sesto stepped into seawater. It filled the companionway to hip height. He sloshed down into it and waded along. The door to the master's cabin lay open.

The desk was knocked askew, and the water was covered with floating clothes and charts, a quill and several hats. They bobbed as he sloshed into the chamber, driving ripples before him.

Raising his arms to keep his balance, Sesto waded unsteadily through the waist-deep water towards the desk. There was someone sitting behind the desk in the high-backed chair, his arms flat across the desktop, his head fallen forward.

Sesto reached the desk. The man looked asleep. He prodded him with the flat of his sword, but there was no response. Sesto reached forward and tugged at the man's doublet front.

The man spilled away before him, arms raised stiffly. There was nothing of him except his head, arms and upper torso. Below the waterline, he was just a chewed and mangled mess of pallid flesh, broken spine and bloated guts.

Sesto cried out and staggered backwards as the corpse up-turned and revealed its horror. He stumbled over something and fell down, submerged instantly in seawater.

The water roared in his ears. It was deep green and cloudy with flesh fibres stripped off the corpse.

Something white glided past him.

He erupted to the surface, choking and spluttering. Whatever was in the water with him was big, far bigger than he was. He saw a hooked fin cut the water and disappear around the desk.

Sesto began to panic.

The desk moved, barged through the water by a heavy force.

He slashed at the water around him with his blade. A long ripple furrowed the water under the cabin windows.

Sesto turned and clawed his way through the water towards the door. He felt a weight of pressure against his legs and turned in time to see a huge, blue-white shape surging towards him, just under the surface, water rolling like boiling glass back across its sleek form.

Screaming, he lunged his sword at it and drove it away. An instant later, it was back, powering all ten paces of itself towards his legs. He saw one black, glaring eye and a flash of thumb-sized, triangular teeth.

There was a loud bang and the water went red, and then began to explode into berserk foam.

'Come thee to me!' Ymgrawl shouted from the doorway, holding out a gnarled hand. In his other paw, a flintlock pistol smoked.

Sesto scrambled towards him as the blue-white shape thrashed out its death agonies behind him.

'YOU WERE LUCKY,' said Luka Silvaro. 'This ship has become a place of death and all the eaters of the seas have gathered to feed here.'

Sesto didn't feel lucky. He was still gagging up filthy water, sprawled on the sloping deck where Ymgrawl had dragged him.

'What chance made it a place of death?' Roque wondered, and the men around them remained silent. They were all thinking the same thing.

There was a low rumble. The day was going, and ahead of the settling evening, a mauve darkness had filled the southern sky. The daily threat of a storm was levelling again, but from the look of the heavens it might actually break this time.

'We must row back, captain,' Benuto said.

There was worry in the bo'sun's voice. If the long-promised storm did indeed break this night, they would be stranded on the island for its duration. 'I would not be here o'er night, so tell,' he added.

Luka nodded at this council, briefly touching the gold ring in his ear and the iron of his belt buckle as luck charms. The sea breeze had got up a little, flapping the trailing lines and tattered yards of the ruined ship, and bellying the intact sails, making them crack and thump. It cooled the Reivers' skins too, but it was not refreshing. More like a warning chill.

'Let us back to the boats,' Luka said dismally. The sight of his old rival's ruin had affected him more than he cared to admit.

With no small measure of grateful relief, the men turned back to clamber into the longboats.

'Captain!'

They looked round. The call had come from Chinzo, one of Roque's men-at-arms, a swarthy fellow with a sock-cap, a drooping walrus moustache and arms like a wrestler. He pointed a stubby, dirty nailed finger at the line of beach in the cove beyond the wreck of the *Sacramento*. Litter from the ship's downfall lay scattered on the sand in the gentle fan of breakers. Sesto could see nothing of significance, but Luka clearly had.

'To the shore, before we return,' he ordered. Many of the men, especially Tende and Benuto, groaned.

'To the shore!' Luka insisted.

THEY ROWED THE longboats across the short stretch of shallows between the *Sacramento*'s sunken stern and the beach, and hauled the sturdy wooden craft up onto the sand. With the boats sitting safe and askew on their keels, the oars piled inside them, the men spread out along the hem of the surf. The breeze was stronger and colder here, blowing straight in between the promontories of the cove from the open sea. Sesto took a look at the dimming southern sky again and saw the glowering darkness as it gathered. The sky at sunset was the colour of amethyst, but there was a fulminous blackness staining through it that was not the approaching night.

The shore party wandered the breakers, studying the debris washed up there. Some pieces of wreckage were limp, drowned corpses, lifting and flopping in the waves. Seabirds, raucous and unwilling to share their loot, flapped and circled around Luka's searchers.

'What did he see?' Sesto asked.

'Who?' replied Luka.

'Chinzo? What did he see? We really should be getting back. It looks like a storm.'

Luka sniffed. 'It is, and we should.'

'Then what?'

Luka led him up the beach to where more debris lay. A torn wine skin. An empty jar. Other nondescript junk.

'See?'

'Litter has washed ashore,' said Sesto, shrugging. 'We could see that from the ship.'

Luka sighed. 'Use those sharp eyes, Sesto. What is this?' He pointed to the pieces of rubbish on the sand at their feet.

'Litter.'

'And that?' Luka pointed down towards the breakers where the others stood.

'More litter, washed ashore.'

'And this?' He pointed again, apparently at nothing but the sand of the beach. Sesto stared and eventually realised that what Luka was pointing to was the vague mark that separated the smooth, wet silt of the lower beach from the dimpled, drier sand that composed the dunes all the way to the threatening gloom of the tree line.

This, apart from at times of gales and storms, was the furthest point the sea came up the beach. The furthest point any piece of litter could have been washed up.

'Someone survived,' Luka said. 'Someone's here.'

VIII

THE FOURTEEN MEN of the shore party spread themselves out
down the length of the lonely beach as the light failed, and
hallooed up into the trees of the lush forest that coated the
steep island above them. The thick, emerald undergrowth
smoked with moisture vapour and rang with the cries of
parakeets and cockatelles. Luka was bent on waiting as long
as he dared in the hope that they might yet find some survivor.

Daylight became a cold, grey half-light. There was no gold
or heat left in the world, it seemed to Sesto, and every hue
and contrast had blanched into a bloodless place of shadows and pale whites. Beyond the promontories and the
spectral hulk of the wreck, the sky was ink black and the
increasingly loud rumbling in the air was now accompanied
by sparking forks of lightning. The wind had picked up and
driven the seabirds from the beach. The waves along the
shore broke harder and more fiercely than before.

'Another quarter hour of light,' Luka told the men, 'then we
row. Zazara, Tall Willm… you stay with the boats and trim
the lanterns. The rest of you, let's look as deep as we dare.'

Sidearms drawn, the rest of the party edged up into the damp fringes of the island's forest. The air was cooling here, but not as fast as out in the open, and consequently thick mists of vapour frothed out of the darkness and trailed between the tree trunks.

Sesto had been into tropical forest before, but always in daylight, when it was a vital place of heat, musk perfume, busy insects and dappled patterns of light and shade. After dark, it was a dank, smoky place of gloom, cold sweat and skeletal leaf shadows. Creeper-coiled trees loomed over him in silhouette, their lank vine loops heavy, like fat, slumbering serpents. There was a stink of cold sap and leaf mould. Unseen leaf edges cut his knuckles and thighs like hanging blades. He could see no further than the width of a deck. To his left, Chinzo and Leopaldo moved forward through the steam, to his right, off in a line, Benuto, Pepy and the scrawny rating known as Saint Bones. There was no sign of Ymgrawl the boucaner, but Sesto knew he would be close by, lurking like a phantom – or a footpad's dagger – close to Sesto's back.

Night insects clicked and ticked in the dripping cold. Gauzy things, some glowing like fireflies, meandered through the vapour. Black, many-legged shapes scuttled across treebark from shadow to shadow.

Luka reached a bank of earth too steep for trees, and struggled up into a small clearing that afforded him a look back over the forest he had ascended through into the cove. It was getting very dark, and lightning was cracking with mounting fury in the south. He could see the melancholy shape of the *Sacramento*, but not the beach, as the forest obscured it.

Roque scrambled up behind him, followed by Tende, Jager and Delgado. Luka could hear the others shouting as they came up through the trees.

The master of the Reivers looked up at the sky as the first spots of rain fell. He'd left it too long, like a fool, like a fool…

At once, the rain began to pelt down, the heavy, stinging drops of an equatorial deluge. A westerly gale, like a wall of frozen air, rushed in across Isla Verde, thrashing the forest cover like a sea in flood. Pieces of leaf and twig flew up into their faces through the slanting downpour. The rain was so heavy, he could no longer see the *Sacramento*, or even the cove. Down below was a tearing, swaying forest and then nothing but blackness and the curtain of rain.

And a screaming voice.

It rose above the din of the encroaching storm for a moment, piercing, and then was lost.

'Hellsteeth!' Luka cried, glancing once at the startled Roque before the pair of them began to slither and leap back down the slope. Tende and the other men followed. The slope was awash already, fluid as mucous, gushing with rivulets. Jager lost his feet and slid down on his belly. Luka slipped a few paces from the trees and tumbled, crashing into a thorny cypress and gashing his cheek and palms. Tende came down alongside him, his boots plastered with mire, rainwater glinting on his black skin like uncut diamonds. He reached out a massive hand and pulled his captain back onto his feet.

Roque scrabbled past them and descended into the forest, shouting out the names of the men still down in the dark.

Deep in the trees, Sesto darted left and right, his sword drawn. The awful scream had come from nearby, but now he could see no one and nothing except the dark leaves and the water cascading down through them. The rain clattered like drumbones across the forest canopy over his head, and all around him, the trees swayed, gasped and creaked in the typhoon wind.

'Hello!' he cried. 'Hello anyone!'

He saw a man up ahead, a brief suggestion of a figure in the turmoil, and battled through towards him. By the time he reached the spot where the man had been, there was no one there.

Had there ever been?

Sesto felt a crawling fear, as if this entire isle might be cursed.

Thunder exploded overhead, and lightning strobed the chaotic forest into a brief, fierce chiaroscuro of black leaves and white air. For a second, that thunder-split second, he saw the figure again, off to his left, and resolved a haggard face in shadow, the white of grinning teeth, the black socket holes of a kaput mortem.

The bony visage of King Death.

Sesto gasped in terror, but at the next flash, the figure had gone. Sesto scrambled away through the undergrowth, hoping he was heading for the beach.

The figure rose up suddenly in front of him, and Sesto slashed out with his sword. The blade rang hard against a cut-less blade.

'Put up thy pig-stick!' Ymgrawl yelled above the storm.

'I saw–' Sesto began.

'What? What didst thee see?' the boucaner snarled, dragging Sesto on by the collar.

'I don't know. Something. A daemon.'

Ymgrawl stopped and checked himself, touching gold, bone and iron – a ring, a necklace and a button – to ward away the evil.

'Care o'er thy tongue, for it spits ill luck!' he hissed. 'Did thee scream out?'

'Scream?'

'Just that past minute or more?'

'N-no! I heard the scream and was looking for the source when I saw the… the…' Sesto swallowed hard and touched iron himself. It was difficult to make himself heard over the raging elements.

They pressed on, assaulted by the storm driven forest. After another minute or so, Ymgrawl hollered out, and Sesto saw Benuto, Saint Bones and Pepy coming towards them, heads down.

'Who screamed?' Benuto yelled.

'Not us, bo'sun!' Ymgrawl replied.

'Where be Chinzo and Leopaldo?' Pepy shouted.

There was another eye-wincing flash of lightning and an ear splitting peal of thunder. The stunning display heralded the appearance of Roque and Jager.

'What see you?' demanded the master-at-arms at the top of his voice.

'Not a hell-damned thing!' Benuto shouted back.

'There!' sang out Saint Bones who, from the top-basket of the *Rumour*, could spy a sail at twenty sea miles. 'I saw a man!'

'Where?' snarled Roque.

'In the trees there, just there!' Saint Bones insisted. 'But he is gone now…'

Together now, the drenched and shaken men moved forward, calling out. They came down the slope, across a gushing stream that had not been there on the way up, through a grove of cycads and swaying date palms, hacking back vines that swung at them from the moving trees.

In the next root cavity, swollen with water, they found Leopaldo. He lay on his back, pressed down into the wet, black earth. From his hairline to his waist, the front of him had been torn away. Some massive, clawed forest beast had done this. Some daemon from the cursed dark.

Ten paces away, Chinzo was sprawled on his side against a tree trunk. His sword lay beside him in the mud, broken in two. He was dead, but there was not a mark on him.

Roque turned the body and Sesto saw Chinzo's face. He knew in a moment that Chinzo, brawny warrior that he was, had died of pure terror. He also knew he would never, ever forget the look on that dead face.

'Get to the boats!' Roque yelled over the constant storm.

'We cannot row in this!' Jager cried in dismay.

'Get to the damn boats anyway!' Roque retorted.

They turned to move.

The figure was behind them.

It was there and yet not there, flickering in and out of the darkness as the lightning flashed. To Sesto – to them all – it looked like a pirate mark come to life: a crude, white figure of dead bones stitched to a black cloth.

It smiled, and the smile broadened, and broadened still into a screaming skull mouth. The howl, partly the sound of a man in agony, partly the sound of an enraged animal, and partly the sound of angry, swarming insects, drowned out the storm. A rotten breath of putrefaction assailed them. The figure raised its arms as it howled, long, bony arms, impossibly long, famine thin, ending in spider fingers as sharp as sail-cloth needles.

It came for them, whip fast, stinking of grave rot. Roque and Saint Bones lashed at it with their swords and both were struck aside, flying back into the air away from it like a vodou bocoor's puppets. Ymgrawl threw himself headlong and brought Sesto down hard, avoiding the next slicing rake of the daemon's needled hands.

Jager was nothing like so fortunate. The daemon slammed its taloned fists together in a clap that caught the rating's head between them. Jager's skull burst like a ripe pumpkin.

Benuto and Pepy, the last men standing, opened fire into the face of death. Both men had three primed pistols apiece strung about them on ribbon sashes, and Pepy had an additional pepperpot piece tucked into his waistband. They fired each gun in turn, dropping them loose on their sashes to grab the next. Every ball hit him with a meaty slap. When his sash-guns were spent, Pepy wrenched out the pepperpot and blasted it at the daemon, point blank.

It killed him anyway, plunging its needle fingers into his face. Benuto fell on his back in terror, crying out prayers of deliverance as the thing stepped up to tower over him.

Luka Silvaro burst out of the storm.

He hacked his sword into the daemon, striking it again and again before it could balance and turn, like a woodsman chopping at a tree.

It reeled at him and lunged but, by then, Tende was at its other hand, swiping with his long-handled Ebonian axe. As it turned, Delgado attacked too, firing a wheel-lock pistol with one hand and thrusting with his tulwar.

The daemon circled and howled again, fending off the three-cornered assault. It slapped and swung with its elongated arms, trying to find a target mark.

Then it pounced. It leapt forward like a cat and buried the screaming Delgado beneath its rending, long-shanked bulk.

'Move!' Luka bellowed. 'Move!'

The survivors started to run. Ymgrawl and Sesto, Tende, Benuto, Saint Bones supporting the dazed Roque, and Luka himself. It seemed to Sesto an act of cowardice and callous fear to use Delgado's fate as a chance to flee, but he did anyway. This was jungle, cursed jungle, and the rules here were dog eat dog and every man for himself.

Delgado's ghastly, fluctuating screams echoed after them as they ran, and then were lost in the storm.

The seven remaining men broke from the forest line and onto the beach. Rain was sheeting down and the storm was locked, frenzied, above the cove. Breakers slammed into the beach. The fleeing men saw lights ahead.

Tall Willm and Zazara were cowering beside the long-boats with lanterns lit. They'd dragged the beached craft right up from the crashing waterline, almost to the trees. The men fell in amongst them, panting and shaking.

'What happened?' Tall Willm piped, lowering his musket.

'Hell happened,' said Ymgrawl.

Luka, shaken to the core, checked the men. Terror and palpitations aside, everyone was intact, except Roque. He was semi-conscious and feverish. One of the daemon's needle talons was embedded in his left shoulder.

'That cannot stay,' Tende muttered. 'Fell magic poison soaks it.'

'Do it!' Luka snapped. He was already looking back down the beach and checking the tree line for signs of daemonic pursuit. 'Ygrawl! Bo'sun! Get into the lea of the boats and load all the guns we have!'

Benuto and the boucaner scrambled under the upturned shell of one of the longboats and started priming weapons in the dry, out of the wind and rain. Saint Bones gathered firearms from the survivors and passed them in under the lip of the boat.

Sesto watched the activity, trying to calm his racing pulse. Tende carefully heated a dirk in the flames of a lamp wick and then swiftly and brutally cut the needle from Roque's wound. The Estalian didn't even cry out. The helmsman seemed reluctant to touch the needle. He grasped it with Benuto's bullet-mold press and tossed it away into the storm as soon as it was out.

'What was it?' Sesto asked Luka, shielding his face from the gale.

'The daemon? Oh, I knew it.' Luka turned away and beckoned to Tende. 'We'll not last the night here,' he said. 'We can't row out until the storm has died, and my marrow tells me that will not be before dawn. In the meantime, that daemon will come and kill us here.'

Tende looked away, troubled by something Sesto didn't understand.

'You know what I'm asking, old friend,' Luka said.

'I cannot, Luka. I have sworn that all away, the day I joined the *Rumour*.'

'But you still know!'

'I know. You do not forget these things…'

'Then for me… for these souls here…'

'Luka…'

'Tende… Remember the covens of Miragliano… Semper De Deos… the temple at Mahrak… the ash grey Shores of Dreaded Wo… all those deeds, all those adventures. I stood by you then. I ask this of you now.'

The massive Ebonian nodded. He walked away from them, and started to pace out a wide circle around the huddle of men and the drawn-up boats. Sesto saw he was kicking the sand, gale blown as it was, to scribe a pattern on the ground.

Tende did this for almost half an hour, all of which time Sesto spent watching the trees and quaking with terror. Every now and then, above the storm, he heard the howl, the insect buzz, the dire sound of the daemon that stalked them.

Tende rejoined them, cutting his left palm with his dagger and marking with his blood the sides of the boats with strange sigils that Sesto shuddered to look at. He marked each man in turn too – Sesto resisted his touch until he was brought up by an angry bark from Luka. With the Ebonian close, Sesto could hear what he had not heard before. The helmsman was muttering soft, necromantic incantations against the night.

Then Tende dropped to his knees in the centre of the circle, chanting louder and more forcefully.

'Have a care!' Benuto cried.

By then, all the men except the comatose Roque were crouching at the edges of Tende's ring, arms ready, watching the dark as the storm blew down across them.

They all looked as Benuto pointed.

The daemon had arrived.

IT WAS LURCHING down the beach towards them on all fours, trotting like a limping wolf.

'Are you set?' Luka called to Tende. The Ebonian helmsman continued to chant, ignoring his captain, his back to the loping fiend that bore down on them.

'Tende! Are you ready?' Luka repeated more urgently.

The thing came on. Zazara vomited in terror and Tall Willm gasped 'Manann's tears!' and raised his musket to fire.

Luka dragged the barrel down. 'No! Don't break the circle!'

The daemon reached them. Sesto felt his bowels turn to ice as it prowled around them, as if not daring to cross the invisible line that Tende had marked. He could smell its fetid corruption. It bounded around the circle on all fours, whining and grinning. It was so big, so thin, so hideous.

'Tende?' Luka hissed, covering it with his pistol.

Tende stopped chanting and rose up to join them, averting his eyes from the daemon. 'My dear friend Luka,' he said, 'I hope you are ready. This is what you asked for.'

Sesto felt his spine crawl as if bugs were scuttling up it. He writhed, his ears popping. The storm raged and–

–ceased. Silence suddenly. No wind. Blackness was still all around. Pelting rain was frozen in the air as if arrested by the gods. The scene was illuminated by a lightning flash that had begun but never ended.

The daemon hesitated.

Incandescent green phantoms came spiralling out of the sea behind it, out of the deep oceans. They flashed and glowed, writhing like snakes in the stilled air, and fell upon the daemon.

It grunted and hissed as they tore into it, pinning its limbs and pulling it down. Some of the lambent green phantoms were like coiled wyrms, others writhed like squids, others like stunted, naked men with heads like goats. Some had no heads at all, just thick outcrops of twisted horns. They swarmed over the daemon, clawing, ripping, bearing down on its struggling limbs.

In the breathless hush, Luka looked out of the circle and said, 'Hello, Reyno.'

The daemon shook and growled under the weight of the glowing phantoms that held it fast. One of the goat heads got its fingers into the daemon's mouth and pried it open.

'Hello, Luka,' the daemon said, its voice like metal scraping stone.

'What happened to you, my brother?'

'Evil happened. Pure evil…'

'Tell me, Reyno! Tell me!'

The daemon gurgled. 'The Butcher Ship did this to me. It murdered my beloved *Sacramento* and slaughtered the crew, and with its final curse made me into this!'

'I'm sorry, Reyno.'

'Sorry? Sorry?' the daemon's aching sob echoed down the unnaturally stilled beach. 'I am sorry for Delgado and Jager and Pepy and all the other sound men of your crew I have preyed on this night. I did not mean to…'

The voice trailed away.

'Reyno? Are you still there?' Luka called. The phantoms Tende had summoned fought to keep the daemon trapped. After a while, the daemon's voice floated back.

'Luka? I can't see you any more. What will become of me?'

Luka looked at Tende. The Ebonian shook his head.

'Reyno? Tell me about the Butcher Ship.'

'What about it?'

'Tell me everything you know.'

'Henri of Breton is the Butcher. Red Henri, the thrice cursed. He did this to me. He did this to me!'

'Henri? Red Henri? How can it be true that my old friend is the Butcher?' Luka snarled.

'How can it be true that your old friend Reyno is a blood-hungry daemon? Eh? Flee, Luka! Flee! Henri's warship the *Kymera* is the butchering ship, and it spits venom from its guns these days instead of shot. Venom! Look at me!'

The wrenching daemon threw off several of the phantoms and rose up before Luka, the remaining phantoms trying to pull him down.

'Luka…'

'Reyno…'

Tende looked at his captain. 'I can't hold him much longer.'

Without looking back, Luka nodded. 'Finish this.'

Tende began to chant.

Luka remained fixed, staring into the daemon's fathomless eyes.

'Goodbye, Reyno, my old friend.'

The phantoms coiled and renewed their attack. They swarmed all over the daemon and began to pull it apart.

The daemon – cursed Reyno – screamed as the phantoms shredded it. Its lingering howl lasted long after time unfroze and the gale began again.

AT DAWN, THE storm passed, they rowed the longboats back to the *Rumour* and the *Safire*, which had rode out the night's tumult at anchor.

As they clambered back aboard, Sesto noticed something inexplicable about Tende. The big Ebonian seemed smaller than he had before. Almost as if he had been shrunk and diminished by the sorcery he had been forced to use in order to save them.

The ships made ready to depart. Prayers and charm offerings were made to the memory of the *Rumour*'s lost souls. Luka rowed back into the cove with jars of lamp oil, and set a torch to the wreck. As if grateful for the cleansing flames, the ship's decks combusted swiftly, and flames leapt up into the billowing yards.

'What happens now?' Sesto asked Luka.

'Now we hunt for the *Kymera*.'

'Just like that?'

'Yes, just like that.'

The *Rumour* turned north-west, the *Safire* at her heels. Behind them, in the lonely cove of Isla Verde, the *Sacramento* blazed the bright tongues of its funeral pyre up into the morning sky.

JUNIO THE STOREKEEPER, may the four winds rest him, had been a man of methodical practice and scrupulous measure, and under his stewardship, the *Rumour* had been fully provisioned with clean drinking water, ale and edibles. But Junio the storekeeper was several weeks dead.

His duties had fallen to Benuto, the bo'sun, and Fahd, the cook, in the way that a drunken man falls between two seats at a table. Gello, the lug-eared boy who had served as Junio's pantryman, had tried to take up the slack, but he had not enough person about him to make himself heard. He was a gawky lad, with freckled skin that the sun punished terribly, and his ears, which abutted his head like a pair of staysails in full weather, were such a source of jokes that he could not appear on deck but to be mocked. To his credit, Gello made several attempts to alert the master to the growing deficiencies, but no one paid him any mind. He had, as it might be said, no one's ear, which was passing strange, as he had ears enough of his own.

Matters finally came to a head on the morning of the twenty-ninth day of sailing. It was before ten of the day, and

the air was cool and brisk. Hot promise of stillness lingered
in the edge of the sky, and the sea glittered, but there was a
firm so'wester and plenty of air to fill the yards. They were
threading through the maze of islets and reefs that decorated the Estalian littoral, as they had been since the grim
matter of the *Sacramento*, and no sail or face had they seen
but for their own.

Sesto, who had been awake for several hours, tucked
away against the foremast with a book of histories, heard
voices raised, and went aft. Fahd was by the deck barrels,
arguing famously with Largo the sailmaker. Neither man
was large: both were wizened and hunched by age, weather
and profession, but Sesto would not have crossed either
one of them. The scale of their invective shamed typhoons
for force. Largo retched out malingering curses and those
barbed Tilean-style insults which slurred Fahd's family
members, the chastity of relevant women and the shape of
several beards. Fahd, in turn, cited dubious parentage and
unfortunate genital quandaries, all the while interspersing
colourful Arabyan oaths, the sort of things that, when
translated, lost all their poisonous force and meant something like, 'I hit you on the head with a spoon, you
monkey!'

Several crewmen gathered to watch the curse-fight, some
clapping, some laughing. Sesto was askance. He sensed it
was about to turn ugly.

Or, at the very least, uglier.

Largo informed the esteemed Arabyan that a donkey bearing such a remarkable similarity to Fahd's mother that it
probably was, in point of fact, Fahd's mother, had enjoyed
a night of uncivilised congress with three of his brothers,
and drew his long, round-nosed hemp blade.

Fahd – declaring Largo a panting dog that had eaten a cat,
and the cat had farted (often) and now Largo also smelled
of cat fart, and he was also a snail with a funny face, which
Fahd would crush with the heel of his slipper, if he could be
half-bothered – slid out his carving knife.

'I think this has gone far enough!' Sesto exclaimed, stepping between them.

'Go boil your arse in birdshite, dung-eater, for then it will
smell as good as your sister's frequently visited underparts,'

snarled Largo, raising the hemp blade, which was as long as Sesto's shin bone.

'I will strike your brow repeatedly with the slack and underused parts of a bear!' Fahd promised, hefting the flesh-slice, which was as wide as Sesto's wrist.

There was a thunderclap of gunpowder, and everyone started out of their skins. Lowering a discharged caliver, wreathed in white smoke, Roque walked into the confrontation.

'Put them away,' he told the combative pair.

Fahd and Largo reluctantly sheathed their blades.

Roque smiled. It was a pleasure to see such an expression on his face. Since the long, hideous night on Isla Verde, he had been pale and withdrawn from his injury, and had lost a great deal of weight. The smile reminded Sesto of the Roque he had first met.

'Explain,' Roque said.

They did. Loudly and against each other, so their words overlapped and turned into shouts. Roque thumbed back the caliver's lock, carefully primed it from his powder flask and then fired it again.

The blast was dizzying.

'Explain… one at a time. Fahd?'

The water butts, explained the Arabyan, were knocking dry, and all the clean drinking was gone. In his opinion, Largo had been pailing up water to stretch and soften his cloth. Not at all, Largo countered when Roque looked at him. The reverse was, in fact, the truth. He had come for a ladle of wet to moisten up a sail hem, and discovered that Fahd had guzzled all the water away for his malodorous stews.

Roque checked the barrels. Nothing came up but sour dredges.

Silvaro was called. He checked the barrels in turn and registered the same. Only then did anyone ask Gello.

All vittals were low, the boy explained. During the tangle with Ru'af, five water cisterns had been holed and drained, and a goodly lot of foodstuffs burned. They were dry, and down to hardtack. 'Something I've been trying to explain,' Gello added.

Belissi, the carpenter, was called to mend the water butts, but that would not fill them. There were wells and springs on some of the islets, though none good enough for more than a pail or two.

Silvaro called to Benuto. Their hunting had to cease for a while. Provisioning had become a necessity.

PORTO REAL WAS the surest bet. Silvaro would have preferred to make for the Isla d'Azure and the pirate-friendly harbour there, but the way the wind was running discouraged such thoughts. Porto Real would have to do. A colony of the Estalian crown, it lay a little to their south on one of the largest islands of the archipelago.

So it was, and not before time, the *Rumour* and the *Safire* came around the Cap d'Orient and turned into the bay, towards the lights of Porto Real. They had been at sea for three and a half weeks.

IT WAS EVENING, equatorially warm and shadow-blue. There were no ships in the harbour. From the rail, Sesto saw over half a dozen brigs and barques careened up on the bone-white foreshore in the dusk, hull-bellies tipped towards the stars like basking sea lions, masts pushed over on the lea like wind blown elms. It had been the same in Sartosa. Sea-faring men, even the toughest of the rogues, had fled the sea this season. The Butcher Ship was out there, stalking any and all. It wasn't safe, for neither pirate nor merchant. Safer by far was to hole up in an island town or a friendly port and drink the summer out, no matter the loss of earnings.

Estalian banners hung limply from yard poles on the quay, as if admitting, with a lacklustre shrug, the sovereignty of the colony town. Batteries of culverin covered the harbour from little headland redoubts, but they were unmanned, though the firebaskets hanging above them had been lit.

The town itself, as it faced the sea, was a mix of lime wash and clay brick, in the Estalian manner. In the higher part of the town, lanes ran up to a little garrison fort, beyond which rose lush green hills.

'Quiet,' said Silvaro simply, watching the harbour line slowly approach.

'Not so,' said Casaudor, and pointed. Figures had appeared on the quay and the runway, and around the heads of the town streets where they reached the harbour-side. Shadows in the dying light, but people nonetheless.

'We must be a rare sight, so tell,' Benuto muttered. 'Like as much, they've not seen a sail in weeks.'

They dropped anchor a few hundred spans from the quay, and the *Safire* nestled in under their shadow. Silvaro called for a boat crew, and beckoned Roque and Sesto to come.

'We may need your airs and graces,' he told Sesto as they went down into the waiting boat.

By the time they came up the eroded stone steps onto the quay, the silent crowds had all but vanished. They could see lamplight coming from the buildings near the harbour, but there were no sounds of laughter or of music.

Roque, Sesto and Silvaro advanced together into the town, unnerved by its hush. The land heat was oppressive, and their clothes stuck to them.

Along the harbour end and down the main street, doors and window shutters stood open. Lamps burned within. In silence, as if weighted down by fatigue in the night heat, men, women and children sat on doorsteps, or lurked inside at tables. Some looked sullenly out at the three new-comers as they walked past. Many did not. Every doorway and window seemed to reveal a little yellow-lit cave in which weary people sat in torpor. Even the dogs lay panting in the dust.

They passed an inn where men sat at tables, clutching thick-lipped glasses full of drink that looked like tar or syrup in the golden light. Everything seemed brown and faded, like an old painting hung too long in the sun. The drinkers were all silent too, and slouched: glasses on tables, hands around glasses, bodies sunk back on chairs.

Silvaro stopped and gestured his companions into the bar. A few heads swung round slowly to watch them pass. A few murmurs. The bar owner stood at the back of the room, unwashed glasses lined up on the bartop. He was leaning against the back wall, as if cowed by the heat.

'Three cups of rum,' Silvaro said in decent Estalian. The barman stirred and picked three little snifter glasses from a shelf. The rum looked almost black in the gloom as it poured into the glasses, and it seemed as reluctant to leave the bottle as the man had been to move.

'You're from the ships?' the bar man asked. He spoke Estalian, but with the rounded vowels of a man born in Tobaro. The islands were home to men of all compass points, no matter the flags they wore. His voice was slow, a tired whisper.

'We are,' said Luka.

'There was excitement when your sails were seen,' the barman said. 'Porto Real is a merchant town, and its lifeblood runs from the sea, but you are not merchants. That much we saw.'

'We are not.' Silvaro lifted his glass and took a sip. 'To the crown of Estalia,' he toasted politely. Sesto and Roque drank too. The rum burned, and its wetness was fat with sugar. It was like watered molasses.

Silvaro put a small silver coin on the bar. 'But there is trade in us. Victuals. Water. We can pay.'

'This can be arranged,' the barman said, picking up the coin.

'Where is the harbour master?'

The man shrugged. 'At this hour? Asleep or drunk or both.'

Roque glanced up and cocked his head. In another second, Sesto heard it too. Hooves clattering on the street outside.

'They'll be looking for you,' the barman said.

Silvaro and his companions went back out into the street. Three riders were slowing their horses to a walk. The men wore the breastplates and comb morion helmets of Estalian soldiers. They were looking out into the harbour towards the shadow of the *Rumour*, still visible in the heavy night.

Silvaro hailed them, and they turned. The leader, a tall man wearing black beneath his polished armour, dismounted and tossed his reins to one of the others.

'Those are fighting ships,' he announced in strong Estalian. 'Plunder ships.'

'They are,' Silvaro agreed, 'and I am their master.'

The man nodded, a formal bow. It was a gesture rather than a courtesy, the sort of movement a man would make before a sword bout. 'I am Ferrol, first sword of the Porto, instrument of the governor. Who is it I address?'

'I am Captain Luka Silvaro.'

There was a brisk, raking sound of steel. Ferrol and his mounted lackeys drew their rapiers with abrupt speed. 'Luka Silvaro? Silvaro the Hawk? Master of the Reivers?'

'Thrice counted,' Luka smiled. He glanced at his companions. Roque's blade was half drawn and Sesto's hand was on his pommel. 'Put them up,' he advised.

He took a step forward, apparently fearless for his own safety. The sword in Ferrol's hand was long and basket hilted, with a straight blade of the finest watered steel.

'Sir,' said Luka. 'I have business in Porto Real, not mischief. Had I meant the colony harm, I would have been dashing the harbourside with chain shot from my two fighting ships, not standing here unarmed.'

'You're a pirate and a rogue,' Ferrol replied.

'I am a captain and a master, seeking victuals from a friendly port, and moreover, I have coin to pay. There is another thing...' Luka reached into his doublet and produced a roll of parchment. He held it out to Ferrol.

The man took it cautiously. He unrolled it and read it over.

'A letter of marque and reprisal, signed and sealed by his grace, the Prince of Luccini. My business is official and legitimate, as my associate here can vouch.'

Sesto moved forward. 'My lord the prince has engaged me to vouch for Captain Silvaro's good bearing. I express respectful greeting to his excellency the governor, and trust the good and ancient friendship that exists between the sovereignties of Luccini and Estalia holds true.'

Ferrol handed the papers back and sheathed his sword. His men put their weapons away. 'Prepare a list of your needs, and a price will be determined. Once it is agreed, I will issue you with a permit to obtain the goods. Your men may come ashore, no more than two dozen at a time. Any trouble will be censured by colonial law. That means me. I am first sword, and also the colony's legal executioner. I will not allow brute behaviour.'

'Nor should you,' said Silvaro. 'I thank you. My crew will be a model of good humour.'

IT WAS EARLY still, not even eight of the clock. The night was as dark and hot now as if a damp cloak had been drawn over the sky with the sun still in it. There was no relief from the humid warmth. Silvaro sent the boat back to the *Rumour* to fetch Casaudor, and to draw, by straws, the first two dozen for shore leave. Roque, Sesto and Silvaro waited for a while in the stifling bar, but the lethargy became too draining, so they purchased a bottle of muscat and retired to the harbour wall, supping in a pass-around and relishing the meagre sea breeze that came in across the water.

Longboats came back from the *Rumour*, three of them this time. Casaudor came up first, clutching the slates of requirements he and Fahd had been drawing up. Gello was with him. Casaudor had job enough being master mate, and had decided to get Junio's apprentice up to speed. Behind them came the lucky straws. Eight men from the *Rumour*, four from the *Safire*. Sesto didn't know the *Safire*'s men, except the ship's master, Silke.

Chance – or more likely rank-pulling – had made sure Silke was one of the first ashore. His broad frame was wrapped in a yellow tunic of Arabyan silk, painted with clover leaf designs in cochineal, and he sported a purple slouch cap over his seven-pigtailed coiffure.

Sesto knew the men from the *Rumour*. Vento, the sailmaker, Zazara, Small Willm (as opposed to Tall Willm, whose straw had been unlucky), Runcio and Lupresso. The sixth man surprised him. It was Sheerglas, the master gunner. Sesto had never seen that spectre of a man above decks, let alone on shore. He wore long robes of black, as if attending a funeral.

'Two hours,' Silvaro told the visitors. 'Then change smartly for the next boats. And make no trouble, or you'll hear from me.'

The men began to disperse into the quiet town.

Casaudor and Gello brought the slates over and were discussing them with Luka when horsemen rode up onto the quay, escorting two carriages. The carriages were ornate and once-fine, their carved decorations covered in gilt that was flaking away in the salt air. Each one was drawn by a six horse team, and their lamps blazed like mast-lightning in the dark.

The outriders were all Estalian soldiers in comb helms, carrying spears upright at the saddle bow. Ferrol dismounted.

He came to Luka and bowed. 'His excellency the governor Emeric Gorge invites you to dine with him this night. He makes the invitation as a gesture of hospitality to the servants of his grace, the Prince of Luccini.'

'I am honoured by the invitation,' Luka said. 'How many does it extend to?'

'All of you,' Ferrol replied.

Luka left Casaudor and Gello to get on with arrangements. A few drowsy looking merchants had been persuaded out of their town houses to haggle prices. The rest of the *Rumour* men boarded the coaches with Luka.

All except Sheerglas, Sesto noted, who had disappeared.

XI

THE CARRIAGES, LAMPS gleaming in the tropical night, took them out of the sleeping town and up into the hills. After weeks of sea life, such conveyance was very strange to all of them. The coaches shook and rattled in a way a ship never did, not even in a tempest. Every rut and crevice in the roadway made them jump and clatter. The coach interiors – faded velvet and polished oak – were well-lit with sconced lanterns, and made little worlds of firelight that reminded Sesto unpleasantly of the tired scenes of melancholy he'd viewed through the windows in the town. He'd managed to get a window seat, and the compartments of the carriages were cramped. The men, some of them the roughest, rudest ratings, were gabbing excitedly. The ride, and the dinner that awaited them – with the island governor no less – was a once in a lifetime jolly.

Sesto looked out at the rolling landscape: dark fields under a moonless gloom. It had been a long time since he'd ridden in a state carriage, or any carriage. Outside, the crickets brisked louder than the beating hooves and the rattle of wooden wheels. Sugar cane plantations and plantain rows, dry and coarse, reached away into the humid night.

He was thirsty. The rum he'd drunk caked his throat like bitumen-caulk. He longed for clean drinking.

THE GOVERNOR'S MANSION stood on the brow of an inland hill, gazing out over the plantations and woodland that fed both it and the island. It was a red brick edifice, palatially fronted and decorated with the influence of Araby, as Estalian fashion had much favoured a century or so before. Red bougainvillea draped the nearby trees. Candles flickered at every window in the facade, and torches and braziers, gushing sparks into the night, had been arranged in the court yard. Moths, in their hundreds, circled the lights. As the Reivers dismounted from the coaches, many of them awestruck at the faded grandeur of the place, they heard music playing from within. Pipes, a viol, a spinnet. This was living like they'd never known.

Ferrol, a striding, purposeful figure in black, led them into the hallway, where they stood on polished marble and gazed up at glittering chandeliers. On the walls, gilt-edged mirrors of stupendous quality and size alternated with portraits of Estalian nobles. Goateed men in ruffs, bosomy ladies with skins like chalk, children in silk pantaloons. Every painted eye seemed to follow them.

'Of all the men I expected to welcome to my home, Luka Silvaro is about the last,' said a rich, soft voice.

The governor of Porto Real, Emeric Gorge, stepped into the hall. He was an old man, completely bald, his dry white skin creased with age and drawn tight across his lean face. His eyes were bright. He wore red velvet doublet and hose, and a cape of white silk that was almost painfully clean and spotless. He opened his arms wide. His fingers, clustered with rings, were pale and thin.

'My lord governor,' Luka said, dropping to his knee.

'Rise up, pirate lord... or should that be privateer now?'

'I am the proud bearer of the marque of Luccini,' Luka said, rising.

'The only reason you are welcomed here, to this house and this island.' Gorge chuckled and winked at Luka. 'I'm lying. The chance to dine and converse with the Reiver lord?

Forgive me, but I count that as a luxury. I trust you and your motley followers can regale me with blood-chilling tales of cut-throat daring?'

'We'll do our best,' Luka said. Quickly, he introduced his crew. Sesto was touched by the humble formality shown by the common dog ratings. Men like Zazara and Small Willm doffed their scarf-caps and bent their knees. The Reivers were on best behaviour.

Silke did not fawn. He wanted it known he was a ship master, second only to Silvaro. He preened and conversed agily with the governor when his turn came.

Gorge reached Roque. 'An Estalian brother?' he remarked.

Roque bowed. 'A son of the sea, rather,' he demurred.

'But you have a noble look about you,' Gorge persisted. 'I am reminded of the Della Fortunas, that highborn family. Is their blood in you?'

'I have only a poor freebooter's blood in my veins,' said Roque.

'Aha! We will see.'

'And this is Sesto Sciortini, a gentleman from Luccini,' Luka said at last.

Sesto bowed quickly. Gorge gazed at him, his tiny, pale tongue wetting his drawn lips as if they were too dry.

'Estalia welcomes its friend from across the sea,' Gorge said in perfect Southern Tilean. 'Come, let us feast.'

THE GOVERNOR LED them into a great hall. The roof was three storeys high, and brazier fires around the walls created that golden fire glow that Sesto now associated with lethargy and torpor. The musicians were playing on the balcony, and servants were placing the last of the dishes on the long trestle tables: roast pork, braised fish, spice-stuffed fowl, bowls of steamed vegetables, baked plantains, sugar-glazed fruit, sausage, curd cheese, plates of rice and shrimp. Gorge ushered them all to seats, and stewards began to track back and forth, filling their goblets – silver beakers inscribed with the Estalian coat of arms – with wine and watered rum.

'I want water,' Sesto said.

'Sir?' the steward asked, poised to pour his jug of wine.

'Water. I'm thirsty.'

The steward nodded, and came back with a glass bell-bottle full of cold water.

Sesto filled his glass and drank deep.

'I cannot deny that times have been tight,' Gorge told Luka as they tore into the salted pork. 'My town lives or dies by the process of trade. Ships come in, ships go out. Porto Real turns over. Six months now, trade has been dead. Before tonight, it's four months since a ship put in.'

'I sensed a malaise,' Luka said.

'How so?' Gorge asked, wiping grease from his chin with his napkin.

'In the town. A strange lethargy, as if the heat had sweltered the life out of the citizens.'

Gorge nodded. 'Porto Real is dying. Without trade it is drying up. You'll find you get a good price for your water and victuals. It's a buyer's market.'

He reached out and took a chicken leg from a nearby dish. Liquid sugar dripped off it as he raised it to his mouth.

'There is an illness too.'

'An illness? Plague?' Luka started.

Gorge raised his hand quickly. 'Be of calm heart, Luka Silvaro! I would have had the quay men raise the quarantine flags if plague had entered Porto Real. No, it's something much more subtle. A malingering weakness. A sapping of strength. It might be the heat, or the draining emptiness of the season.'

'I saw it in the faces around me,' Roque said.

Gorge nodded. 'We have been craving newcomers. New arrivals. Fresh blood, so to speak. Anything to enliven our lives. Commerce and intercourse have run dry.'

Luka raised a fat scallop to his mouth on his twin-tined fork. Cooking butter ran down the handle over his fingers. He bit into its flesh. 'Because of the Butcher Ship?' he asked.

'Because of the Butcher Ship, precisely,' Gorge agreed, watching as Luka devoured the scallop. 'That hideous thing is out there, and no ships dare sail. It is a monster, dare I say it… a vampire, sucking the life out of a sea that was once thronging with trade.'

'The Butcher Ship is the reason I have been awarded my letter of marque,' said Luka.

Gorge was impressed. 'You are charged to kill it? Well then. Good luck, Silvaro.'

'Have you seen it?' Luka asked.

'I have heard stories. Better men than you have died facing it. Once, at nightfall three weeks ago, I was called to the quay because yards had been seen. A daemon ship, scarlet like blood, coursed in, took a look at us, and sailed away. I am certain it was the Butcher Ship. The very sight of it terrified me.'

Luka nodded.

'And you're going to hunt it out and sink it?'

'That's the plan,' said Luka Silvaro

Sesto took a swig of his drink. He'd finished the water now, and the steward had been topping him up with wine.

He swilled down some of the wine, and then took a helping of sausage from the nearest dish.

He felt very tired suddenly.

SESTO WOKE WITH a start. His mind was as blurry as a fogbound dawn. He thought he'd been woken by a cry of pain or fear, but it was quiet now.

There was a taste of spices in his mouth, the flavoured meats and sausage of the governor's table. He remembered the meal now, the heat, the cloying damp of the night. He had no memory whatsoever of making his way back to the harbour, let alone returning to the *Rumour* and his bed. The Estalians deserved respect for the potency of their wines.

A sobering anxiety abruptly washed through him. He had no memory of returning to the ship, because he had not done so. Without even opening his eyes, he knew he was still on dry land.

Sesto struggled upright. The room he was in was so pitch black he could not even estimate its size, but from the heat, and the stridulation of the crickets outside, he felt sure he was still in the governor's mansion house. The sounds of snoring breath around him told him he was not alone.

He tried to feel his way around, and bumped into first one and then a second prone body. Neither one roused. Then his hands found the edge of a sideboard cabinet or a table, and from there, the wall. He picked his way along the wall to a corner, then along again until his fingers settled on the metal latch of a door. Cautiously, he drew it open.

The hallway outside was gloomy, but tapers burned in brackets towards the far end, and he started to be able to see his surroundings. He pushed the door open wider and began to resolve features of the room he had woken in. It was a state room of some size, furnished with low chairs and two chaise longues. The Reivers, who had come with him to the banquet, were sprawled about the room, on the floor, lolling on furniture, all sleeping soundly. What was this? Had they all imbibed so much the governor's men had thrown them in this room to sleep it off?

Sesto realised he was mistaken. He counted the sleeping shadows again. Not everyone was here. There was no sign of Small Willm, Runcio, or one of Silke's crew.

Silvaro lay nearby, and Sesto shook him to wake him, to no avail. But for his low, raspy breathing, the captain was as limp as death. Sesto tried to wake Silke, and then Roque and Vento. Not a man of them would respond.

Sesto went back out into the hallway, and at once heard approaching footsteps. He pulled the door shut, and slipped into hiding behind an embroidered arras. Immediately, he felt foolish. Why was he hiding when there was no real cause to suspect danger? He reached to touch the hilt of his sword, so that the metal might give him good fortune. His scabbard was empty. His knife had gone too.

Now he had cause. If all this was innocent, why had his weapons been taken from him?

Figures approached, marching urgently. It was Ferrol, and four of his guardsmen. They carried oil lamps. They opened the door of the stateroom and went inside. Sesto had to strain to hear them speak.

'What about Silvaro?' one of the men seemed to suggest. Sesto couldn't hear all of Ferrol's answer. Part of it ran '...says he's sick of pirate salt... like mongrel dogs... thoroughbred Estalian...'

There was movement, and then the guard party emerged from the room, dragging Roque and Zazara, Estalians both. Ferrol closed the door and went off down the corridor behind the men and their slumbering loads.

Sesto took off after them, following at a cautious distance. The windows that he passed revealed to him that night was still on the island, though from the pale edge of it, dawn was not too many hours away.

Ferrol and his men disappeared through the great doors into the banquet hall. Sesto followed, pausing to unhook a pair of crossed sabres that hung on the wall beneath an Estalian roundel. His hosts had wanted him weaponless, so caution suggested a weapon would be good to have.

He reached the doors. They had been left ajar, and he was able to peer in.

What a sight he saw. The musicians and servants had long since departed, but the banquet had not been cleared. Tables of plates and half-eaten fare had been pushed back and dishes piled up. Seven men of the colonial guard, black clad and comb-helmed, stood around the walls of the room, both watching and waiting.

Emeric Gorge stood in the middle of the room. He had stripped to the waist, his arms and upper body as pallid white as a stinging jelly. His back was to Sesto, and his arms down at his sides. A guardsman knelt at his right hand and another at his left, as if each was kissing the backs of Gorge's hands in ritual homage. Roque and Zazara, sleeping still, lay near the doorway.

Small Willm, Runcio and the man from Silke's crew lay in a heap at the far end of the room. Somehow, the limpness of their bodies told Sesto they were more than asleep. Even a slumbering man does not relax and fold so completely.

'Enough!' said Gorge, and the two men rose, wiping their mouths on black handkerchiefs. As Gorge turned, Sesto saw with horror that his inner wrists were wet with blood.

'Another!' he said. Two guards moved from the wall and scooped up Zazara. They dragged him to Gorge, and held him up as Gorge pulled the Reiver's head back by the hair and held a small crystal bottle under his nose.

Zazara woke, coughing and spluttering. He looked around, bemused, not really comprehending his surroundings. The guards let him stand.

Gorge stoppered the crystal bottle and set it aside on a table, then walked back to the blinking, woozy Zazara.

'Estalian,' he murmured. 'A better vintage…'

Gorge seized Zazara by the upper part of the left arm and the hair, and wrenched his head aside so his throat was exposed. Gorge's widening mouth was suddenly full of long, sharp teeth, like a wolfhound or a striking snake.

Zazara cried out briefly as Gorge clamped his bite down into the Reiver's neck. He shook, but Gorge would not let go. Zazara convulsed. Sesto watched with total revulsion and a rising terror. He saw little, macabre details. Gorge's thin, pale frame was at odds with his grossly swollen pot-belly. Zazara's feet twitched because he was actually held off the ground by Gorge's great strength.

Gorge released the Reiver and Zazara collapsed. Blood ran down the governor's chin. The guards picked up Zazara's corpse and threw it with the others.

'Better,' said Gorge, his words slurred by the great teeth that pushed out his lips. 'Quickly, the other now. The noble one.'

Outnumbered as he was, Sesto could not just look on any more. Two guards were dragging Roque towards the governor.

Gripping his sabres tightly, Sesto backed up to crash open the doors.

XII

HE WAS STRUCK such a blow from behind that he burst the doors open anyway, and sprawled onto the floor. He'd lost his grip on both the swords. When he reached out to snatch at one, a black boot pressed the blade firmly to the flags.

Ferrol stood over him. 'One woke early,' he said.

'I had a notion that one had not supped as much of the red lotus as the rest,' murmured Gorge. He smiled down at Sesto and the smile was terrible. 'Welcome to the feast, gentleman. I will be with you shortly.'

Gorge turned away and woke Roque with a sniff of the crystal bottle. The master-at-arms jolted awake, and struggled at once with the men holding him. They kept him pinned tightly.

Gorge yanked Roque's head over by the hair, and lunged at his throat. Roque howled as the monster's bite ripped into his neck.

But the feasting did not go as before. Gorge suddenly lurched away, retching and spitting, coughing blood out onto the floor. The men released Roque and he fell to his knees, clutching at his wounded throat.

'What is it? My lord?' Ferrol asked, hurrying to Gorge's side.

'This one has filth in his blood! Vile pestilence! Like sour milk or turned wine!' Gorge retched again, and a great measure of noxious blood spattered across the tiles.

All attention was on the governor. Sesto reached out again for the fallen sabre.

'You should be careful who you bite,' mocked a voice from the shadows. Like a phantom, Sheerglas melted into the lamplight, his black robes swirling around him like a piece of the night itself.

Gorge turned to face him. His men drew their rapiers.

'I could smell you in the town,' said Sheerglas. 'Your stink is everywhere. It has been hard, hasn't it? Thirsty times for you and your little coterie of servants.'

'Who are you?' Gorge asked.

'One who knows,' replied the master gunner. 'How long have you ruled here, daemon-kin? Longer than any other colonial governor, I'll be bound. Those portraits in the hall. They're not your forebears, are they? They're you in other ages. You, and your legion of consorts.'

Sheerglas took a step forward, and some of the guards moved in around him. Sesto heard several of them growl, like dogs facing off against a rival male.

'It must have been so easy,' Sheerglas murmured, keeping his gaze on Gorge. 'A constant traffic of merchants and visitors, a town packed full of strangers. Every ship that came brought fresh liquor to quench you. But the traffic stopped, and you were forced to break your own rules. You had to find your nourishment from the local population exclusively. And my, your thirst has left them weak and drained. Much longer, and Porto Real would have started to die. Hurrah, then, for a ship! Fresh blood at last.'

Gorge had stopped spitting blood out. He raised a bony finger and pointed at Sheerglas. 'Kill him,' he said.

The guards rushed Sheerglas.

Sesto leapt up, recovered both sabres, and ran to Roque, who was kneeling still, and shaking with pain. But he had seen the business well enough.

'Can you stand?' Sesto asked.

Roque snatched one of the sabres from Sesto and stumbled determinedly towards Gorge. Sesto ran with him. They plunged their blades into the backs of the two guards who had remained at the governor's side. Death blows.

But they didn't die.

They turned, eyes dark beneath the brims of their silver comb helmets, and swung their rapiers at Roque and Sesto.

Somehow, Sheerglas had not fallen under the weight of the men who had rushed him. Indeed, like a shadow, he seemed to separate himself from them, sending several tumbling to the ground. He had drawn no weapons. A bladesman rushed him, and Sheerglas sidestepped, catching the wrist of the thrusting sword-arm and breaking the elbow joint with a savage upward blow of his other hand. The guard screamed and fell back, and Sheerglas took the Estalian rapier from his hand, drifting around like smoke to engage three more of the black-garbed soldiers. Sparks flew from the flickering blades.

'Their heads!' Sheerglas yelled above the din of steel. 'You cannot slay them unless you take their heads off their shoulders!'

Sesto, driven back almost to the door, parried the whipping strokes of the guard and dodged aside as fast as he could. The guard's sword tip struck the wooden door and stuck for a second.

Sesto whirled and parted his neck. The man fell. There was a sudden, sharp stench of burning. By the time the body hit the ground, it was nothing but boots, rotting black clothes and a rusty comb morion filled with dust.

Half revolted and half delighted, Sesto ran forward and lopped the head off the guard engaging Roque. Again, brimstone corruption seared the air as the man became ashes.

'My thanks,' said Roque. Together, they turned and laid into the soldiers attacking Sheerglas. The master gunner had already dispatched two of them. 'Keep them busy,' he hissed. Before Sesto could question the remark, Sheerglas had again flickered out of view, slipping into the shadows. He reappeared like a swirl of mist in front of Gorge. Sheerglas tossed away his borrowed sword and threw himself at the governor. They grappled furiously. Sesto heard the devilish snarling again.

He and Roque were miserably hard-pressed. Five guardsmen still remained, including Ferrol. Sesto was not the greatest swordsman in the world, and Roque was slowed by his injury. Only fury and fear kept them fighting the blades away. Roque managed to turn a rapier aside and sweep his sabre into a throat. Another of Gorge's deathless followers found the dust of the grave at last. But now Ferrol was onto Roque and driving him back.

Sheerglas and Gorge struggled on. With inhuman force, Gorge threw the master gunner across the hall, and he crashed into some of the trestles, shattering dishes and cascading platters onto the floor. He leapt straight back up, vaulting into the air so his black robes billowed out like a bat's wings, and came tearing back down onto Gorge, throwing him sideways. The governor's pale body demolished another table and overturned two chairs.

Gorge recovered as swiftly as Sheerglas had done and pounced at the master gunner. The leap was far further than any mortal man could have managed. He tore into Sheerglas, fangs wide, and brought him over into a further row of feast tables. Bottles smashed, wood splintered. A pewter beaker clattered to the floor and rolled away.

Sesto cried out as a blade ripped across the back of his hand, and another tore a long gash in his cheek. He parried furiously. He and Roque could not hold the swordsmen off any longer.

Sheerglas threw Gorge over onto his back and sprang on him, pinning him for a second.

'Bastard!' Gorge rasped.

'Fiend!' Sheerglas replied. He seized a snapped leg strut from one of the broken trestles and rammed it down into Gorge's chest with both hands.

Gorge screamed. His mouth opened so wide that his lips tore. Poisonous, rotten light shone out of his throat, out of his eyes, and out from around the stake through his chest. He thrashed violently. Then in a flash of flame, like a misfiring cannon, he exploded and disintegrated.

One by one, the Estalian guards burst apart like smoke, their empty clothing and armour falling to the floor. Ferrol was the last to go.

Silence. Nothing but the smell of mausoleum dust.

Roque and Sesto backed away, panting. They looked at Sheerglas. He rose to his feet, and let ash spill out between his fingers.

'It's done,' he said. 'Take the bottle there and wake the others.'

Roque limped to the table where Gorge's crystal bottle stood and picked it up. He looked at Sheerglas for a long moment, then hobbled out of the room.

SESTO FOLLOWED SHEERGLAS out into the entrance hall.

'We owe you thanks,' he said.

The master gunner shrugged.

'I say it was lucky that you came ashore tonight. Lucky you picked a straw. You don't often leave the ship, do you?' Sesto asked.

'Once in a while,' said Sheerglas.

'Why tonight?'

'Same as all of us. I was in search of clean drinking.'

He looked back at Sesto and gestured to the bloody gash on his cheek. 'You should bind that.'

'It's only a flesh wound.'

'I know. But it's also tempting.'

Sheerglas walked away. In the great mirrors of the hallway, Sesto saw only himself reflected.

THE SEA AIR was cool, and they had made fair going, but in the lea of the land, the islands were heady and humid: jungle draped cones that trilled with birdcalls and the ratchet of insects.

Around nameless rainforest atolls they meandered a snaking course. Luka Silvaro knew every tideway and channel by heart, with no need of a chart or waggoner. The Southern Littoral of Estalia had been his particular hunting ground of old. When he had been a pirate, not a privateer, that was.

'This is where the treasure ships would come,' he told Sesto, late one afternoon while they stood on the stern deck of the *Rumour*. The sky was turning coral red in the west, and seabirds chased and wheeled in their wake. Fahd had just cast a bucket of slops over the rail. 'They would be tired and breathless from the ocean crossing, like sprint horses run too hard, too long. Their bellies would be heavy. Lustrian gold, Arabyan spice. Here, they had a choice. Sustain their sprint another eight days, running a straight line east all the way to Tilea, or rest and water in these southern islands.'

'What measure of good did that do them, if the likes of you were out hunting for their souls?' Sesto asked.

'Plenty,' replied the former pirate lord. If he'd sensed any rebuke in Sesto's remark, he made no show of noticing it. 'In the early days, they would run straight. Running the jaws we called it. On the last of their vittals and the last of their man-strength, they'd break backs for Luccini or Miragliano, hoping to give us the slip. Those were the days of the big pirate ships, you understand. Sixty-pair guns, eight hundred tonnes. Sacadra the Jinx, Bonnie Berto, Banehanded Ezra. The pirate lords of legend, Manann spare their souls. In open sea, a black flag could spy a treasure galleon from twenty-seven miles... and vice versa. It was a game of chase and stamina, one the heavy treasure ships often lost, more often than not.'

Luka Silvaro paused and toyed with the fat gold ring around his little finger. 'So the prey learned to come in close to the shore and work up into the islands.' He made no bones of the word 'prey'. It was quite matter of fact. 'In amongst the islands, they were harder to spot, and they had a chance to draw breath and reprovision after the arduously long crossing. Working their way through the islands – threading the teeth, it was called – they could choose when and where to make their break into open sea. It improved their chances.'

He patted the polished rail of the *Rumour* affectionately. 'That's why, in this modern age, we prefer the slighter hunting ships. We have learned to stalk the islands, and spring upon the prey in lagoons and shallow bays while they are watering. It is a trick the corsairs have learned too. Their galleys could never catch a four master galleon fat-yarded in a blow.'

They were now nine days south-west of Porto Real, in amongst the last thickets of green islets before the bony reaches of the bare, dagger atolls that spiked out to the end of Known Land and heralded, like a shattered archway, the great, dark oceans of the mysterious west. Sesto knew well the blood was up now, the hunger for the hunt. It was like old times for Silvaro and the rogues who had shipped out with him before.

Three times they had put in at cove settlements along the island chain. A boucaners' enclave, a small Estalian port town and a sovereign-less fishing village. In each one, the story had been the same. The Butcher Ship was close by. This was the heart of its hunting ground. Every few weeks or so, its great, ruddy hulled, scarlet sheeted shape would sail into the little harbours and train guns. Sometimes a warning cannonade would be fired. The locals, in fear of their lives, were forced to load up every ounce of provision and clean water they had to hand and row it out as ransom for their continued existence.

In the first part of the morning of the next day, Sesto heard voices arguing in Silvaro's cabin. There was no doubting the voices belonged to Silvaro himself and to Roque, the master-at-arms. Sesto didn't dare approach. He sat down with his back to the base of the mainmast and waited. Ymgrawl sat down beside him. Long-limbed and scrawny, Ymgrawl just folded himself up into a sitting position. He took out a tanner's knife with a hooked tip and began cutting away at a yellow-dry whale's tooth.

'They're arguing,' said Sesto at length.

'Aye.'

'Do they often argue?'

'Thou knowst as good as I. No two better friends on the seas.'

'Then what?'

Ymgrawl fixed Sesto with his narrow, flinty stare. 'The Butcher Ship. Roque can'st credit this to be the truth. Too easy, saith he.'

'What do you mean?'

'The Butcher. 'Tis a monster. Like a force of creation. Roque saith it would not threaten for supplies. It would as like raid and burn and take its will.'

'Then what is it we hunt?'

Ymgrawl shrugged.

THE FREEPORT OF Santa Bernadette was said to be the last living place in the island chain, though Ymgrawl boasted he knew of others. It was at least the last place of any real size. They came upon it in the heat of the afternoon. Across a bay, twinkling with bright, reflected sunlight, lay the inner curve of a dense, green island. Between sea and jungle lay a stripe of white washed buildings.

The bay was too shallow even for the *Safire*, so they cast out anchors at the mouth, and three armed boats were prepared and lowered.

It was a long, sticky row to the shore. Sesto travelled in the lead boat with Luka, hearing the bare-chested ratings around him grunt and pant as they heaved to the stroke call. Sesto watched Luka prime and cock a pair of wheel-lock pistols and a short-muzzled caliver, and began to wish he'd brought a deal more than his rapier. Maybe his little Arabyan gun would have been a good idea.

They beached and dragged the longboats up onto the gritty sand. At Roque's gesture, men drew swords and pistols, and scurried forth up the head of the beach towards the stucco shacks and limed buildings that drowsed under the hem of date and palm.

'There's none here on it,' reported Fanciman, one of the armsmen, returning to Roque.

The master-at-arms had crouched down, touching a dark patch on the sand. He sniffed his fingers. 'Wet with lamp oil,' he said.

'What does that mean?' Sesto asked.

''Ware those huts!' Roque shouted, rising. The men up the beach, about to burst into some of the dwellings, paused.

Sesto hurried after Luka and Roque as they crossed to the nearest building. It was an old blockhouse, built of timber and mudbrick, its white plaster crumbling.

Luka pushed open the door with the snout of his caliver. The wood-planked door, gnawed away at the edges by the ministry of sand and sea, creaked in a little way and stopped. Luka was about to nudge it again, when Roque raised a hand.

The Estalian crouched low to the side of the doorway and made the others stand back as he prodded the door the rest of the way in with his sabre's long blade.

The gunpowder boom scared birds out of the trees and its echo rolled up and down the warm air of the beach.

Inside the hut, a blunderbuss had been set to a chair and its trigger tied with fishing twine to the door bolt.

'A trap,' said Roque, examining the makeshift weapon.

'A trap for what?' mused Silvaro.

Outside, a thin rattle of gunfire sounded.

They ran out of the hut. Bullet-balls and short-haft arrows were pelting down the beach from both the north and south ends, coming out of the trees. Already, three of Luka's landing party had fallen, wounded. There was a heavier boom from some field piece, and a geyser of sand vomited up from the ground not ten paces from where Luka and Sesto stood.

'To arms! To arms!' Roque shouted.

Sesto heard a soft, clicking rush. Flames licked along the beach edge in a line, growing into a furiously burning wall. The oil Roque had scented was a fire-trap dug into the ground. Someone had carefully – desperately, Sesto thought – prepared this welcome.

Another cannonball whizzed overhead and cracked wide the gables of the blockhouse they had entered.

'Manann's mercy! I've had my fill of this greeting,' Luka growled. 'Into cover!'

One of his men, obeying blindly, ran into a hut and was blown in two by the fowling piece strung to its door. Three more ran ill of a covered pit between two huts. The stretched, sand covered canvas snapped away beneath their weight and plunged them into a staked darkness. Their howls were almost unbearable.

From the cover of the trees, men charged them. Dozens of men, carrying spears, hatchets and machetes. Their skins were black, and white skull marks had been daubed on their faces, aping the look of King Death himself. They howled and ululated, and beat on drums and copper kettles. Sesto thought them quite frightening. They had the pirate landers pinned on a narrow stretch of beach between the huts and the crackling wall of fire.

'Damn this…' roared Luka. He raised his caliver and fired at the first savage who came running at him. The blast walloped the man over onto his back. Luka cast the caliver aside, and drew his pistols, greeting the next two assailants with similar fates.

Roque, his voice brooking no disobedience, brought the Reiver party into a knot, forming two walls that faced each head of attack. A salvo of locks crackled and puffed white smoke, and skull-faced men dropped hard onto the sand.

Then blades came out and it came down to steel.

Luka, the largest man on the beach, was raging with temper now. He drew his curved shamshir and a stabbing dagger and hurled himself at the line of charging foemen.

'With him! With him!' Roque shouted.

Sesto drew his rapier, trembling with fear, and dashed out after Luka.

He met a man coming at him with a woodaxe, little more than a hatchet, and stuck him clumsily through the throat. Then he felt rather bad about it. For all his howling and warpaint, the man had seemed more scared than he was.

Luka and four of his most thuggish retainers – Fanciman, Tall Willm, Saint Bones and Saybee – led the brunt charge into the straggled southern line of attackers, and gave fearful account. Luka ripped a man open with his shamshir, then impaled another on his dagger. He kicked at a third, then slashed at him once his sword was free. Tall Willm gutted a man with his sabre. Saybee, the massive lee helmsman, swung a double-toothed axe forged in the Norse lands and felled two men like trees. Strung around with various flint- and wheel-lock pistols on ribbon loops, Fanciman seemed never to need to reload. Saint Bones, his devilish rapier dancing, sang Sigmarite hymns as he slew.

To the north hand, Roque did the lion's share of the bloodletting, flanked by Tortoise Schell and Pietro the Hoof, two of his favoured armsmen.

And that was enough.

The attackers broke off and scattered, fleeing up the beach to both compass points. Their ululating had become howls of fear. They left weapons, drums and kettles on the sand behind them, along with twenty-four dead or dying men, six of which Luka alone had dealt with.

The Reivers themselves had lost three, with four more wounded. One of the wounded was a man dragged, bloody and wailing, out of the stake-trap. Some of the stakes came with him, stuck through his legs. The hot afternoon stank of blood and sweat. Flies buzzed around them, suddenly swarming from the damp, leech haunted forest beyond the huts, drawn by the reek of fresh blood.

'One lives yet,' Roque announced as some of his men dragged a bleeding, shivering savage to face Luka.

The man was thrown to the ground at Luka's feet. He didn't dare look up. A pistol ball had shredded his right ear and blood was pouring out of the mangled flesh onto the sand, where the drops quivered proud like rubies before slowly seeping in. Sesto could see that where the man's dark skin had been smudged away, his flesh was as pale as any mainland Tilean's.

Luka shook his head and knelt down to face the man, who whimpered and tried to turn away.

'You thought we were the Butcher Ship, didn't you?' Luka sighed.

XIV

THE SUN SANK fast, as it does in the tropics, and a cool ocean snap blew in across them, spurring the last dregs of smoke off and away from the glowing, glassy embers of the oil trap. A thin crescent moon came out, sharp as a claw extending, and stars lit their tiny lamps. In the dark foliage of the island forest, nocturnal insects began to thrill and peep and knock.

Sombre and half-hearted, kerchiefs tied around their mouths, the landing crew dragged the bodies of their enemy into a stack at the northern tip of the beach. No formal words were made, but some of the men came, one by one – Saint Bones, Fanciman, Pietro the Hoof, Roque – and muttered things to the dead, casting coins or rings or other trinkets into the heap.

Wards of protection, no doubt. The Reivers were cutthroats, but this action had a sour taste.

Once the moon had cleared the tossing silhouettes of the island's trees, Luka took a flaming torch from Saybee and threw it on the heap.

The flames burned bright, white with heat, yellow with fat.

Sesto walked as far away from the pyre as he could get.

Down by the south end of Santa Bernadette's beach, he discovered Roque, alone, drinking from a flask of jerez.

'A bad business,' Roque said, aware of Sesto in the night shadow behind him. He held out the flask.

Sesto took a sip. The sweet, heavy fortified wine tasted like silk.

'Mistaken identity,' the Estalian mariner went on, looking out into the sea, watching the waves roll up in gentle curls along a sandy waterline made glassy by the moonlight. Little red crabs scuttled and jumped on the mirror of sand, their calliper claws leaving marks that lasted just a heartbeat before the next sudsy curl smoothed them over.

Roque took the proffered bottle back. 'This Butcher. He makes butchers of us all.' Roque suddenly knelt and twisted the flask down upright in the dry sand to stop it upsetting. He leaned forward and washed his hands in the breakwater. It was too dark to tell if there was any blood on them, too dark to see if any was scrubbing off. Sesto was sure the act was essentially ritual. Or at least the contrition of a man's unhappy soul.

Roque had not been right since the dreadful night on Isla Verde. Only Sesto and Sheerglas knew that the fiend Gorge had rejected Roque for having spoiled blood. They had not spoken about it.

To his dying day, Sesto would believe there was nothing more terrible to witness than a self-avowed killer trying to make amends for his own sins.

'I heard you argue,' said Sesto nervously.

'Then your ears are as big as the fool-boy Gello's!' Roque snapped.

'Forget I spoke, sir,' Sesto said, and turned away.

'Sesto!' Roque called. He got up, recovered his flask, and hurried to the young man's side.

'What?'

'Forgive me, sir. I forget myself in a gentleman's company. It has been a long time since–'

'Since what? Since you were at court, Señor Santiago Della Fortuna?'

'Yes. That is perhaps what I meant.'

'So you are that man? That famous discoverer?'

'Sesto, Sesto… That man is long dead, years dead. That man is also here. Make of that riddle what you will.'

'What happened to you?'

'I have sworn not to tell it. I… Let me just say, I travelled wide, made my name and fortune, and then pushed my luck against the fates of the fickle oceans too far. In Lustria, in that abominable land. Such things I saw… The scaled ones… they–'

He took a deep swig.

'Five years I was lost. Five years I will not speak of. It was as a low oar-slave on an Arabyan corsair galley that Luka found me. Found me, saw my worth… the man who stands before you on this beach tonight was born again, whole, at that moment. All that he had been before was melted away and lost.'

Sesto pursed his lips. 'You argued with Luka today.'

Roque nodded. 'We stalk the wrong prey. There is a tyrant ship out in the waters of the islets, but not a butcher. And today we–'

He fell silent.

'I killed a man today,' Sesto said.

'Three myself, and none deserved it. If you killed, Sesto, you know this pain. The Butcher's taint makes even the best of us brute killers.'

The notion surprised Sesto somewhat. That curious pirate code again, no doubt. The notion that there were degrees to which one could be a killer.

THE BALEFIRE BURNED on at the far corner of the beach. Nearer to the huts and shanties, driftwood bonfires had been built and lit. Their crackling heat and parched smoke billowed around the huts and drove off the night flies and mosquitoes.

Luka had a bellyful of wine in his skin, and sat morosely at a plain timber table in the main hut. 'Dead for a peso octo, all of them,' he muttered as Roque and Sesto came in. 'Dead by our hand for trying to stay alive.'

Roque plonked his jerez on the table and Luka immediately helped himself.

'Living here in terror of the Butcher,' Luka mumbled darkly. 'Living here in living terror of the monster out there.

They put their all into scaring it off when it next came. The last of their oil, the last of their shot. They painted their skins black and skulled, and made the noise of savages, all in the desperate hope that it would drive the evil out. But the evil was us, and we killed them anyway.'

'Leave him,' Roque whispered to Sesto. 'In this black mood, he's a danger even to himself.'

But there was a noise from outside the hut that roused Luka before the pair could slip away.

Saint Bones and Garcia Garza had appeared, dragging with them a man they had found hiding in the woods. The last survivor of the battle had died of bloodlet before he had been able to talk.

'Sigmar have mercy on me!' the man protested. He was a scruffy churchman from the Empire, his skin tanned by many years spreading the true word under a heathen southern sun.

'Sigmar can save his mercy,' Luka told him. 'I'll not harm you.'

'You are pirates!'

'Not at all. We are privateers, and we carry a letter of marque and reprisal to prove it.'

'But you… you slaughtered and you–'

'We were attacked, sir. By you and your fellows. We would have given quarter had we known.'

The man bowed his head and started on a prayer to Sigmar that seemed to Sesto to run in time to the beat of the crickets.

'Tell me of the Butcher Ship,' said Luka.

'It is our bane. It comes upon us at each new moon and demands all we have.'

That story again, four times heard now.

'Where does it go?'

'Go?'

'Go, from here?'

'South, and then we see it gybing east. They say it lurks in a cove within the Labyrinth.'

'Does it now? Which cove?'

'Some say Angel's Bar, others the Greenwater Sound.'

'Thank you, father,' Luka said. 'You may go free, and tell your brethren here that none of my men will harm them. This I make as a pledge to your god, Sigmar, so he might claim my poor, barbarian soul should I break it.'

The churchman got up, and started away.

'Father? My good father! One last thing…'

At the edge of the firelight, the man froze, fearing the very cruellest of pirate tricks.

'Father… What say you are the dimensions and character of the Butcher Ship?' asked Luka.

The balding, bronzed Empire man turned back slowly. 'It… it has three masts. A great barque of three hundred and a fifty paces, with sixty cannon in two gun decks. Its hull and sails are red as blood. Green fire burns where it should have a figurehead. The men who crew it are not men, they are night-beasts.'

'I see. Go in peace, father.'

Gratefully, the man disappeared into the night.

'The *Kymera*?' Roque asked.

'It fits the description. The *Kymera* is a great barque, two hundred and twenty paces, and it mounts forty guns. But the churchman there was no mariner. A fearful man makes monsters of the truth. Just look at Belissi.'

Some of the Reivers gathered around laughed at this.

'Mother mine!' mocked Fanciman, querulously.

'So?' Roque asked.

'Be it the *Kymera* or some other bastard barque, we cut our way down into the Labyrinth to war with it. One thing's for sure, we'll not find it in Greenwater Sound.'

'Why not?' asked Sesto.

Luka tapped the side of his nose with a long finger. 'Old habits, old skills, Sesto. We're hunting prey that's threading the teeth. Greenwater Sound bottoms out at two fathoms. No barque, be it three hundred and a fifty paces or two hundred and twenty, could find harbour there. Angel's Bar, however, has no floor any man has ever managed to leadline.'

IT WAS DARK still as they rode back out to the ships. They left the miserable bonfire at the beach end blazing into the cold tropical night.

Before dawn, a fair wind came up, fresh and true, and the *Rumour* and its consort turned south and east, deeper into the archipelago.

IT SEEMED AS if they might run out of sea. So Sesto thought on the second day out from Santa Bernadette. The islands, cased with fuming green foliage, were more densely packed here than ever before. The two ships edged their way down channel throats and narrow runs, luxuriant green jungle spilling down like emerald cliffs to either side. Bright macaws and parrots darted from island to island overhead, and the *Rumour* and its consort were wont to glide through passages fraught with mist. The water was bright turquoise, speaking of a bottom perilously close to the ship's keel. This was the Labyrinth, a dense maze of islands that buffered the Estalian Littoral.

In bays swathed by rainforest, they anchored and rested. Vento and Largo had to chase chattering monkeys off the rigging, which they had mistaken for trees. Fahd's speciality became monkey stew. Each dawn, they had to mop the decks and rails clear of the dew left by the curling dawn fog. Blades rusted quickly in this place, and guns choked and plugged. Roque kept drill after drill running to maintain the battle readiness of Silvaro's company.

On the fourth day, the *Rumour* led the *Safire* down a reef channel and around a bay, beneath overhanging banks of beard-moss and draping bougainvillea, towards a fathomless cove named after angels.

It was early and there was scant wind, so the going was slow. At the head of an inlet that Silvaro said led straight out into Angel's Bar, they dropped anchor, and Casaudor was sent out in a longboat to spy around the inlet's turn.

'Why do we wait?' Sesto asked.

'No wind, so tell,' replied Benuto. 'If we force a fight, we'll want the wind with us, to press our advantage of speed.'

On the mid-decks below them, Roque was bringing out the armsmen now, setting pavis and targettes along the rail on the starboard side-rests. On the slopes of the hull, gun ports were being hooked open. Sesto could hear Sheerglas's command whistle shrilling from the gundeck as he ordered up his pieces. The *Rumour* was rolling up its sleeves for a fight.

Casaudor returned out of the early morning mist. He stood in the prow of the longboat, the six oars behind him slowly beating the sap-green water, and sprang up the side as soon as he was close enough to take hold of a rope.

'Is it there?' asked Silvaro.

Casaudor nodded. 'Like a dream in the mist. It lies at anchor, massively dark of shape and sail. A green fire smokes at its prow.'

'The Butcher Ship?'

'I know not, but it looks the very devil of a thing. And if it is the Butcher, then the Butcher is not the *Kymera* after all.'

'What do you mean?'

Casaudor looked grim and spat out of the side of his mouth for good fortune. 'The old churchman was not exaggerating. This monster is three hundred and fifty paces from stem to stern, and along its double gun decks nest sixty guns.'

THE OMINOUS NEWS spread. Many fully expected Silvaro to turn them around and quit such a confrontation, especially if this was not the prize they were after. Indeed, on the *Safire*, Silke began to make preparations to come about, until Silvaro signalled him otherwise.

'If we get wind, we'll go in at him,' Silvaro told his senior men. Several muttered oaths. 'Oh, he's a big bastard, by Casaudor's account, but we are two, and we are quick, and we have surprise on our side. Besides, I have to know. If this is the Butcher Ship, I have to know. And for the soul of Reyno, if no other, I have to strike.'

Roque nodded grimly. Casaudor too assented. The bo'sun in his crimson coat seemed too concerned with the mechanics of the fight to bother over the outcome.

Sesto sensed there was another reason behind Silvaro's decision. The Reiver lord wanted vengeance for the blood he had been forced to spill on the beach of Santa Bernadette.

A STRONG EASTERLY rose quite suddenly an hour after Casaudor's return, and though they were close-reached by it, Silvaro made use of it at once. According to the first mate's report, the enemy lay with its head to the wind.

The blow lifted the mist away from the inlet like a drawn curtain, and the tree covered spits were revealed on either side, like barricades of jungle. Half-sheeted, the *Rumour* stole down the inlet's sound, and the *Safire* spurred in, about forty lengths back on the starboard quarter. Both of the *Rumour*'s armed watches gathered at the starboard rail, pikes ready at the shield wall, and the calivermen took their places. Bottles were handed around and swigs taken.

Unlike some rogue crews, the Reivers would not go into battle drunk and roaring, but it was custom to toast for success and fortify nerves, and drink away the curse of the sea daemon. Sesto accepted a drink from a bottle as it was passed along. His hands were shaking.

Silvaro called for more sheet and more speed. Then he walked down from the poop and approached Sesto, who was preparing his little Arabyan wheel-lock.

'When we get into it, keep your head down. I'll not have you killed for nothing,' Silvaro ordered.

'I took a life on Santa Bernadette,' Sesto replied bravely, despite his shaking hands. 'For that I'll claim at least one back here.'

Silvaro paused and pursed his lips. Sesto's words had clearly struck a chord. The Reiver lord nodded and tugged a long-barrelled flintlock out of his belt, handing it off, butt first, to Sesto. The damn thing was monstrously heavy.

'Then take this, sir. It'll be more use to you than that little, shiny toy.'

Ruefully, Sesto put his little, ornate pocket pistol away and clapped a firm hold of the mighty handgun.

Silvaro was about to offer some other remark when the man up in the topcastle suddenly hallooed. He was pointing to starboard, into the trees that rushed past on their right hand.

Sesto looked, wondering what the matter was. Then he saw it. His heart sank. What he had first taken to be tall tree-tops he now saw to be the royals and skysails of a most massive ship running east with them on the other side of the spit. The sails were red. Their enemy must have taken the opportunity of the rising blow too, and was now riding his way down out of Angel's Bar, from anchor. Due to his great size, the tops of his main masts stood up above the jungle trees. And the man in his topcastle had, without doubt, spied the *Rumour* and the *Safire* in the inlet.

Their surprise was gone. In another five minutes, they would both run clear of the spit into the open waters of the bar and be clean on, beam to beam. Side on to a sixty-gun leviathan, the *Rumour* would be rent to matchwood.

'Loose some sheets! Loose some there!' Casaudor yelled, seeing the awful fate that bore down on them.

'Belay that!' Silvaro roared.

Casaudor looked at his captain as if he was mad. 'We must turn and run! They have us!'

'No, sir!' Silvaro snarled. 'We will not break now! More sheet! Full sheet, you laggards! Full sheet and more besides! We will beat this unholy giant to the spithead!'

Trembling, Sesto realised Luka Silvaro's intention. The *Rumour* was a sleek, fast vessel – a 'slighter hunting ship', he had called it. He meant to out-race the enemy barque before the spit was done, and come around across its bows. But the barque was huge. Its plentiful sail cloth could push it ahead at a tremendous speed.

The *Rumour* raised full running sail and filled its canvas fat with wind. For a moment, it paced ahead of the red topsails behind the trees. Then the red sails began to catch up again.

They slid above the tops of the forest, ominously suggestive, like the fin of a great fish cutting the water, hinting at the monster hidden below. The enemy had raised the black flag, showing an hourglass that expressed the fact that time was running out for its intended victim. In response, with a curse, Silvaro hoisted his jolie rouge.

Vento's ratings monkeyed up and down the ratlines, extending a pack of studdingsails before the main course and main top, and a flying jib before the fore staysail. At once, the additional sheets caused the *Rumour* to fly and gain water at the expense of its lumbering foe.

A length they had on it, then a length and a half. The end of the forest spit was in sight, and the deep, bottomless open water of the Bar yawned out before them.

With less than a half minute to go before they cleared, Sesto looked back and saw with dismay that the *Safire* had fallen away far behind down the inlet. Silke, it seemed, had chosen to sit this one out. And that, most as like, spelt doom for the *Rumour*.

As the *Rumour* cleared the spit into open water, it had two and half lengths on the massive barque. They thundered out into the cove and immediately began to gybe to starboard.

Sesto got his first look at the enemy racing up to meet them. He had imagined many things supporting the red tops seen over the trees, but this was worse than any of them. It was a colossal, dark ship, more than three times the size of the *Rumour*, its tight-yarded sheets red as dried blood.

A lambent green fire burned in a metal lantern affixed to the bow. Dark shapes – daemon bodies, Sesto supposed – swarmed on the decks and up the ratlines.

It was coming at them head-on as they turned about across its front. Their starboard side was flat-on to its racing bows. Did it mean to ram them?

The lurch of the fast-running *Rumour* was great now they had come into open swell. Sesto was forced to hang on as the deck pitched and rose.

He heard a whistle shrill and then felt the boom-shake of guns firing below him.

A full side let out at the enemy. Sesto couldn't hear the impacts, but he saw splashes in the sea beside the barque, and puffs of splinters and pieces of rail fly off from its bows. Its inner jib snapped and flapped away like a streamer.

Sheerglas's gun teams fired again, loosing chain shot this time. They had the range now, despite the rapid, cross-passing movement of the ships. All the enemy's jibs shredded off, along with the fore starboard ratlines. Dark shapes tumbled away into the rushing sea. The royal stay-sails ripped aside or were torn into holes, and the top part of the foremast came down like a stricken tree.

White smoke puffed out on either side of the hellish green lantern. The enemy had bow guns, heavy cannon by the look, and it had used them. A water spout leapt up beyond the Rumour's bows where one shot went wide. The other tore the luff edge out of the Rumour's biggest studdingsail and caused the loose canvas to snap and crack wildly in the blow. Severed yards whipped back and forth above the deck, despite Vento's efforts to team them in and control them. One savagely snapping line decapitated a rigger and sent him tumbling away off the upper ratlines into the sea. His blood fell like rain on all below.

'Again, Sheerglas!' Luka yelled.

Working like devils, sweating in the hot, dark confines of the gundecks, the master gunner's teams succeeded in rattling off a third salvo as the Rumour came about, broad-reached, around the mighty foe.

This did the most damage yet. Sesto winced as he saw parts of the bow quarters splinter and hole. Pieces of red wood fluttered up into the air, high above the level of the main sails.

Then it was all commotion. Silvaro bellowed orders that Benuto bellowed louder. Tende and Saybee hauled the wheel round together and the ratings mobbed up the lines to bring the sheets to true. Roque gave a piped command that sent the armed watch over from the starboard to the port to re-establish their armoured wall there. The Rumour was turning now, its speed dropping suddenly as they went almost head to the wind. Silvaro was striving to keep the smallest possible profile towards the barque. Now they were all but bow-on as the barque presented its starboard side to them.

The barque fired its starboard guns. It was a huge salvo, and for a moment, the hull of the ship disappeared behind an expanding cloud of firelit smoke. The broadside recoil rolled the barque heavily to its port line, and it began to loose sheets to close into battle.

The sea to either side of the *Rumour* blossomed with cannon splash, and two heavy culverin balls smashed into the port bow just above the water line. The deck shook.

Silvaro edged the *Rumour* around just a hint so that Sheerglas had his port guns at a tight present. They flashed and fired. Hull boards and gunport hatches blew out into the water, and smoke laced the space between the two ships. Another thundering broadside came from the devil barque. The *Rumour's* foresails exploded into shreds and several men on deck were slaughtered. Sesto could smell blood again. Blood, sea salt, sea wind, powder smoke.

The barque had dropped all speed, and was edging around, trying to out-turn the *Rumour*.

'In close! In close!' Silvaro ordered.

The call seemed like suicide. As they came in shy of the barque's starboard side, its cannons flashed once again, and the *Rumour* shuddered as hull wood burst and rails blew away. The foremast was in tatters. Sesto saw at least one of Vento's riggers hanging, dismembered, from the foremast's torn ropes.

The order was not madness. The barque's gunports, though plentiful, were high up on its waist, and once the sprightly *Rumour* got in close enough, the enemy couldn't angle its heaviest guns low enough to target the *Rumour's* hull. Still, their shots ripped through the sails. Few were more than shreds now. Sheerglas used the foremost guns to drench the enemy with grape shot. The calivermen on the rails and rigging and the men with the swivel guns began to pink at the closing foe. Cannons barked and flashed sporadically from its dark red sides. They had calivermen up too. Tortoise Schell, a cut-less in his hand as he waited for a chance to board, was killed stone dead by a caliver ball. Rodrigo Sal and Dirty Gabriel were shredded by chain shot that smashed through the pavises. Vento was impaled with splinters from the foremast along his left arm and chest, and fell twenty feet onto the deck. Largo ran aloft with his gold comb-morion in place, and spat arrows from his horse bow at anything moving at the enemy's rail.

They were at close quarters now, both ships almost dead in the water and shrouded by a gagging envelope of gunsmoke. Grapples flew out from the *Rumour*, and poles reached to their extremities as the vessels, great and small, wrapped one another in a tight embrace of battle.

The *Rumour* and the Butcher Ship came side to side, stem to stern. Just before their fenders crashed and grated against each other, Sheerglas fired a final retort and stove in the enemy's hull in six places just above the line of flotation.

Screaming, the Reivers began to mob and charge across onto the barque. They scrambled across boarding planks, clambered over nets, or swung out on yard ends. Ferocious hand-to-hand fighting broke out along the barque's starboard rail.

Sesto saw Silvaro storm across, and Casaudor and Benuto too. Even Tende had left the tiller and was leaping across the deep gap between the fighting ships, his Ebonian war-axe lofted in his hand. The caliver and swivel gun men, along the *Rumour's* battered side, blasted away at the heads of the enemy crewmen.

Sesto grabbed hold of a boarding line in the thick of the mayhem and steeled himself to go over.

Ymgrawl grabbed at him. 'Are thee mad? Thou stays here!'

'The devil you say!' Sesto cursed, kicking the lean boucaner's hands away. 'I have a debt to pay!'

Pushing off, Sesto swung over onto the barque.

XVI

THE REIVERS HAD made it look so damned easy.

Sesto hadn't counted for the sheer drop between hulls that yawned below him, or the effort such a swing involved. Nor had he realised how hard it would be to hold on to a rope. When, more by luck than judgement, he landed hard on the barque's deck, he was almost impressed with himself, and privately swore that he'd never do such a thing again.

Abruptly, he had more pressing matters to deal with. A member of the rival crew – a howling, bearded thug dressed in red leather – charged at him, swinging a cut-less.

Badly balanced after his landing and all but falling over, Sesto tried to pull out the grand flintlock Silvaro had given him.

He got it free, but before he could actually fire it, the enemy cut-less dashed it to the deck.

The brute in the red leather kicked Sesto over and swung up his curved blade to finish him.

Then he fell over, hard, blood bubbling out of a neat little hole in his forehead.

Sesto lowered his ornate Arabyan piece. It had proved its worth, to him, at least.

SILVARO, ROQUE AND Casaudor, with a gang of Reivers, had almost fought their way down the mid deck to the barque's wheel when the tide of battle turned, decisively at last.

It had been hard slugging and brute blading all the way along. The decks were plashy with spilled blood, and Roque and Silvaro were both covered in bloody scratches and gashes, their shirts shredded. Casaudor, somehow, was untouched, though his coat was stained with the gore of others.

Then they heard the rolling thunder of guns. They saw the flash and fizz beyond the port rail and felt the wet deck beneath them shudder and protest.

The *Safire* had stormed out of the inlet, having deliberately hung back to allow the enemy to pass clear. Now it came in, fast as an arrow, sheets fully fat, giving out cannonade after cannonade from its starboard guns.

It sped up along the barque's port side, firing and flashing and adding to the smoke fog.

No man could argue with the situation. The great barque was vanquished.

The Reivers had won.

'YOU PRETENDED?' LUKA Silvaro hissed. He was incredulous.

'We did. It seemed to be the thing… I mean to say, it worked.'

'It worked. Did it?'

'Yes, sir…'

They stood in the barque's master cabin. The air was still filmy with smoke, and blood and water dripped down from between the deck boards above. Luka stood at one end with Roque and Sesto. At the other, under the blown-out window lights, a powder burned and bleeding man sat in a chair he had been forced into.

'By what name was this barque known?'

'It is the *Demiurge*, lord.'

'And by what name are you known?'

'I am Pieter Pieters, of Bretonnia born. I was master mate of this craft. My captain was Henri the Little, also known as

Bearded John. I saw you kill him in the tiller house, lord. I saw your sword sever his neck not fifteen minutes past.'

'So I did. His blood stains my shirt. And his neck-bone put a dink in my favourite shamshir.' Luka's voice was full of boiling threat. 'Bearded John I know. And the *Demiurge*, consort to the *Kymera*, the vessel of Red Henri of Breton.'

'The same, lord.' Pieters coughed up a good deal of blood and fell slackly back in the chair.

Silvaro paced forward and dragged the dying man up by the hair. 'And you say this is… pretence?'

'Lord?'

'You pretended to be the Butcher Ship?'

Pieters leaned forward and set his elbows on his knees. 'It was easy enough. The whole of the sea fears the Butcher Ship. We clad us up in red and set a chemical lamp at our bows for effect. Every port we came to gave us vittals with no argument. We ruled the Labyrinth and the Littoral with fear. They were terrified of us. Reputation is everything.'

'It is indeed,' said Silvaro. 'So what do you know of the real Butcher? Is it Henri?'

'It is, sir.'

'The *Kymera* is the Butcher Ship?'

'It is, sir.'

'Do you know how that might be?'

Pieters dropped his head. 'It was the end of last season, shortly before we were due to return to Sartosa. We were a company of four – the *Kymera*, the *Demiurge*, the *Alastor* and the *Diadem*. One day, Henri sighted a Tilean treasure ship, returning from Lustria or mayhap Araby or mayhap the dark continent of the south, heading across the Bay of Tilea at great speed, and gave chase. All of us were soon outdistanced by both Henri's powerful galleon and the fleeing prey – which was moving with unnatural speed. We never saw Henri again, though we expected him to turn back for us once he'd made his kill… or the treasure ship had escaped.'

'And then what?'

'What? Nothing! Henri never came back. What terror or toxin he found on that treasure ship, I cannot say. It was like unto a magic ship, a daemon-cursed mast, running against the laws of nature across the sea. Henri was a fool to chase it, and a greater fool to touch it. What it has made him, I dread to think.'

'Though you were happy to live off his new reputation,' Silvaro sneered.

'It was a living until you came along,' Pieters said.

Silvaro turned away.

'One thing I must ask,' Pieters said. 'When you came for us, you flew the jolie rouge. Does that mark still stand now?'

'I forgot about that,' Luka Silvaro said, turning back. His shamshir whistled as it slid through the air. Pieters's head bounced heavily off the deck boards.

'Yes, it bloody does still stand,' said Silvaro and strode out of the cabin.

XVII

AT SOME DAMNABLE hour of the pre-dawn – so late and yet so early that gods of the sky and sprites of the pit alike had taken to their beds – a chamberlain woke Juan Narciso, the Marquis of Aguilas.

The marquis, a loose-tempered man in his forty-fifth year, was about to order the man beaten for rousing him, when he heard the bell towers of the city below the Palacio ringing all of a frenzy.

'What?' he coughed. 'What is it?'

'My lord,' bowed the chamberlain. 'Sails, my lord, sails have entered the bay.'

Juan Narciso closed his eyes, sighed a silent prayer, and said, 'Fetch my robes.'

AGUILAS WAS THE southernmost of the old port cities on the eastern flank of mainland Estalia. Sea trade had been its primary industry for centuries, and its deep harbour had seen a busy traffic of treasure ships, merchantmen, privateers and warships over the years. But its relationship with the oceans went deeper than that: it was the birthplace of ships. The shipbuilding docks and dry-yards of Aguilas were a womb where many ships of the Estalian navy had been conceived and brought to term. Not for nothing was the standard of the city-state emblazoned with a full-sailed barque and two leaping dolphins.

The late summer dawn was pumice grey when the marquis and his retinue arrived at the wharf. Behind them, the great city climbed away up the slopes of the bay: the sea quarters, the market places, the higher streets of the old town, the refined districts where the gentry lived, all the way up to the crown of the volcanic plug where the Palacio sat, lowering across the bay. The church bells were still ringing their alarms, and most citizens had taken to their cellars, or begun to flee up into the hills and olive groves of the Del Campo. Some, however, inquisitive even in the face of death, had gathered at the dockside. They bowed as the marquis's men shouldered a path through them.

The harbour waters were empty, and had been so for many months, since the start of the curse. Only the *Fuega* sat at anchor, pugnacious and regal.

On the dockside and along the wide harbour wall, detachments of the city and marine guards had assembled, and the culverins had been primed.

As Juan Narciso approached, he heard the occasional rattle of armoured men held to attention, the flap of the banners, the snort and stomp of reined-in horses. He smelled gunpowder and fear.

Captain Duero of the marine guard approached and saluted. 'We are set to repel, excellency.'

Narciso nodded. He swallowed. 'Is it…?'

Duero shook his head. 'I cannot say, excellency. Captain Hernan awaits signal to slip anchor and meet them.'

'Hold the signal,' Narciso said. 'A spyglass?'

One was brought. The Marquis of Aguilas trained it out beyond the harbour mouth, beyond the lips of the fortified seawalls. A glimpse of those reassured him. Aguilas was a city of war as much as it was a city of trade. Its sturdy defences had withstood many a raid and several notable sieges by the fleets of Araby.

There, far out, like phantoms in the deep water of the sound, he saw the ships. Two of them. A great barque with a smaller consort ship, a brigantine, perhaps. They had slackened their sheets and seemed unwilling to venture in towards the harbour and the range of the city's cannons.

'Are they known?' Narciso asked.

Duero shook his head again. 'Their names and brands cannot be read from this distance, excellency, though I'd make them as Tilean vessels. Should we raise a signal from the breakwater wall?'

'If they're in no hurry to come in,' said Narciso, 'I'm in no hurry to greet them. Gods, but I wish we knew them.'

'Begging your pardon, my lord marquis,' a voice called from back down the quay. 'Begging your pardon, but I think I know them.'

Narciso turned. A young man, Tilean by his accent, had pushed to the front of the gaggle of citizens held back by the marquis's bodyguards. The man made a bow when he saw Narciso notice him.

'Bring him here!' the lord of Aguilas ordered.

Two heavy troopers in comb morion helms grabbed the young man and pulled him up along the flagstones into their lord's presence. The young man bowed again. His clothes were fine, Narciso noted, but he was shabby and he smelled unwashed. There was a neglected air to him.

'Look at me,' Narciso ordered. 'These ships. You know them, do you?'

'I believe I do, excellency,' the young man said. He spoke Estalian well – very well, Narciso had to admit. In fact, despite his Tilean twang, the young man spoke it as well as one of the finelyeducated courtiers of Tilea. He had schooling in diplomatic convention and manners.

'Then tell me,' Narciso said.

'The barque, excellency, is named the *Demiurge*. The brigantine is called the *Rumour*.'

'Indeed…'

'My lord!' hissed Duero. 'Those are known pirate vessels, both!'

'And how do you know that?' Narciso asked the young man.

'Because their master told me so, excellency,' the young man said gently.

'You admit to consorting with pirates?' Narciso asked.

'No, my lord. But I admit to this–' The young man reached in under his coat. Immediately, Duero struck him to the ground. The guard captain roughly searched the young man's clothing.

'A weapon?' Narciso asked.

'No. No, excellency. Just this.' Duero held out a fold of parchment.

'If you'd but let me explain,' the young man said.

Narciso shook open the papers and read them. 'Letters of marque and reprisal. Signed by the Prince of Luccini.'

'Yes, my lord marquis,' said the young man. 'May I get up?'

Narciso nodded.

'His highness the prince has charged those vessels with a task that I imagine will meet with your lordship's full approval. We require supply and, more particularly, the crafts-manship of your famed dockyards. It was considered foolhardy to simply sail into your harbour and face the mis-guided wrath of your guns. A more discreet approach was deemed to be in order.'

'I see. By whom?'

'My master, Luka Silvaro.'

'That rogue? Could he not come here himself?'

'I did,' a voice from the crowd said. 'But I fancied the Mar-quis of Aguilas might just hang me without asking questions.'

At a sharp nod from Duero, twenty musketeers turned and trained their primed weapons on the crowd, which ebbed back in dismay.

'Who said that? Show yourself, pirate!'

'Would you shoot down your own citizens, excellency?' the young man asked.

'To find that blackguard? Yes!' Narciso snarled.

'No wonder, then, that he has hidden himself,' the young man said. 'Two things you should know, sir, before you give your captain-at-arms the order to fire. One, the marque has charged Luka Silvaro to hunt and destroy the Butcher Ship, against pardon for his crimes.'

'And the second thing?' asked the Marquis of Aguilas.

'You should know that I am Giordano Paolo, sixth and youngest son of the Prince of Luccini.'

* * *

'WHY IN MANANN'S name didn't you tell me before?' Luka growled.

'There was no need,' Sesto replied.

'No need?'

'No need at all.'

They were in an apartment in the palacio, Sesto sitting on a bench overlooking a courtyard garden where songbirds trilled and fluttered, Luka pacing behind him.

'I thought you were some courtier, some diplomat sent... dammit! You should have told me!'

'Why?' asked Sesto.

'Because! Because it puts pressure on me! Guarding the life of the prince's own blood!'

'You were under pressure before. To keep me alive. It doesn't matter what blood runs in my veins. With me dead, you'll never get your pardon, even if you scupper the Butcher.'

Luka Silvaro stopped pacing. 'True enough, I suppose.' He looked at Sesto. 'So what do I call you now, princeling?'

'Sesto,' Sesto replied. 'There's no reason the crew should know.'

Silvaro shrugged and nodded.

It had taken them a week and a half to limp up the Littoral from the engagement at Angel's Bar. Both the *Rumour* and, especially, the *Demiurge*, were badly wounded. Casaudor and Benuto had argued that the great barque should be left behind, especially seeing as Silvaro had executed every man jack of its crew according to the code of the jolie rouge.

Roque had supported Silvaro's notion that they could use every ship they could find. The *Demiurge* was a fighting man-at-arms, and full-crewed and gunned, could menace anything on the seas. As they needed to find a friendly port to repair the *Rumour* anyway, it seemed only fit to skeleton-crew the *Demiurge* and bring it along. With the *Safire*, the trio would make a handsome pack to hunt the Butcher Ship to its doom.

And so they had limped up the mainland coast, the *Safire* running protection for the two crippled vessels. Aguilas had been decided upon early as the only viable port of call. There, they might be repaired, re-victualled, and the *Demiurge* recrewed. It was the only harbour they could reach in decent time that could furnish the services they needed.

Providing, of course, that Aguilas was receptive.

That had been why, two days out, Silvaro and Sesto had switched to the *Safire* and sailed in to an uninhabited bay three leagues south of the Aquilas Bay, to enter the city on foot and broker the agreement.

'They may still hang us,' Luka said.

'They may,' Sesto replied. 'Well, you certainly. They would not dare hang me. What, and risk my father's reprisal fleet?'

Luka grinned. 'You're learning the selfish streak of a true pirate, Sesto, you know that?'

'Must be the company I've been keeping.'

They took a glass of wine each and walked up to a terrace that overlooked the harbour bay. Below, signalled in, the *Demiurge* and the *Rumour* had both come into dock. Out in the sound, the distant shape of the *Safire* was now turning inwards with the wind. It was a bright day, softly lit by a golden Estalian sun, now the dawn vapours had gone.

'Just one other ship down there,' Sesto pointed. 'An Estalian man-o-war.'

'The *Fuega*. Yes, I saw it,' Luka replied. 'A grand old dame of the sea, an Estalian galleon, forty-gunned, mean as a bludgeon. I saw her straining in the harbour there, keen to slip out and take us on. Ah, the times I've tangled with old ladies like that! The backbone of the Estalian navy, the scourge of pirate men. Slow and fat, like a dowager duchess, heavy on the turn, but packed full of spite and thunder. Those close gun-decks, tight spaced. They can do a wonder of hurt. That's why men of my inclination switched to smaller, faster craft like the *Rumour*. Why fight what you can outrun?'

'Why indeed?' Sesto smiled.

There was a knock on the chamber door, and a chamberlain entered.

'His excellency is ready with his answer,' he announced.

THE GRAND HALL of the palacio had been laid out for a midday feast.

'That's a good sign,' Sesto whispered to Luka. 'It's a mark of Estalian hospitality to provide a fine luncheon for those they would have terms with.'

'Uh huh,' Luka whispered back. 'May I remind you of our last taste of Estalian hospitality? Porto Real?'

'The glass is always half empty for you, isn't it?' Sesto sneered.

'Half empty of poison,' Luka replied quietly. 'Besides, this may be the celebratory feast they plan to enjoy once they've signed our execution warrants.'

'Oh, ye of little faith,' Sesto said. 'By the way, leave all the talking to me.'

A fine gathering of nobles and uniformed officers had assembled around the long table. One, Sesto noticed, was a hard eyed, dark haired man in beautifully crafted half-armour and puffed crimson sleeves, his skin tanned and prematurely lined by years at sea. His glaring eyes never left Silvaro.

A band of fifes, guitarras and drums announced the arrival of the Marquis of Aguila.

Splendid in his gold-thread robes and silver crown, attended by a train of liveried servants, Narciso took his seat at the head of the table. He lifted a goblet in a hand clustered with jewelled rings of dark Lustrian gold.

Sigmar's bones, but he wants to impress, Sesto thought.

'Raise your cups and bid our visitors fair welcome,' Narciso declared.

The standing courtiers took up their goblets. Silvaro reached for his, but Sesto slapped his hand.

'Not yet!'

'But I'm thirsty…' Silvaro whispered back.

'Luka Silvaro, sometimes called The Hawk. And… Sesto Sciortini, noble cousin. To both of you, we utter our welcome.' Narciso sipped, and his courtiers did likewise. Sesto noted that the hard eyed man in the crimson sleeves simply put his goblet to his lips but did not swallow.

Now Sesto took up his glass, and nodded to Luka to do likewise.

'Excellency, your greeting humbles us, as does this array of good fellowship,' Sesto said loudly in Estalian. 'We accept your welcome, and pledge to your continued health and wise governance.'

Sesto and Luka drank. Luka finished his cup.

'Now you're going to have to mime,' Sesto whispered.

'What?'

'We answer your friendly response with all good humour,' Narciso called. 'And we pledge in turn to your health.'

The lord and his courtiers sipped again.

'And to you, excellency, for this warm companionship, we raise our cups in true fealty,' Sesto answered, toasting again. Luka awkwardly mimed supping from his empty cup.

'We are gratified by your arrival, and we offer to you all sundry rewards that Aguilas has to offer,' his lordship toasted again.

'Manann! How long's this back and forth going to last?' Luka whispered to Sesto.

'Twenty minutes,' Sesto whispered back. 'And to you, excellency,' he declaimed aloud, cup held aloft, 'we are bowed by your beneficence and your largesse.'

Silvaro stuck his empty cup out behind him and jiggled it until one of the waiting wine stewards refilled it. He brought it back in front of him.

'All right, I'm good,' he whispered. 'Whose turn is it now?'

Twenty minutes later, they all took their seats. The stewards began to serve the first course of the meal.

'To begin with,' Narciso said, nibbling at a quail's drumstick, 'let us get the greater matter over. We accept the provenance of your letters of marque.'

Across the table, the man in the crimson sleeves snorted.

'We greet you as brothers,' Narciso continued, 'for your aim matches ours. The Butcher Ship is a deadly scourge, and we would see the common seas rid of it as soon as possible.'

'Luccini concurs, my lord marquis,' Sesto said.

'It is a foul blight on trade,' Narciso said. 'A foul, foul blight. Therefore, we have agreed to your requests. Your vessels – the *Demiurge* and the *Rumour* – both will be repaired and refitted in our yards. And at no cost. We will supply the materials and the craft, as our contribution to this united cause. Within a fortnight, your ships will be ready to set out to finish this grim task.'

'The generosity of Estalia, and most particularly, Aguilas, is gratefully noted,' Sesto said.

Luka mumbled something.

'What was that?' the man in the crimson sleeves asked.

'My comrade merely suggested that it was good that our nation states should ally themselves against a common foe this way,' Sesto replied quickly. 'A joining of forces. After all, in good faith, we sailed our ships into your harbour, under your guns. If we had meant menace, we would have been destroyed.'

The Marquis of Aquilas nodded. 'A gesture of trust that convinced me. Pirates always look for the shallow way, in my experience. The callous trick. But you played not false, and submitted your vessels to Aguilas's harbour guard.'

'As luck would have it…' Luka muttered under his breath.

'Again!' said the man in the crimson sleeves, stiffening. 'Another low dissent!'

'Hernan! Hernan!' Narciso said. 'Settle down. My cousin, dear Sesto, these have been hard times. Trade has dried. Ships have been lost, many ships. The once-busy waters of Aguilas harbour are now empty and slow. One ship alone we keep here, the formidable *Fuega*, Captain Hernan's vessel. The last of the old war pack. Hernan would have the *Fuega* set out to stalk this devil ship, wouldn't you, captain?'

The man in the crimson sleeves coughed and nodded. 'Yes, excellency.'

'We can't have that! We can't have the last fighting ship in Aguilas gone. Who would protect us then? Of course, the shipyards have laid down the keels of other warships, but it will be a year or more until they are complete. Repairing your vessels arms us much faster.'

'And we will rise to your defence,' Sesto said.

'You'll need crew,' said a courtier nearby.

'Of course,' said Sesto.

'That won't be easy,' the man in the crimson sleeves said bluntly. 'Able mariners have fled the port. Only rats and rating-dregs remain.'

'My kind of crew,' Silvaro said, biting the end off a skewer of meat.

'Crew will be found for you,' Narciso assured smoothly. 'But what of a commander? Will you captain the *Demiurge*, Master Silvaro?'

'No, excellency,' Luka said through his mouthful. 'The *Rumour* is mine.'

'Aye, so it is,' hissed the man in the crimson sleeves.

'But I'll find a commander to take the *Demiurge*,' Luka said breezily.

'Well, sir, if you have a hard time looking,' Narciso said, 'you might consider my nephew Sandalio here. He's an aspiring captain, trained on the sail. Aren't you, Sandalio?'

A very plump, pig-eyed boy at the end of the table at the marquis's right hand belched and grinned. 'I tho very mutch am,' he lisped. 'I thrtive to therve the offith of my uncle.'

'Yes, Sandalio's your man,' Narciso said.

'I'll remember that, lord,' Silvaro said. 'And if I don't find a worthier captain amongst my crew–'

'Then I hope you don't,' Narciso said. 'Sandalio would serve you well.'

'I'd sooner sail into hell than give a ship to that buffoon…' Silvaro whispered to Sesto.

'Hear him! Another slight.' The man in the crimson sleeves pushed back his chair and rose to his feet.

'Sit down, Hernan!' Narciso said.

'No, lord,' Hernan said quietly. 'This man, this pirate, is an affront to our good company here. I know his crimes. I know his ignominy. Five years ago, we clashed in the Straits of the Gorgon and he left me aflame with sixty dead.'

Silvaro frowned. 'The Straits of the Gorgon? The *Scalabra*? Was that you, Hernan?'

'It was, sir.'

'Well, joking apart, I bested you on that fair afternoon and I'll do it again. Sit down.'

Captain Hernan did not. He hurled his glove at Silvaro so hard it spilled the dish of food into Silvaro's lap. Slowly, threateningly, Silvaro rose.

'This is a nothing,' Sesto cried. 'We can forget this old animosity!'

'Of course,' agreed Narciso. 'This is just an aberration.'

'No, it's not, my lord,' Hernan said.

'No, it's really not,' Silvaro agreed. 'Our arrangement not withstanding – and I pray to the gods that it stays in place – Captain Hernan and I have a matter of honour to settle.'

'Oh gods…' Sesto murmured.

'When?' asked Narciso, taken aback. 'Where?'

'Right here, my lord,' said Hernan.

'Yes,' smiled Silvaro. 'And right now.'

XVIII

THE TWO MEN strode out through the tall side doors of the grand hall into the walled flower garden outside. The rest of the fine company, bemused for the most part, got up from the table and followed them. Juan Narciso had a troubled frown on his face.

Sesto ran ahead and caught up with Silvaro.

'In the name of the gods, stop this foolishness!' he whispered urgently.

'Too late,' Silvaro replied.

'I'm a prince. I could order you to stop this,' Sesto said.

'You could try that,' Silvaro admitted.

'I order you to stop this now!' Sesto cried.

'Well, look at that,' Silvaro replied, still walking. 'It didn't work.'

Silvaro and Hernan arrived in the centre of the flower garden, a paved area out in the bright sunshine, with a small hour dial in the centre. The air was warm, and heady with the perfume of the brilliant blooms in the beds around.

'Here suit you?' Hernan asked.

'Here's fine,' Silvaro replied.

The guests and worthies from the dinner crowded around the outer paths of the garden, beyond the flower beds and the low box hedges. Some had brought their drinks.

Hernan stripped off his half-armour, tossing the pieces to a waiting soldier. Then he drew his sabre and made a few practice slashes in the air. It was a fine weapon, as fair an Estalian blade as Roque Santiago Della Fortuna's.

Silvaro took off his coat, handed it to Sesto, and then looked over at the waiting nobles. 'Might I trouble one of you good fellows for a sword? I never seem to have one on me when a duel comes along.'

Captain Duero of the marine guard looked over at the Marquis of Aguilas, who nodded slightly, then drew his own sabre and offered it, grip-first across his arm, to Silvaro.

Silvaro took it. 'Thank you, captain,' he nodded, and tried its weight and balance. A good sword, service-issue. A professional's weapon. Nothing like as fine as the blade in Hernan's hand.

Silvaro stepped carefully across one of the flowerbeds, relieved one of the guests of his wine glass, took a swig, and handed it back.

'Thank you, sir, I was a little dry.'

He turned to face Hernan, who stood waiting, sword held at a forty-five degree angle to the ground. 'Ready?'

Hernan nodded.

Silvaro looked over at the marquis. 'My lord?'

'Begin, if you must,' said Narciso. His excellency glanced at the chamberlain beside him and said, 'Go fetch a priest.'

Silvaro cleared his throat, shook out his shoulders, and said to Sesto, 'Stand back. If I die, the ship's yours.'

Shaking his head, Sesto retreated to the other side of the flowerbeds.

'All right then,' Silvaro said, assuming a ready stance. 'Take your guard.'

Hernan lunged forward and the blades struck against each other three times, fast as a snake strikes. Silvaro broke and circled, and they came together again, their swords lashing and parrying so rapidly it was difficult to follow. The chime of metal upon metal rang like a furiously shaken hand bell. Such was the speed and expertise displayed by the two men that when they broke to circle for a second time, the onlookers let out a round of applause.

Keeping a skip in his step, like a dancer, Silvaro circled the little yard, making sure he didn't box out any route of evasion by getting too close to the sundial. Sweat beaded his brow already. It was hot in the direct noon sunlight. Hernan seemed as cool as ice, following Silvaro step for step.

Silvaro pressed the attack now, sweeping in at Hernan's right quarter guard, and the drive led to the longest rally exchange of the duel so far. Seventeen blows traded in four seconds, blade slithering against blade. Silvaro turned his last half-parry into a low lunge that grazed his sabre down the length of Hernan's blade and in through his half-guard. But at the last second, Hernan brilliantly twitched his wrist out and over and hooked Silvaro's swordpoint away. Silvaro had to skip backwards to avoid being run through by the riposte.

They circled again. Silvaro was breathing hard.

'My compliments, captain,' Silvaro said. 'Your hand is good and your eye better. You've read your Bresallius.'

'From cover to cover.'

'And you've studied your De Poelle.'

'I studied *under* De Poelle,' Hernan replied.

'Ah. Well, I'm in trouble then, aren't I?' Silvaro said.

'Who, might I ask, did you study under?' Hernan asked.

'Study under?' Silvaro laughed. 'Enemy fire, mostly.'

They closed again, and rang out five, hard *chings* from high, sweeping cuts, before sliding their blades together until the guards locked and they were pushing and shoving like wrestlers.

Hernan's expertise favoured blade-play, but in more physical competition, Silvaro's size and strength had the advantage. Hernan was shouldered backwards, and found himself forced to break in a clumsy, frantic fashion, almost colliding with the sundial in his haste. Silvaro followed him with a savage slice that lopped the gnomon off the dial.

Yet again, they circled one another. To Sesto, it looked like Silvaro was slowing down. The Estalian was still tight and quick, energised, but Silvaro looked sluggish. He'd clearly been relying on the fact that if he closed with his adversary and brought it down to brute strength, he would

win. Hernan would not be fooled into a wrestling match
again.

'You know,' said Silvaro, wiping the back of his left hand
across his dripping brow, 'I had all but forgotten that day on
the Straits until you mentioned it.'

'I'm not surprised, pirate,' Hernan scowled. 'So many
ships you've left burning in your wake.'

Silvaro shrugged. 'Maybe. But it's coming back to me now.
Quite a scrap, as I recall. The wind was up, a fair westerly
snap.'

'South-westerly,' Hernan corrected.

'Yes, you're right. Ideal for a long run around the Straits.
And you in waiting. The *Scalabra*. A big bastard of a ship,
that.'

'She was a sweet engine of war, ready to sink a motherless
dog like you.'

Hernan lunged and forced Silvaro into a double parry
that kicked sparks from the blade edges. Silvaro feinted,
thrust in at the lower right quarter with a dazzling down-
point cut that drew gasps from the crowd, but which was
squarely blocked and turned away by Hernan's nimble
hand.

'I suppose then,' Silvaro said, 'it rather begs the question... why *didn't* you sink a motherless dog like me?'

Hernan narrowed his eyes, but did not reply.

Their blades flickered together again, a passing clash as
they rotated their circling.

'After all,' said Silvaro, breathlessly, 'you had me outgunned, outrun and caught against the wind. But at day's
end, you were the one afire.'

Hernan growled in barely contained rage and ran at Silvaro. Their swords rattled against each other, fifteen passes,
twenty, Silvaro desperately short-parrying each deadly
thrust and lunge. By luck, more than skill, Silvaro kept the
Estalian's blade at bay and his skin intact.

He broke again, but Hernan kept pressing. Sabre rang off
sabre. Hernan pivoted forward, bested Silvaro's guard with
a half-lunge and fast riposte, and sliced round to take Silvaro's head off.

Sesto winced. Silvaro back-stepped, ducked like he was
bowing to an emperor or a dancing partner, and the stroke

missed. He speared his sabre up again, and Hernan had to give ground, fending off the long lunges with three anxious, low chops of his watered steel. For a second, all grace and skill had evaporated and the fighting had become brutal and dirty.

'I had only one chance that afternoon, Captain Hernan,' Silvaro rumbled, 'to ram against the wind and then gybe hard behind your stern before your guns could range me. But you knew that. You came in tight, loosing sheets, cutting me off. It was a brilliant move.'

Sabre glanced off sabre. Hernan made two extended parries to knock Silvaro's determined swordpoint away.

'But you came in too broad, too early. You were ambitious, reckless. I like that in a man. It was bravura seamanship. Only the very best could have out-guessed you, and only the very best of them out-sailed you too.'

Silvaro turned again, and sliced at Hernan's upper right quarter, forcing the Estalian to move to his left, his blade raised to defend.

'But that's what I am, Captain Hernan.'

Driven to his left, Hernan suddenly found that he and the sundial wanted to occupy the same place. He crashed into it and fell.

Silvaro pounced, kicking Hernan's sword away and placed the tip of his sabre against the sprawled captain's throat.

'I left you burning, yes, but I could have sunk you to the seabed if I'd had a mind too. I spared you that day, Hernan, because I admired you and your skill.'

'Gods receive me…' Hernan gasped.

Silvaro pushed the tip of his borrowed sabre against Hernan's windpipe until a bead of bright red blood appeared. Then he took the sword away.

'That's why I spared you then, and that's why I spare you now. With the Butcher Ship abroad, Hernan, you're too good a fighter to lose.'

Silvaro tossed his sabre from his right hand to his left and then extended his right down towards Hernan.

'I don't want you to like me, Captain Hernan. I don't expect you to. But this season, it seems, we're on the same side. What do you say? Can we set our quarrel aside for the time being?'

Hernan took Silvaro's hand and allowed himself to be pulled to his feet.

Silvaro turned to the audience around the edges of the flower garden. 'Show's over!' he cried. 'Let lunch and drinking resume!'

Loud clapping broke out around the flower beds.

'There's always next year,' Hernan hissed at Silvaro.

'I look forward to it, captain,' Silvaro replied. 'A reckoning. You can hold me to it. I just hope we're both still alive to see it.'

'The Butcher Ship?' Hernan said.

'The Butcher Ship, sir, indeed.'

XIX

THE NEXT MORNING was fair and breezy. Sesto woke early, but found the Aguilas dockside already bustling with activity. Gangs of shipwrights, chandlers, carpenters and labourers had arrived, bringing with them carts of tools and wagons laden with seasoned oak, green-cut deal and pine, cauldrons of pitch and bundles of tarred horsehair. Hoists had begun to unload the materials, and the air was full of shouts and the drumming of hammers and mallets. A smell of hot sawdust and stewing pitch lingered on the wind.

Sesto pulled a light cape around his shoulders and walked along the quay, observing the work. Up in the yards of the *Demiurge* and the *Rumour*, teams of men clambered amongst the swifting tackle and the shrouds, little monkey-shapes against the bright sky. Acres of holed and burnt sailcloth were being lowered to the decks, and torn rigging lines re-spliced or wound in. Along the body of the wharf, victuallers had already begun stacking the barrels of salted meat, biscuit and dried fruit that the longshoremen would soon be transferring to the holds. Sesto saw Fahd standing amongst a group of free merchants, sampling the spices they had brought on their handcarts, haggling over the price of cinnamon, nutmeg, cloves and white pepper. Elsewhere, Benuto and the boy Gello were examining the quality of planked timbers, and Vento was supervising a team of men as they rolled out new rope along the flagstones and paced the measurements.

At the far end of the quay, Silvaro, Roque, Silke and Casaudor were inspecting the first of the would-be recruits. Captain Duero's men had scoured the taverns and stews the night before, and drummed up as many potential ratings as could be found. Some of the recruits looked like experienced mariners, if a little old. The rest were just scared-looking youths.

Dodging past a wagon bringing in fresh blindage screens for the *Rumour*'s damaged pavis, Sesto spotted Ymgrawl. The old boucaner was sitting on a mound of hemp-rope, eating something out of a muslin bag.

Sesto wandered over to him. Ymgrawl was breakfasting on little sugar-dusted twists of fresh pastry. The arrival of the three ships had brought traders down to the quay in droves, eager to make money from the newcomer crews. Cobblers, tailors, knife-sharps, musicians, tinkers and a good few bawds had congregated along the landward side of the docks, creating a noisy, ad-hoc market. The best of the trade went to the vendors of food and drink, the bottle-men, the confectioners, the barrow-cooks and the fruit-girls. After a long time on meagre sea-rations, the Reivers flocked to them, hungry for the delights of sugar-sticks and oranges and sweet loaves, the temptations that had lingered in their dreams night after night.

Ymgrawl was consuming his pastries with an expression of almost beatific content. Sesto smiled when he saw there were actual tears of pleasure in the boucaner's eyes. To a citizen of the land, the little pastries would be an everyday inconsequence, a snack for the sweet-toothed. But to the raw dogs of the open sea, they were wonders, extraordinary treasures beyond compare, luxuries that a Reiver might sample only a handful of times in his life.

Ymgrawl saw Sesto approach and, reluctantly, offered him the bag.

'My thanks, no. I've already eaten,' Sesto lied. He hadn't the heart to deprive the boucaner of even one of the delicacies.

Ymgrawl rose and, finishing his breakfast, walked the quay with Sesto.

'They're pressing new crew,' Sesto remarked.

'Aye,' replied the boucaner. The pastries all gone, he was running his grubby fingers up and down the inside seam of the bag to capture the last crystals of sugar. 'But they'll need them a captain.'

'I thought Casaudor, or Roque.'

Ymgrawl shook his head. 'Thee thinks it wrong. Silvaro'll not part with his master nor his arms-chief. He'll look wider abroad.'

They passed by old Belissi, the master carpenter. He had set up a small bench on the quay and was planing down a rough block of pine, crooning as he worked. Sesto saw that the old man was shaping another crude copy of his false leg, like the one he had cast into the sea as an offering the morning they had departed Sartosa.

'What is that about?' Sesto whispered to Ymgrawl.

Licking his thin lips, Ymgrawl had been staring at the traders down the quay, considering whether or not to purchase a second bag of pastries. Turning away, he took out his clay pipe instead, and tamped smelly, black leaf into the bowl.

'Belissi? Him?' Ymgrawl muttered. 'Ah, the old curse, that which hath followed him.'

'Curse?' Sesto echoed. With a start, he realised he had touched the iron of his sword-grip against ill-fortune. So easily the customs of the Reivers filtered into his blood.

Ymgrawl nodded, lighting his pipe from a tallow stick he'd poked into a nearby brazier. 'We're all cursed, thee and me and every man of us. That is how the sea regards our breed. But Belissi, he is accursed more than most. Upon his first voyage, many year ago, his ship it were taken unto ruin by a dragon-fish.'

'A what?'

Ymgrawl shrugged. 'A sea-beast, a leviathan. The seas are deep, mark thee, and many a scaly monster lurks down in the court of King Death. The bull-whale, the krakoon, the serpent, the sea-lizard. And, oft times, they wake and rise and make their ravage upon the waters of the surface. Some are so great, men mistake them for islands, and land there upon them, and kindle fires. Some are mighty swallowers of vessels. Vouchsafe thyself, Sesto, that thee never sail against one.'

'Have you seen one?' Sesto asked.

'In my time, aye. Twice. At a great distance. The horned back of a serpent, breaking the waves. And also, a thing of many, oozing arms, each one longer than a tall ship's mast. No closer I'd care to get.'

'But Belissi did?'

Ymgrawl blew a cloud of peaty smoke out around his pipe-stem. 'That he did. A dragon-fish. But the men of his ship, they fought against it. And Belissi himself, with a harpoon, speared it, and hurt it to its mortal guts. A hero he was, and cheered much by his fellows.'

'And?' asked Sesto.

'No sooner had the dragon-fish sunk away, staining the water with its rank blood, than the water churned again, bloody and all, and the dragon-fish's dam rose, vengeful, to the air.'

'What are you saying?' Sesto blinked. 'The monster's mother?'

'The monster's mother, aye!' Ymgrawl hooked his pipe out of his mouth. 'Nine times the size of the first, and lusting to avenge its child. Its fury took the ship athwart, its wicked jaws consumed man after man. Belissi was the sole survivor, adrift upon a rag of wood, the mother having taken off his leg. By some miracle, he was picked up and saved. That is why he made his trade as a carpenter, to spend his days working with the one substance that had saved him from drowning. But he knows that one day, the mother will return to exact the rest of her price. That's his curse. So he makes an offering, every time he casts off from main land. A leg, to soothe the mother in the sea, made of the precious wood that wardeth Belissi's life.'

'Then this is… mother mine…?' Sesto asked in all seriousness. 'I've heard others in the company joke and mock at Belissi's expense, as if no one believes a word of it.'

'Only a fool would,' Ymgrawl said.

Sesto started and saw the old boucaner wink at him. 'Ah, you devil! I honestly believed you!'

Ymgrawl chuckled.

They heard some commotion down the dock and hurried forward to discover its nature. Silvaro had been summoned, and the senior officers of his company came with him. Benuto, the boatswain, in his shapeless hat and crimson coat, was coming down the boarding plank from the *Safire*, followed by two Reivers who were manhandling a third figure between them.

'We found him hiding in the chain locker, so tell,' Benuto told Silvaro. 'Smelled him, more like. He's been there a while.'

The two crewmen shoved their captive to his knees. The filthy man fell hard, as if he couldn't quite break his fall with his hands.

'Manann's oath,' Silvaro said. The man looked up at him, his face dirty, thin and pale.

It was Guido Lightfinger.

'I HAD HOPED never to clap eyes on you again,' Silvaro said.

Guido swallowed and made no reply.

Silvaro turned to look at Silke, who glanced aside uncomfortably. 'You knew he was stowed in your vessel, didn't you?'

The master of the *Safire* pursed his lips and then nodded reluctantly. Sesto knew from the talk of the crew that Silke had been a particular crony of Guido's, although at heart he was an equivocator who was content to side with whoever had the upper hand. 'Yes, sir,' he said. 'You made no order that he couldn't be brought along...'

Silvaro snorted. 'Yet you anticipated my displeasure enough to keep him hidden!'

Silke shrugged and toyed with the end of one of his fussy, plaited pigtails. 'I find it's always wise to anticipate you, Silvaro,' he replied. 'Look, I didn't expect Guido to even want to come with the company after... after your falling out. But he begged me. Begged me on his knees. And, my duty to you not withstanding, I have a bond of friendship with him. I did not see the harm...'

'Did you not?' Roque said mockingly.

Silvaro looked at Guido again. 'Is what Silke says true? Beg, did you?'

'Yes, Luka,' Guido croaked.

'Why?'

'Better to hide in the bilges and be of the company still than rot as a cripple-vagabond in the backstreets of Sartosa. I thought perhaps, after due time, once the voyage had progressed and your mood mayhap had softened, I might emerge and–'

'And what?' Silvaro glowered at his half-brother.

'Rejoin the company proper,' Guido said quietly.

Silvaro burst out laughing, and some of the other Reivers around joined him in it. 'As what, Guido? You can't haul rope or even stand to the wheel with the few fingers I've left you!'

'I can hold a sword,' Guido said.

'That's what I'm afraid of,' Silvaro replied, no longer laughing.

A large crowd had gathered around the altercation: Reivers and dock workers, some civilians, and even a few of the marine guards, drawn by the confrontation and the raised voices.

'Clap him in irons while I decide what to d–'

Roque cut Silvaro off. 'There's one thing he can do,' he said.

Silvaro looked at the lean Estalian. 'What?'

'Well, I like him not at all, and trust him less, but credit where it's due,' Roque said. 'Guido is a fair and able shipmaster and–'

'Manann's oath!' Silvaro exploded. 'Are you suggesting I make him the captain?'

'He is skilled, and he has much to prove,' said Roque. 'Better him than that idiot bloater of a nephew you say the marquis is trying to press upon you.'

'Enough!' Silvaro exclaimed. 'I'll not consider that dungworm for anything, not anything, unless he's first been prepared to take the test.'

THE TEST – AND the very mention of it sent Guido's face paler yet – was evidently of such great import, the Reivers began muttering and oathing.

'Tomorrow!' Silvaro declared. 'From the *Safire*!' There was a chorus of approval.

'What is this test you speak of?' Sesto asked him.

'A measure of trust, courage and fortitude,' Silvaro answered glibly, 'that assays the mettle of a man as a white-smith assays the metal of an ingot…'

'That's all very well, but what–'

'Any wretch, like Guido, who has fallen out of favour with his company or crew, can repair his fortunes by submitting to the test. He lets the sea itself become his judge. If he fails, he is consigned to his fate. If he succeeds, then he is worthy of trust. It is a test that cannot be cheated. The sea's verdict is always true.'

'Yes, but–'

'Come with us tomorrow,' Silvaro said, 'and see for yourself.'

LATE THE FOLLOWING afternoon, with repairs still proceeding on the *Demiurge* and the *Rumour*, the *Safire* put to sea. Aboard it, along with Silke as his crew, were Silvaro, Sesto and a gang of men from the *Rumour*.

And Guido Lightfinger. His arms bound, he stood alone on the foredeck, shivering as he gazed out to sea, or perhaps into his deepest thoughts.

The sloop made fine going. The late afternoon was hot, the sky a transparent blue, but there was a good wind. The *Safire*'s golden hull slipped through the water like a splicing fid, and they came out of Aguilas Bay, into the sound, and then turned north east up the coast for a few leagues.

At last, with the sun just beginning to sink, Silvaro ordered them to drop anchor in a calm stretch of water a mile or so from the coast. Sesto could see the coastline, the copper crags of the Estalian interior, the dark fringes of forest and scrub. Seabirds swirled around the sloop, and there was a gentle chop. The waters looked almost violet.

Activity began, and Sesto watched with increasing fascination. Fahd had accompanied them, bringing several wooden casks that stank of offal. With the help of Curcozo, Silke's brawny first mate, the old cook hauled one of the casks upon a line over a yard arm, holed its bottom with an awl, and then let it swing free over the port side of the *Safire*.

Blood began to leak out. Silke's men worked the rope up and down around a fiddle block, sometimes swinging it down to drag the cask into the waves. An oily slick of blood began to stain the sea beside them.

Fahd went to the rail with the other casks, opened them, and began to fish out chunks of spoiled meat with a marlinespike, and toss them into the sea.

Sesto crossed to the port rail to watch, wrinkling his nose at the stink of the bad meat and sour blood.

'There,' muttered Ymgrawl at his side, and pointed.

The first of the eater-fish had appeared, summoned by the blood. In increasing numbers, dark shapes converged on the slick, sliding beneath the water, some the size of longboats. Occasionally, there would be a splash or a flurry of water as some of the great fish disputed a chunk of meat. Once in while, a great fin, grey like a blade, broke the watertop.

Fahd threw out more meat, and the feeding began to turn to a frenzy. The water, stained red, boiled and frothed. Tails and fins appeared more frequently, writhing and thrashing.

'That'll do it,' Silvaro ordered. Two men came forward and, using rope mallets, fixed a timber plank to the ship's rail with iron nails, so that the better part of the plank – some four spans – reached out over the seething water.

'Name of a god...' Sesto murmured, beginning to realise what the test was to be.

One of Silke's men, a little crook-back Estalian by the name of Vinegar Bruno, produced a small tambour drum and a bone stick, and began to beat out a lively rowdy-dow-dow. Some of the men laughed. Others, like Silke, remained silent and grave.

Roque brought Guido forward. Lightfinger was shaking now. Silvaro nodded, and Roque fetched a snifter of jerez so that Guido might fortify his nerve. Roque had to hold up the glass so that Guido could swig, for his arms were still bound.

Once the glass was empty, Roque bowed to Guido and stepped back. Largo, the sailmaker, then came forward, and slipped a cowl of dirty sailcloth over Guido's head, masking his face entirely. Sesto heard Guido moan. With quick, sure fingers, Largo sewed up the back of the cowl until Guido's whole head was sealed in a canvas bag so tight that the material stretched around his nose and chin.

'Ready?' Silvaro called.

Guido nodded. Silvaro waved his hand, and two well-muscled ratings shuffled forward, picked up Guido between them, and set him on his feet on the ship end of the board. It shivered under his weight. Sesto swallowed. The plank was little wider than two feet placed side by side. Guido teetered for a moment, trying to find his balance, his shoulders turning and shifting because he could not use his arms as counterbalance.

Vinegar Bruno beat the tambour harder and faster. Over the side, the great, sleek eater-fish, half-seen and menacing, continued to thrash and churn the surface. Guido and his precarious board were eight spans above them.

'He'll walk to his death!' Sesto gasped.

'Aye, if he's guilty,' Ymgrawl replied. 'He must walk to the end of the board, turn, and make his way back. If he does this, the sea hath judged him innocent and true. If he falls, then the sea has found him wanting. But he must go right to the end of the board, thee hear. If turneth he back too early, guessing it awry, then he is forfeit too, and Silvaro will put a pistol ball in his chest afore he can step back onto the deck.'

Sesto could not take his eyes off the trembling figure on the plank.

'Get on with you!' Silvaro yelled. The drumming rose in urgency, and some of the men were now clapping in rhythm.

Guido Lightfinger took his first step. The board quivered. A second step, Guido tilting and switching at the hips to maintain his balance against the vibration of the plank and the roll and pitch of the ship itself. Another step, another frantic twist and shimmy of the hips and shoulders. The further Guido walked down the plank, the more it bowed under his mass, and the more exaggerated its shudders became.

Sesto looked down for a second, into the dark, roiling water, in time to witness a great maw rise for a moment through the bloody foam, huge teeth ranged around a vast pink cavity. Then it was gone again. Three or four fins circled below the plank like the sails of toy dinghies.

Guido was now three quarters of the way along the test-ing board. His creeping progress had slowed yet further, for the plank was bending significantly as he neared its end, and he was in danger of simply sliding off. He slipped his feet forward, little by little, no longer raising them off the board, feeling his way with his toes.

'He's going to stop,' Ymgrawl whispered. 'If he turns now, it'll be too soon.'

As if suspecting the same thing, Silvaro had drawn a wheel-lock pistol and armed it ready. But Vinegar Bruno's drumming continued frantically, like the pulse of a racing heart, and Guido pushed on, struggling to stay upright.

Little more than a single pace from the end of the plank, Guido slipped. An especially heavy piece of swell had rolled the *Safire*, and that motion was transmitted, amplified, to the man on the end of the flexing plank. Guido's balance went. He overcorrected with his shoulders, then started to pitch the other way. So, instinctively, he stepped out with his left foot to steady himself.

But there was nothing under his left foot.

For a second, he wavered. The men fell silent. Even the drumming stopped.

Somehow, Guido corrected himself, shifted his weight, and hopped back on his planted foot. The hopping put a wicked spring into the board, but he found his footing and remained upright.

An unabashed cheer went up from the deck. Even Silvaro nodded in respect. Guido remained still, waiting for the springing to subside, retaining his tenuous balance.

One more pace remained. Again, Guido seemed about to turn, but the eager drumming struck up again, goading him, and he took that final step.

He was right at the end of the plank. Slowly, he lifted his right foot to make another step forward.

Everyone held their breath. Even the drumming slowed, becoming nothing more than a hovering, expectant rattle.

Guido put his foot back down, and slowly shuffled around until he was facing the *Safire*. Another cheer. He began to edge his way back along the board.

The return trip was not without risk. Twice, he swayed dangerously as the swell yawed the ship. But Guido kept his

balance, and at last fell off the rail-end into the waiting arms
of the ratings.

There was much chanting and hullabaloo. Rum was
brought out and Guido's name and luck toasted. Fanciman
took out his fife, and Alberto Long his fiddle, and they set
up a boisterous reel against Vinegar Bruno's tambour beat.

Roque cut Guido's bonds, and Largo slit open the canvas
cowl and pulled it free. Guido's face was death-pale, and his
hair was plastered lankly to his sweaty scalp. He took the
cup of rum Silke pressed into his claw hand, and sank it,
and the refill too. The third cup he raised to Silvaro, who
toasted him back with a grudging nod. Then Guido went to
the rail with a bottle of rum, threw it into the sea as an offering of thanks, and spat at the eater-fish below who had been
cheated of his flesh.

Thus it was that Guido Lightfinger became master of the
Demiurge.

'WE HAVE NOT yet had the opportunity to become acquainted, Master Sciortini,' said Guido Lightfinger.

Ten days had passed since the nerve-wracking test, and in that time, Guido had changed a great deal. Fed and cleaned up, he struck a much more robust figure than the snivelling wretch that had been dragged up out of the *Safire*'s chain locker. He was groomed and shaved, and wore newly-purchased boots of Estalian leather, black moleskin breeks, a white blouse and a long coat of steel blue shagreen. A polished, hooked blade protruded from his left cuff in place of his lost hand, held to the stump of his wrist by a metal cup that strapped to his forearm. Glinting gemstones had been threaded into the beading of his chin-beard, and he wore a Tilean captain's hat, a tri-corn of purple felt, that shaded his eyes.

But the changes to Guido Lightfinger ran deeper than that. The real difference lay in his manner and his bearing. His confidence was back, his silky arrogance. After much debate, following the test, Silvaro had agreed to give Guido probation as the master of the *Demiurge*. Sesto knew this,

more than anything, was down to the fact that Silvaro
wished to avoid having to take on the marquis's nephew.
But, off-guard in conversation with Sesto, Luka had admitted that Guido was a good master, and a skilled war-captain,
who knew how to clash with the best, and survive.

'Just stay out of his way,' Luka had advised.

Sesto had done just that. It had been a busy period, the
workforce of Aguilas labouring round the clock to refit the
ships. Guido had spent much of his time aboard the *Demiurge*, testing his new-pressed crew, drilling them hard. He
had purloined a good number of Reivers into his crew,
mainly those who had old loyalties to him. From Silke's
crew, he had stolen Curcozo as his mate, Vinegar Bruno,
Alberto Long and seven more. Silke had complained, but
Reivers had been traded between the *Rumour* and the *Safire*
to balance the company.

Silvaro himself had been absent for several days, travel-
ling up the coast with Casaudor and a detachment of guards
under the charge of Captain Duero. They had ridden from
port town to port town, village to village, gathering intelligence, collecting rumours. There had been sightings of the
Butcher Ship. At one little place that based its industry upon
the catching and curing of mackerel, the dread barque had
been seen across the bay just two nights before, gliding
north in the twilight like a phantom.

On the eighth day after the test, Guido had taken the
Demiurge out for the first time, into the sound, for trials and
sea-drills. Newly cleaned and painted, with clean sheets as
white as the clouds, it made a splendid sight as it swept
majestically out of the harbour. No longer was it the dark
hulk, the false *Kymera*, that had faced them down at Angel's
Bar.

Sesto had kept himself to himself, spending time in the
library of the palacio as the Marquis's guest, studying
almanacs and waggoners and other rare volumes concerning the nature of the sea and all that is in and under it. His
escort was Captain Hernan, who proved to be a man of
immense wit and fine learning. Hernan eagerly assisted
Sesto in his endeavours to discover if any clue to the nature
or sorcery of the Butcher Ship might be contained in the
marquis's priceless collection.

Only once, as they paused in their scholarly work and took a glass of jerez, did Hernan raise any protest.

'My lord,' he said to Sesto, 'how can you sail with a bastardo like Silvaro? You seem to me a gentleman of fine manners and noble birth. Yet you consort with the Hawk himself.'

'Luka is a dangerous man, captain,' Sesto conceded, 'but this is dangerous work. What is the saying... I'm sure you have it here... "Set a reiver to catch a reiver"?'

Hernan nodded. 'And a daemon to catch a daemon?'

'I understand your animosity, captain. Gods know, it is justified. But it has been my experience that to know Luka Silvaro is to know an honourable man.'

'He is a pirate, sir.'

'Yes, he is a dog of Sartosa. But if all pirates were like him, they would not have earned the name of dogs.'

Spending his days at the palacio, dining with Hernan, or the marquis, or both, Sesto returned to the *Rumour* only to sleep. The marquis had offered him accommodation for his stay, but Sesto had developed a strange yearning to sleep on the water within the oak embrace of the ship.

On the seventh night after the test, late, after the midnight watch-bell, he had started up from his cot at the sound of screams. Grabbing up a cut-less, he ran down the lamplit companion way in his night shirt. The screams were coming from Roque's quarters. Men had gathered, sleepy and alarmed, Ymgrawl amongst them.

'Stand thee back,' Ymgrawl said.

'Get to my heel,' Sesto ordered firmly, and opened the door himself.

In Roque Santiago Della Fortuna's small cabin, a lamp was still lit. By the light of it, Sesto could see the lean Estalian on the floor, wrapped in his sheet, twitching and clawing at the deckboards as if gripped by some terrible nightmare.

'Roque?' Sesto hissed, shoving back the men who crowded in behind him. 'Roque Della Fortuna?'

Roque screamed again, and the scream turned into a gurgle. He fell limp, then looked up at Sesto blearily. 'What? Who comes here?'

'You cried out, sir,' Sesto replied.

'I did?'

'Aye, loudly, as if a sea daemon had thee in his red-hot pincers,' Ymgrawl said.

'Get back to your berths,' Sesto ordered. 'You too, Ymgrawl. Go dream of sugar-dusted pastries.'

The men shambled away. Sesto closed the door, and poured two glasses of rum from a flask on Roque's table, as the master-at-arms clambered back into his crumpled bedding. Sesto handed one to Roque. The Estalian was rubbing his left shoulder, where the daemon's talon had punctured it on the Isla Verde.

'Bad dreams?' Sesto asked.

'Bad dreams, sí,' Roque replied, sipping his rum. 'Every night, it seems, though tonight must be the first wherein I have cried out and woken the company.'

'What do you see, in these dreams?'

Roque shook his head. 'I have not the words, Sesto. No words to do it justice. Blood, there is blood. Pestilence. I see the future, I think. Fire and sword, fire and sword. Wholesale war. And darkness. Such suffocating darkness. Is that what is to come, Sesto? A grim darkness of the far future where there is only war?'

'I know not,' Sesto said.

Roque shuddered. 'Worst of all, there is a dryness.'

'What?'

'In my nightmares, a cloying dryness of sand and dust and desiccated life. Like the dry soil of an old tomb. It pours into my mouth, my nose, my ears, burying me, burying me for untold centuries. I wizen and shrivel, my sinews crack like hearth wood. I... thirst.'

'Bad dreams indeed. The worst of mine usually involve me discovering I am stark naked in the middle of the Grand Summer Dance in front of a thousand grandees of Tilea.'

Roque sniggered. 'I would not wish my dreams on anyone.' He rubbed his shoulder again. 'Sesto,' he said, 'I believe I may be cursed.'

'Cursed how?' Sesto asked innocently.

'By the daemon on the Isla Verde. By the thing that was Reyno Bloodlock. The Butcher Ship had transformed him, and in turn, he left his mark upon me, deep in my flesh.'

'Tende cut it out...'

'The talon, not the curse. I am damned, Sesto. Every night, the dreams haunt me, dragging me into the sand and the dry dust. I sometimes wonder if it would be for the best for Luka to shoot me dead, or maroon me on some barren atoll where I might harm no one but myself.'

Sesto refilled their glasses. 'Ymgrawl says every man of us is cursed. He says that it is the natural state for men of our breed.'

Roque peered at Sesto in the golden lamplight. 'The boucaner says that? Well, he's an old dog and a knave, and I would take a pinch of both snuff and salt before I believed any of his words.'

'He's not seen me wrong yet,' Sesto said quietly.

Roque sat up straighter on his bolsters. 'So, you think I'm cursed?'

Sesto shook his head. 'I'm just saying, Ymgrawl believes we all are, in our particular ways.'

'Like Belissi, with his mother mine?' Roque laughed. 'Our lives are tormented by superstition and charms, Sesto. If Belissi feels better about a voyage just because he tosses a false leg over the taffrail at embarkation, good luck to him. Some men favour gold in the ear, others a garnet worn on the trigger finger and–'

'I know, I know. Perhaps, then, some curses are worse than others.'

Roque stared at him. 'What do you know?'

'I don't know if I should tell you this,' Sesto said. He paused. 'No, in fact, I think I must.'

'What, sir?'

'At Porto Real. That horror we endured at the governor's mansion.'

'What of it?' Roque asked quietly.

'You were drugged, sir, and you did not witness it. But the monster preyed upon you too, as it had done on our brothers at arms. It meant to drink your blood.'

'It… bit me?'

Sesto nodded. 'It did.'

'I wondered. I had a raw wound in my throat. I thought it was from the swordplay.'

'No, sir. Gorge bit you and… and he rejected you. He howled that your blood was tainted, spoiled. It made him vomit.'

Roque rose to his feet and poured another glass with a shaking hand. 'Who knows this?' he snapped.

'Myself, and Sheerglas. Only the two of us, and we have not spoken of it to any man.'

'My blood is so foul a vampyr would not drink it?' Rogue said, distantly.

'Or too noble, perhaps?' Sesto suggested.

Roque smiled at the effort, but the smile was thin. 'I'll sleep now, Master Sciortino. Go back to your rest. Please, I implore you, speak of this to no one. I will find the measure of my curse and decide what to do. Luka, especially, don't tell him. I need his trust.'

'I understand.'

Sesto put down his glass and moved to the door.

'Sesto?'

'Yes, sir?'

'In it all, in the midst of it, the hack and cut, if you see me… wavering. Wavering or hesitating. Please, make your strike sure and clean.'

'I will, Roque,' Sesto promised, and let himself out.

ON THE TENTH day after the test, Sesto rose and dressed, and considered taking a carriage up to the palacio. But he knew Silvaro was due to return, and thus lingered on the quay-side, watching the city armorers load cannon, shot and powder kegs onto the *Demiurge*.

And that was how he came to encounter Guido Lightfin-ger, face to face.

'We have not yet had the opportunity to become acquainted, Master Sciortini,' the voice said.

Sesto turned and found himself facing Guido and his entourage of senior crewmen, who had been promenading on the dock.

'Master Lightfinger,' Sesto bowed.

Guido waved his men on and remained with Sesto. He held out his claw of a right hand and Sesto took it gingerly.

'My brother sets a great store by you,' Guido said, conversationally.

'Yes, master.'

'Guido, please. We're all of the company here. I understand you are our passport to amnesty and reward?'

Sesto shrugged. 'I serve my duty, as given to me by the Prince of Luccini. I am merely the witness to the bond of the letters of marque and reprisal. I am no one special.'

Guido laughed. 'I beg to differ, Giordano Paolo. Ah, the look on your face! Secrets don't remain secrets long amongst a company of pirates, princeling. It pays to have spies everywhere. These things you will learn if you consort with Sartosans long enough. But, be assured. I mean you no hurt. Why, you are the very mascot, the trophy of our endeavours. Without you, we Reivers will not be able to claim our grand reward! Master Sesto, look not so abashed. I, and the men under my command, will guard your life with our very blood, if needs be.'

'I thank you for that, sir.'

'So you do, so you do. Well, "Sesto", what think you of the *Demiurge*?'

Sesto regarded the great barque hauled up at the quayside, the armorers hoisting powder kegs up into the waiting arms of the deck crew.

'A very fine fighting man-o-war, sir,' Sesto said.

'Isn't it?' Guido smiled. 'I do so like to show it off. I'd enjoy parading it to you, sir. Would you take supper with me this evening, aboard? I have retained a rather fine cook from the kitchens of the Palacio, and he promises to serve a fine lamb stew, wafer bread and blackened lobsters, set in their cases with cream.'

'Well, that's very tempting, sir.'

'I insist!' Guido said. 'I absolutely insist. We dine at the end of dog-watch. Please, I hope you'll come.'

'Then I will come too,' Ymgrawl said.

'No.'

'No? Why no?'

'Because he's invited me as an honoured guest and you–' Sesto's voice trailed off.

'I'm but bilge-dregs. I understand that, right enough.'

'It's not like that,' Sesto protested. 'I can take care of myself.'

LAMPS WERE TWINKLING in the dusk all along the quayside as Sesto walked to the *Demiurge*'s boarding ramp.

The sound of jigs and reels issued forth from the taverns along the dockside, and riotous laughter dribbled out like the last bubbles of air from the lips of a drowning man. The night air was scented with pork fat, roasting mutton, paprika and ale.

At the foot of the ramp, Curcozo was waiting for him. The big man executed a little bow.

'Come aboard, sir,' he said in low, mellow tones. 'The master awaits.'

Sesto followed the master mate up the ramp and into the belly of the *Demiurge*. Voices were singing drunkenly from down below, and the smell of stove smoke drifted down the low companion-ways. The ancient decking creaked under him with the to and fro of the tide.

The stateroom, behind the *Demiurge*'s gilded sternwork, was lit with a hundred candles and shone like gold. Through the gallery ports, nothing showed but the night. Guido was waiting, along with a dozen of the ship's senior men, glasses in hand. The candlelight twinkled off the cut crystal. The table was laid as perfectly as any banquet hall in Luccini.

'My dear Sesto!' Guido cried, and moved forward to press a crystal goblet into his hand. 'Let us toast to the future! To just rewards! To great conquests!'

Sesto raised his glass.

SILENT AS A shadow, Ymgrawl crossed the quay, drawing his tanning dagger and folding his finger around the deep choil at the back of the blade. He looked up at the *Demiurge*, and considered the best way in. Along the anchor say, that would be it. A shinny up there, and over the bower anchor into the–

'Looking for something?'

Ymgrawl turned, bringing his dagger up. But Curcozo and his sailmaker's mallet were much faster.

ALBERTO LONG WAS laughing uproariously at something Handsome Onofre had said. In the wafting, golden light, Sesto tried to remember what that might have been. His head was spinning. Too much wine, though for the life of him, he couldn't remember his glass being refilled even once.

He got up, unsteady. Guido's laughing face loomed at him, then Alberto's, then Kazuriband's, then Onofre's, then Guido's yet again.

'I feel…' Sesto began.

More laughter. Sesto fell on his face and upturned the table.

THEIR BACKSIDES WERE sore from the saddle, and dust caked their throats. Luka Silvaro rode around the headland into Aguilas after dark, Casaudor at his side, Captain Duero and his men straggled out behind. The path was dusty and the roadside thickets thrilled with cicadas.

From the brow of the road, Luka had a good view of the Aguilas harbourside, glittering with lights. Even from this distance, he could make out the faint refrains of tavern music on the hot night wind.

Something was wrong. He could taste it. He could–

Down below, in the harbour, there was a sudden bright flash, a huge wash of orange flame. A moment later, the thump of the blast came to him on the air.

Luka cried out and spurred his tired horse on down the roadway, urging it into a gallop. Behind him, Casaudor and the marine guardsmen did likewise.

Flames lit up the dockside below him, flames that were suddenly quenched. Luka saw his precious *Rumour* foundered against the quay, half-sunk. Steam and smoke came boiling out of its underside, flaring white in the evening sky. There were only two ships at the quayside. The *Safire*, and the ailing *Rumour*.

Luka glanced east, and saw the *Demiurge* making fine sail out of Aguilas Bay, past the anchored *Fuega*, out into the sound with full sheets, heading towards the setting moons.

'Guido!' Luka yelled. 'You bastard! Guido! I'm going to follow you to hell for this! To hell and back!'

A POWDER CHARGE HAD been used to hole the *Rumour* below the waterline. Scuppered, she slumped in the water at an angle, beside the dock. Steam still rose from her hatches. She would not be going anywhere for a good while.

Luka dismounted, threw his reins to Duero, and walked slowly towards the *Rumour*, ignoring the commotion and the figures dashing around him. Bells were ringing, and the city guard had been raised. Members of the Reivers company, summoned from taverns and stews, joined their captain to stare in disbelief at the crippled brigantine.

This was infamy. Guido had surpassed himself. To steal the *Demiurge* and fly was crime enough, but Guido Lightfinger, knowing his half-brother would come after him, had purposefully wounded the *Rumour* so she could not sail.

Luka was shaking with rage, and there was worse to come.

'He hath taken Sesto,' Ymgrawl said. The gnarled boucaner was clutching a bloody wound on the side of his head.

'What?'

'Sesto was aboard the *Demiurge*,' Ymgrawl replied. 'I could not stop him.'

'What happened to you?' Silvaro asked.

'That bastard Curcozo happened,' the boucaner said bitterly.

'Silke! Silke!' Silvaro yelled into the smoky darkness. The master of the *Safire* appeared, clearly agitated by the night's events.

'Make the *Safire* ready to sail. At once, you hear me?'

'Yes, Luka,' Silke nodded, and began shouting orders to his men.

'You'll take the *Safire* after Guido?' Roque asked.

'It's a damn fast ship. With luck, I might catch the *Demiurge* up, despite its lead.'

'And then what?' Roque asked. 'The *Safire* cannot take on a barque that size alone.'

'It can and it will,' Silvaro snapped. 'I'll find a way. Roque, with the fury I have inside me right now, I could take the *Demiurge* with just a longboat and a pistol.'

Roque raised his eyebrows. 'I don't doubt it, Luka,' he said.

Luka turned away and began to pace, his mind racing. What truly troubled him was not Guido's treachery – he knew what the man was capable of. The hurt Luka felt was the mystifying betrayal of the sea itself. They had conducted the test, and the sea had judged Guido trustworthy. Had the sea lied, or had Guido found some way to cheat even the rolling, eternal waters? And if the former was true, then the sea and King Death had deserted Luka Silvaro entirely.

'Assemble a company of men-at-arms, under your command,' Luka said to Casaudor. 'You'll come with me aboard the *Safire*. Roque, take charge of things here. See what you can do to get the marquis's help in making swift repairs on the *Rumour*.'

Roque nodded, though he knew such work would be a serious undertaking. Their beloved *Rumour* might even be beyond saving.

'I will come with thee,' Ymgrawl said to Silvaro. It wasn't a request. It was a statement of intent. 'I have business with Curcozo.'

IT WAS ANOTHER three hours before the *Safire* cast off and sped away into the night. There was a good wind, and Silke ordered the crew to rig not only the main sail, but also the great lateen, which ran off the long bowsprit.

Making great speed, the water hissing off her white bows, the *Safire* shot out into the open sea like an arrow from a longbow.

THE NEXT DAY was half over when Sesto awoke. His head hurt so badly he hardly dared to move for a few minutes, and when he did, he was sick.

He was on an unmade bunk in a small, dark cabin. It was cold, and there was such a tang of salt in the air that he didn't need the motion of the deck and the constant rheumatic creaking of the timbers around him to tell him he was at sea. At least the rolling sensation was real and not just a symptom of his malaise.

Sesto couldn't remember where he was or what he was supposed to be–

Suddenly, it all came back. He rose up, was sick again, and then sat in silence trying to clear his head, a cold sweat on his body. Guido, the dinner aboard the *Demiurge*…

He was on the *Demiurge* now, he knew that at once. Despite the aromas they had in common – salt, tar, smoke, grease – all ships had their own distinct scents. The *Safire* had a clean, waxy smell with a hint of camphor and linseed. The *Rumour* had a much more robust odour, a musky flavour of gunpowder, turtle meat and spice, undoubtedly because of the permeating smells of Fahd's pungent cooking. This was the *Demiurge*. It stank of dirty bilges, cloves and onions.

Sesto knew he had been drugged, and supposed he had been kidnapped. His pistol and his sword had gone. But he was not tied up or restrained, and the door to his cabin was not locked.

He went out into the dark companionway and made his way up onto the deck, his legs automatically compensating for the heavy roll of the deck. There must be quite a swell, Sesto thought.

On deck, he narrowed his eyes against the harsh light. It was a bright, blustery day, cold, with a great white sky. The grey sea, foam capped, was rolling hard, and the *Demiurge* was crashing through it, full sailed. There was rain in the air, and Sesto closed his eyes and let it wash his face.

He looked around. There was no sign of land. Just the raging sea all around.

'Did you sleep well, master?'

Sesto turned. Handsome Onofre, ropes across his shoulder, was grinning at him.

'Where is Guido?' Sesto asked.

'Where a captain should be,' Onofre said.

Sesto pushed past the man and walked down the mid-deck. The crew was busy with the sheets, hauling in teams. Whistles blew and orders to haul were barked in relay along the gangs.

A few men looked at him as he went past.

Guido was on the poop deck by the wheel. Kazuriband, the helmsman, was easing the heavy wheel by the king-spoke, and Curcozo, the master mate, stood at his captain's side. They all gazed with some amusement at Sesto as he climbed into view.

'Master Sciortini,' Guido said, with a mocking half-bow. 'How nice of you to join us.'

'I don't believe, sir, I was offered any choice.'

Guido nodded. 'True enough.'

'You've abandoned Luka,' Sesto said.

'More than abandoned,' Curcozo muttered, but did not finish the observation.

'My half-brother and I do not get on, Sesto. I thought it best that we broke our arrangements and went our separate ways.'

'You thought that once he'd given you a ship and a crew.'

Guido looked scornfully at Sesto. 'Do you expect me to feel guilty? I'm a pirate. This is what we do.'

'And what exactly is it that we're doing?' Sesto asked.

'We're heading home.'

'To Sartosa.'

'No, Sesto. Not Sartosa. To your home. To Luccini.'

Sesto smiled and shook his head. 'To claim the reward from my father.'

'Just so.'

'For a task you have not completed.'

Guido grinned. 'The prince needn't know that. Not until he's paid us and we're long gone.'

'I must be missing something,' said Sesto. 'I know you need me to pull off this shameful deceit. But you must realise I'll not support your story for a moment.'

'But of course. Unfortunately, by the time we reach Luccini, you will be very ill. So ill, you will not be able to talk. Your father will be relieved just to have you back alive. Onofre is very handy with philtres and poisons, as you found out last night. Your malady will be very convincing.'

'Luka will come after you,' Sesto said.

'No, I don't believe he will.'

Sesto stared at Guido for a moment, then turned away and left the poop deck. Shaking and ill, he wandered the *Demiurge*'s upper decks for over an hour, contemplating his options. More than once he considered hurling himself into the breaking seas to rob the vile Guido of his winning card. But Sesto didn't want to die. And, for all Guido had said, he was sure Luka would come. Not for him, but for revenge. Luka would want Guido dead for this.

Sesto decided to bide his time and see what fate brought. It would be a week at least before they reached the Tilean mainland. In that time, things might change. Sesto might even get his hands on a blade and slide it between Guido's ribs.

He was standing at the mainhead rail beneath the cracking canvas of the foremast, gazing out into the grey chop and the rain, when he noticed a figure curled up miserably beside the bower anchor.

'Belissi?'

The old carpenter wriggled over and peered up at him. 'Master Sesto, sir,' he said.

'Manann's sake, Belissi,' Sesto said. 'I thought you were Luka's man. I never imagined that you'd throw your lot in with this gang of rogues.'

'Oh, you mistake me, sir,' Belissi said. 'I am not a part of this. Not at all, as King Death is my witness. I was working on the hatch coamings until late last night, and laid myself down to sleep where I was, so that I could take up my tools again first thing. When I woke, I found we were at sea. Imagine my consternation. That bastard

Curcozo found me, and he and Alberto Long were all for slicing my gizzard and tossing me over the rail, but Guido said not to. He said I could live if I swore to him and plied my trade. There's still many fixings to be done to this old barque.'

'You poor fellow. We're prisoners both, it seems.'

Belissi nodded. 'Aye, sir, but not for long I fancy.'

Sesto realised the old carpenter was distressed, and not just because of his situation as an unwilling crewman in Guido Lightfinger's company. He was fearful and despairing.

'What do you mean?' Sesto asked.

'I mean we have put to sea, young sir. Put to sea from the mainland and I have not made my customary offering. She will be angry for that, you see.'

'Who will?' Sesto asked, dreading the answer he knew he was about to hear.

'Mother mine,' said Belissi. 'I have not made my offering to soothe her. She will be coming. Coming for me and all the souls of this doomed barque.'

Sesto went and found Handsome Onofre, and demanded a jug of rum. Onofre, faintly amused and assuming Sesto wished to drown his sorrows, produced one from the stores. Sesto returned to the mainrail head and plied the one-legged carpenter with the sweet liquor to calm his nerves.

'Can you not fashion another leg of wood now and make your offering?'

Belissi shook his head. 'Too late now, sir, too late. Mother mine is quick to anger.'

They sat for an hour or so, passing the jug back and forth, though Sesto took only the smallest sips. Belissi became quite drunk, but at least he seemed to relax.

The wind took up more furiously, and the *Demiurge* lurched and juddered massively as she scaled the heaving waves. Sesto heard a cry.

It came from the foretop castle. The lookout there was singing loudly. 'Sail! Sail at the close reach!'

There was activity on the poop deck, and orders shouted that Sesto could not hear above the buffet of the wind. He got up and looked out, but could resolve nothing in the spray and the chop. The distance was a boiling grey torrent, masked in haze.

'Here,' Belissi said, pulling himself upright and offering Sesto a small brass spyglass from his tool sack. Sesto extended the instrument and stared out into the murk.

And there it was, just above the line of the horizon.

A massive black ship.

Night settled uneasily about Aguilas town. A full day had passed since the *Safire*'s nocturnal departure. Putting all concerns about Luka, Guido and their bloody chase into destiny out of his mind – for he knew it was now far beyond his power to influence – Roque had settled to furious industry. Three hours of the morning he had spent in a meeting with the master shipwrights, Captain Hernan, and officers of the marquis's court, negotiating the urgent repairs to the *Rumour*. The marquis declined to involve himself personally, but Hernan was not backwards in conveying his excellency's displeasure.

'Pirates cheating pirates, back-stabbing one another. This is exactly what we expect from ungoverned scum like you,' Hernan announced. 'You fight and feud, and betray each other, and behave like sewer rats. The marquis believes he should not have become involved with you, despite your letters and seals. Aguilas has provided labour and material in good faith, and now that effort is overturned. It is an offence.'

Roque had been tempted to ask the captain if he thought Luka a good swordsman, but he bit his tongue. Silvaro bested you, he wanted to say, and I am a much finer fencer than he. Shall we duel to settle this?

He forced himself to act with the diplomacy he knew Luka would have expected from him. He apologised and apologised again, reaffirming the Reivers' single-minded intention to seek out and destroy the Butcher Ship. Eventually, Hernan was assuaged, possibly because Luka had been smart enough to leave a true-blooded, articulate Estalian like Roque behind to seek appeasement. By noon, the work to lift, pump and repair the *Rumour* had begun.

At dusk, Roque left the harbour. The work was to continue around the clock, the dock gangs labouring by lamplight. Roque left Benuto in charge, and walked up through the old town with Tende.

'Where are we going?' the Ebonian asked.

'For a quiet drink,' Roque replied.

They stopped at a dining house in the high old town, and shared a dish of rice and shrimp and a bottle of musket. Around them, along the quiet narrow streets, stood the whitewashed haciendas and walled gardens of the grandees. Orange trees hung heavy with fruit and filled the air with their scent.

'I'm cursed,' Roque said after a long silence. 'Reyno's daemon touch… it is in me and won't let me go.'

'I know,' said Tende. 'I expected as much. Do you want me to kill you? I know several painless ways.'

Roque shook his head. 'No, no, old friend. But I thank you for the offer. Listen to me now. The curse of the Butcher Ship is in me, irrevocably. In my blood, my dreams, my soul. I am damned. Sooner or later, it will come out and consume me.'

Tende nodded. 'King Death will have a place for you at his high table, Roque.'

'Yes, I think he might,' Roque smiled. 'But before that great day dawns, I yet have a connection. A daemon-link to the Butcher Ship we seek.'

Tende shrugged his massive black shoulders and sank a cup of musket. 'You do, you do.'

Roque sat back and folded his arms. 'Well, I could just wait for my doom to overcome me…'

'Or?'

'Or… use that link. Use my curse. If I am connected to the Butcher Ship through its infectious magick, surely I should be able to employ that fact to our benefit?'

'How do you mean?' Tende asked, guardedly.

'We need to find it. Hunt it down. When Luka returns… and I have no doubt he will return… we will have just scant weeks to locate our quarry before the season ends and the winter sets in. I want to turn the curse that is in me back on itself. I want to divine where the Butcher Ship is.'

Tende breathed out and shook his head. 'You're talking about powerful voudon, the very worst black magicks. I can't do that for you, Roque. I know that's why you asked me here, but I simply can't.'

'You managed it well enough on Isla Verde.'

Tende poured himself another drink. 'Aye, that I did. Against my better judgement. And see how it sapped me.'

There was no mistaking the fact that Tende was now conspicuously smaller than he had been when he first beached at Isla Verde.

'I know that,' Roque said. 'You mistake me. I would not ask that of you, friend. I brought you here because… I just thought… you might know a place.'

THE WITCH DWELT in a mouldering townhouse at the west end of the bay. Her garden yard was lit by hundreds of candles, and Roque noticed the odd marks and sigils scribed onto the stones of the gate.

Glass chimes and strings of mirror beads hung from the yard's trees, tinkling in the night air.

'Wait here,' Tende said, and wandered inside.

Ten minutes passed, fifteen. Roque stood by the gate and fingered the pommel of his sabre. Moths darted around the candle lights. A fox, its fur as white as arctic snow, crossed the road and glanced at Roque with mirrored eyes, before vanishing into the cricket haunted thickets.

'She'll see you,' Tende said. He had appeared out of nowhere.

The Ebonian led Roque into the house. The hall was lined with shelves on which animal skulls gazed blindly into the gloom. Herbs hung from the ceiling, and there was a smell of spice, unguents and incense.

Two girls, astonishingly tall and astonishingly voluptuous, stood at the end of the hallway. Both were so nearly naked that the wisps of lace that dressed them seemed like an afterthought. They both kissed Roque on the mouth and drew back the silk screen.

Tingling, his heart racing, Roque walked into the circular room beyond. The witch was waiting for him. She was surprisingly young, dark-skinned, and wore her hair gathered up in a silk scarf. She laughed as she saw Roque, and beckoned for him to sit down. Her small card table was covered in a purple cloth of silk, upon which the signs of the zodiac had been embroidered in silver thread.

Roque sat, trying to ignore the fact that the beautiful witch's hands were old and wizened.

'Many troubles,' she said. 'Ouch. So many. Dark things flow in your soul, sir. I hear them calling to me. Oh. Such evil things.'

Roque smiled, humouring her. 'I don't need the patter, dam,' he said. 'Save that for the common punters who like a show.' He took a felt purse from his belt, teased out the strings and shook twenty gold doblons onto her table.

'I'm paying well enough. Just do your craft.'

'Oh,' said the beautiful witch. 'Right then, if that's the way you like it.'

'It is. None of this atmospheric rubbish. Just plain business.'

'Show me your hand.'

Roque held out his left hand. She took it and examined it, and Roque forced himself not to flinch from the touch of her wrinkled fingers.

'What your friend told me is true. You are cursed. Gods! I feel ill just touching you. What is it you want to find?'

'The Butcher Ship. I wish to know where it is.'

'Wait, wait… ah, yes… close to here. Just up the coast, northwards. Such darkness. Such woe. I smell flowers.'

Roque started. He smelled flowers too now, the perfume invading the little room. The candle flames fluttered as if a presence was entering the chamber with them.

'Ohh,' the witch said. Then 'Mhhhm,' and 'Ahhhh.'

'I see him!' she said abruptly. 'He has plant boxes! The names are writ on the lids in Tilean!'

'Plant boxes?' Roque asked.

'Yes, yes! Mhhh! I see a name. Salvatore... Salvadore... something like that. He is looking for something. Oh, so bright! So vivid! An orchid. The Flame of Estal! Ohhh, so bright! So-'

She took her hands away from his. 'Well, I hope that helped.'

'That's it?'

'Yes,' the witch said. 'A very clean reading.'

'That's it?'

'That's all the spirits showed me.'

'Really?'

WALKING BACK DOWN to the harbourside in the night air, Roque glanced across at Tende.

'You realise that cost me twenty doblons? Twenty doblons?'

'Money well spent.'

'Manann's tears, that's the last time I ask you for a favour.'

'SAIL HO!' THE crow yelled down.

The *Safire*, two days out from Aguilas now, was thumping through the heavy chop, racing like a greyhound.

'Do you see it?' Silvaro asked Silke, who was fumbling with his spyglass.

'I see a dark ship...' Silke began.

Silvaro pulled the glass out of his hands and trained it against his own eye.

'There it is. Run out the guns. Put the crew to quarters.'

'Aye, sir,' Silke said.

'Name of a god, but she's coming on strong,' Silvaro said, still gazing. 'Such a big bastard, and heading right for us.'

'The *Demiurge*?' Casaudor asked.

'No, not her.' Silvaro focused the glass again. 'Holy saints! In the name of King Death and all who follow him, it's the *Lightning Tree*.'

XXIV

IN THE MIDST of that wild, open sea, Luka Silvaro came face to face with Jeremiah Tusk for the first time in five years.

Sporting their pirate marks, the two ships – the dainty *Safire* and the massive brig *Lightning Tree* – dropped all sheets and drifted around each other as Luka went across in a longboat with Casaudor and Ymgrawl. Rowing was hard work, but the sea was too lively for the ships to come to close quarters. A jacob's ladder dropped to them and they clambered up the dark green hull of the *Lightning Tree*.

'Luka!' a voice creaked out against the wind. It was dry and reedy, but carried with great force. Tusk's crew, savage, shabby men all, stood back and made an avenue for Luka and his companions to approach the binnacle box where Tusk himself stood.

Jeremiah Tusk was, in Luka Silvaro's opinion, the last of the legends, a throwback to the old days of high adventure. By far the oldest pirate master still operating, Tusk had begun his career in the days when the likes of Ezra Banehand and Metto Matez were still scourging the sea, and he seemed somehow to carry that old, bloody tradition with him. He was a pirate lord in the old sense of the phrase, and so much more than that. A traveller, and an explorer too, he had in his time been to all points of the compass, and on occasions served as a privateer for Tilean lords, Estalian marquises and even, it was said, Arabyan despots. He had opened trade routes, found new passages, and been the first man of the Old World to set foot on some alien shores.

He was also Luka's friend. Well, perhaps friend was too strong a word. But they were bonded in blood, and many times had worked together, as comrades in arms.

'Let me look at you,' Tusk said. 'Ah, the grey shows in your hair now, Luka. You're getting long in the tooth like me. Truth is, I heard you were dead.'

'I heard much the same about you, Jeremiah. Word is, you are another mark on the tally of the Butcher Ship.'

Tusk spat on the deck to avert ill-luck. 'No,' he said, 'I've been away.'

Tusk had always seemed old to Silvaro. By his own admission, he was a good thirty years older than Luka, which made him remarkably long-lived, not just for a man pursuing such a risk-heavy career, but for any man, full stop. Facing him now, Luka realised that Tusk was at last showing the cares of his long years. A tall, slender man, he now had the hint of a stoop to his frame, and the lines of his face were deep. He wore, as ever, a long black coat, calico trousers and a shirt of white lace, and these garments seemed loose upon him, as if age was eroding him away. His long hair, back-swept, was white as snow, and fluttered in the wind. He walked with the aid of a narwhale's spike as a cane. Where his right hand had once been there was a hefty hook of bone, the gently curved tooth of a walrus. Many were the times Luka had seen that blunt device crack skulls in open combat. Jeremiah Tusk's eyes were as dark and hard as anthracite, and seemed to be the only part of him that had not aged a day.

'Away?' Luka smiled. 'Did you make your trip at last?'

Tusk nodded. 'All the way south, around the Horn of Araby. Just as I said I would, one day.'

'And how was it?'

'Eventful,' Tusk smiled.

Luka had often begged Tusk to record a narrative of his exploits, for his life had contained so much more than any one man should have been capable of. His stories, his secrets, the strange facts of his enterprises, were priceless gems and should have been bound up in a book like the ones in the Marquis of Aguilas's library, for future generations to learn from. But Tusk was always tight-lipped, and desired no glory from posterity. 'My stories will die with me,' he'd once told Luka, 'except those that are remembered by the likes of you and told on to others.'

'Around the Horn,' Luka murmured. 'By Manann, Jeremiah, I'm proud of you.'

Jeremiah Tusk grinned and embraced Silvaro warmly. 'Ah, but it's good to see you. You too, Casaudor, you old rogue. Is he still beating you regularly?'

'When the mood is on him,' Casaudor smiled, and accepted an embrace himself.

'And worthy Ymgrawl. Still standing, I see.'

'Just as thee are, sir,' Ymgrawl chuckled, and clasped his hands around Tusk's left hand as it was offered.

'I was concerned we would not meet anyone,' Tusk said. 'Gods, but the sea is dead and empty. I go away, and when I come back, the waters are void.'

'It is the Butcher Ship, Jeremiah,' Luka said.

'We've heard tell of that,' said Manuel Honduro, Tusk's mixed race master mate. 'At the ports we've come to, along the tip of Araby.'

'It is a devil,' Casaudor said. 'It preys on all. It is a daemon-thing.'

'It is also the *Kymera*,' Luka said.

There was a long pause in which nothing stirred except the wind and the creaking, pitching deck. 'Henri's ship?' Tusk asked.

'The same. Cursed and cursed, and cursed again,' Luka said.

Tusk shook his head sadly. The crewmen all around him spat or touched iron, or made warding signs.

'I knew the *Safire* the moment I saw her,' Tusk said, pointing with his spiral cane at the sloop off the starboard. 'Pretty little thing as she is. But where's the *Rumour*?'

'It's a long story,' Luka said.

'Come below and tell it,' said Jeremiah Tusk.

LUKA AND TUSK went below to the master's cabin, leaving Casaudor and Ymgrawl on deck, swapping news with the *Lightning Tree's* company. Luka had forgotten how much he loved his visits to Tusk's private cabin. It was cramped and untidy, piled high with curios and relics of his travels: books, pieces of bone, artefacts, weapons, tribal masks and shields, stuffed animals, mounted heads, musical instruments and an endless list of wonders. Luka imagined that the inside of Tusk's head looked something like this.

'Get us both a drink from there,' Tusk said, limping in and indicating a wall dresser with his bone claw. 'There's rum, porter, some of that damn Kislevite laughing water that makes you gasp. Oh, try that there. In the flask wrapped in bamboo. There, man, in front of you.'

Luka dutifully poured the clear liquid into two small thimble glasses from Tusk's drinking case.

'What is it?' he called dubiously, sniffing it.

'It's called sarkey, and they drink it in the islands of Niipon.'

'You got as far as Niipon?' Luka asked incredulously.

'No, man. I got as far as a trading port where merchants from Cathay were selling it. It's a fine brew. I'm quite partial to it, though that's my last bottle. The Niiponese, I'm told, drink it by the cup, like tea.'

'What's… tee?' Luka asked. Tusk just laughed and sat himself down at the long oak table. He shoved aside plates and pewter bowls and a ragged cluster of charts and waggoners.

Luka brought the drinks over. They raised their glasses and sipped.

'It's good,' Luka said.

'Very fine. Oh, now, you must try this.' Tusk rummaged in the piles of bric-a-brac he had just shoved aside, and produced a bowl filled with what looked like jerky.

'Salt meat?' Luka said.

'We cured it ourselves. It's fine crackling.'

Luke tried a piece and agreed it was. 'What is it?'

'River horse,' Tusk said, chewing on a piece himself. 'Great brown beasts, they are, fat as hogs, and savage when roused.

We caught ourselves a good deal of game on our voyage. Needs must. We were down on provisions, so we developed a taste for things. Snake is good. Alligator too. But others, pah! In the south, my friend, there is a horse that is striped black and white–'

'Surely you jest?'

'No, and it is as cantankerous as a mule. Never, ever eat one. Even cured, it tastes like tree bark. I'd sooner eat rat.'

'Or snake.'

'Or snake indeed.'

'This river horse… What manner of beast was it?'

Tusk shrugged, and reached over to pull out a heavy black ledger. He flipped open the handwritten pages, pages full of curious drawings and odd designs. 'The river horse. There, see?'

'It's an ugly thing. What name did you give it?'

'Uh, river horse…' Tusk replied, as if that had been a trick question. 'The locals taught us how to hunt it. They were a manner of man with very black skins, like coal.'

'Ebonians?'

'No, blacker yet. And dressed not in any cloth or modesty, but they knew the land and the means of it well. They were fine hunters. DeGrutti sketched the beasts we found. These are his recordings here. See, he gave the river horse a pompous name in the old tongue. Hippo, which is horse, and potamus, of the river.'

'That's an idiot name. No one will ever remember that. I'll call them river horses, I think, as you do.' Luka turned the pages of the ledger, marvelling at the pictures. 'My, DeGrutti is a man of fine penmanship. These beasts are astonishing. This thing! Its neck's so impossibly long.'

'Yes, that. We called it a long-neck.'

'Makes sense,' Luka noted, flipping on through the pages. 'How is DeGrutti?'

Nicholas DeGrutti was a scholar of natural physic from Tilea who had joined Tusk's crew a dozen years before to study the wonders of nature that might be revealed by the *Lightning Tree's* voyages. He had become Tusk's best friend and confidant, though he was no pirate, and Luka had enjoyed listening to the man tell his tales.

'Nico?' Tusk said sadly. 'He's dead. The river horse killed him.'

'Oh,' said Luka, and put his half-eaten piece of jerky back in the bowl.

'Not that particular river horse,' Tusk laughed.

'Even so,' Luka said. 'My appetite seems to have fled.'

'So tell me your news,' Tusk said.

Luke began his tale, speaking of his capture and his return, his deal with the Prince of Luccini, his feud with Guido, and, of course, the Butcher Ship. Their glasses were empty by the time he had finished. Tusk gestured for Luka to refill them.

'So Guido cheated you again? I'm not surprised. My only wonder is that you've not killed him already.'

'That is the purpose of this voyage,' Luka said. 'Whatever Guido has done to me in the past, nothing can match his crime against the *Rumour*.'

'But how will you close and finish against a barque of that dimension with only the pretty little *Safire*?'

'How did you know the *Demiurge* was a great barque?' Luka asked.

Tusk smiled. 'Because I met it yesterday. In open waters. It was heading east at a terrible pace. I went to it, hoping for news, but it liked not the look of me, for it shot out across my bows with a full side. I left it alone. I have no interest in hunting any more.'

'But it was the *Demiurge*?'

Tusk nodded. 'Half a day ahead of you, Luka. But even if you catch it, I don't know how you propose to beat it. It has you outgunned four to one.'

'Five to one, actually. I simply trusted the sea to show me a way when the time came.' Luka looked at Tusk.

Tusk understood the look and shook his head. 'Oh no. No, no. no. Luka, don't ask this of me. I'm too old and–'

'There is the matter of three times,' Luka said.

'I thought it was twice,' said Tusk.

Luka shook his head. 'No, three times. At Sartosa, during the bar fight. The man with the adze. Secondly, off the coast of Luccini that summer, the revenue men. One had a concealed pistol. Thirdly, when we tangled with those corsairs off the point of the Back Gulf. Three times, Jeremiah.'

Tusk shook his head. 'Three, is it? Damn. I should never have stopped to greet you.'

'What's the matter?' Luka chuckled. 'The fire gone from your blood?'

Tusk's response stopped him in his tracks. 'Yes, Luka, it has. The fire has gone. As you meet me today, I'm sailing to my cross.'

'No… no, surely not?'

Tusk nodded. 'I'm old, Luka. Too old, as it goes. This last voyage is my final trip. I'm done with the sea. I'm sailing to my cross and that's the end of it.'

Luka sat back, deflated, miserable. 'I can't believe this,' he said. 'Jeremiah, I thought you and the *Lightning Tree* would carry on until the end of time.'

'This is the end of time,' Jeremiah said softly. 'Of my time. I'm old, Luka. My bones are heavy and my limbs are slow. I'm dying, my friend. I just want to find my cross, pay off my valiant men, and lay my head upon a soft pillow.'

Luka rose to his feet. 'I will honour that, of course. Jeremiah, this news makes me sad to my heart. The sea will miss you. I'll make to my sloop and be out of your way.'

'The *Safire* is a lovely ship,' Tusk said. 'But she'll never take that barque.'

'I'll trust the sea to show me a way.'

'Luka?'

'Yes, Jeremiah?'

'Is it really three times?'

'Yes, sir.'

Jeremiah Tusk rose to his feet. 'Then I suppose my cross can wait a little while longer.'

'IT'S JUST A chisel,' Belissi whispered.

'But its end is sharp,' Sesto replied, taking the tool and hiding it under his cape. 'It'll make a hole in his chest as well as anything.'

Belissi wasn't listening. He was gazing out at the choppy waters, watching for something Sesto didn't want to imagine.

It was the third day of the flight. By Curcozo's estimation, they were crossing the mid-waters of the Tilean Sea already. The days were still white and sunless, the wind still boisterous. The sea raged, heaving and galloping. Full-sheeted, the *Demiurge* pressed on for Luccini.

Holding the chisel against his hip with one hand, Sesto began to walk back down the deck towards the poop, fighting the roll of the ship. He had made up his mind. He was going to kill Guido Lightfinger. The chisel would stab through the man's breast well enough. Of course Curcozo, Alberto Long, Vinegar Bruno and Handsome Onofre would then cut him to ribbons for his action, but what of it? He'd die well, vindicated.

Sesto could see them on the poop deck now, Guido shouting orders into the blow. He'd have to get close. Close in, like ships at close quarters. Then a single, sudden stab...

'Sail! Sail!' the lookout bellowed from above.

The crew turned to look sternwards.

Gods, and there she was. Coming on like a dart across the turbulent sea. The *Safire*, her lateen bulging fit to tear. Fast, fast, faster than the lumbering barque *Demiurge*.

Luka was coming. Just as Sesto had predicted, Luka was coming to end this affair.

Sesto's jubilation suddenly ebbed. Guido was calling up his gunners, and there was a series of audible claps as the gun hatches lifted along the lower decks and the guns ran out. The *Safire* was so small, so slight, how in Manann's name did Luka hope to turn this fight?

Sesto clambered up onto the poop, in time to hear Guido give the order to come about.

Guido looked over at Sesto. 'Think he's come to save you?' Guido snarled. 'Think again, my prince! He has no hope! Come about! Come about again! Turn to make him!'

Curcozo was relaying orders. Kazuriband heaved on the wheel hard, with the help of the lee helmsman.

'If my half-brother bastard wishes to make this a fight, then I'll take it right to him!' Guido bellowed. 'If he has the temerity, I have the wit and the power! The *Demiurge* will blow him out of the sea!'

There was a distant crump and bang. Smoke fogged the prow of the *Safire*. Her forward chasers had fired.

Sesto heard the cannonballs whiz overhead, cast long. He ran back down to the mainhead and pulled Belissi upright.

'We have to find some cover!' he said.

'Is she here? Is mother mine here?'

'No, for the gods' sake! No, she isn't! But Luka is. We have to find cover!'

The *Safire* fired again with its bow cannons. This time, the whistling balls punched through the mizzen yards and left acres of canvas loose and snapping in the wind.

'Turn!' Guido yelled. 'Turn and gun them!'

The *Demiurge* slowly came about, until it was side-on to the chasing sloop.

At Guido's orders, it fired a broadside.

The entire ship juddered at the release. Smoke washed back over the deck in torrents. Sesto dragged Belissi down and covered his head.

The *Safire* came on still. If it had been wounded, it showed no sign. It fired its long-cased bow chasers again, and this time the side rail of the poop deck exploded, killing four of the ratings nearby.

The *Demiurge* fired another broadside at its attacker. After the thump and the roar, after the jolt of the deck, Sesto was able to see the *Safire* again as the smoke cleared.

It was damaged. The lateen jibs had gone, exploded off the long bowsprit. Canvas, loose, ripped back across the foredecks, unmanaged and rogue. The *Safire* began to lag. Its foreguns flashed again. Plumes of water burst from the sea short of the *Demiurge*'s flanks.

Guido's crew cheered.

Above the shouting, Sesto heard a call. Up in the rigging, a man was singing out, his warning drowned by the cheering.

'Sail! Sail again!' the man was yelling. 'To starboard!'

Sesto turned to look. A vast emerald brig was turning against them, running with the wind. As it came side on, a mile away, it fired its guns.

A crackle of flame, a spit of soot. Then the hell arrived. The starboard side of the *Demiurge* was bombarded with cannon fire. The rails shattered, the hull splintered. Sheets ripped wide and men died.

The *Lightning Tree* swung in closer and fired again.

STRUGGLING TO STAY upright in the heavy swell, Luka Silvaro stared ahead. In the grey light of the day, through the rain, he watched as the *Demiurge* and the *Lightning Tree* closed with each other, gun ports spitting. Jeremiah's ship, expertly steered, had the better of the clash. Its side guns, three decks deep, belched tongues of flame. Water spouted up from the sea. Pieces of wood scattered into the air from breaking rails. The *Demiurge* faltered, stricken.

Another salvo, and Guido's ship began to limp.

'Get us up close!' Luka bawled.

They were side-on to the *Demiurge* now, and the *Safire*'s guns were doing dreadful harm to the barque's hull. Black smoke lifted up into the air and was carried away by the headwind.

'Closer!'

'We cannot!' Silke yelled. 'Not in this sea!'

'Damn the sea! Get me in to blade-length!'

As the *Lightning Tree* pounded its starboard side with chain shot, the *Demiurge* shuddered as the *Safire* came up against its port. Guido's men tried desperately to lower booms and fenders to stave the sloop off, but the ships ground together. Despite the fierce chop, grapples were thrown across, and tie-ropes, and the ships mashed against one another.

Luka Silvaro prepared to lead the boarding charge.

GETTING ABOARD A ship riding in such heavy seas was task enough, but doing so in the face of fierce resistance was quite another thing. Guido's men stood at the port side pavis of the *Demiurge* with poles, billhooks and hot oil. A row of caliver men crackled drizzles of shot down from the *Demiurge*'s rigging, and several of Silke's crew fell before they'd even left the *Safire*.

The *Demiurge* was a massive brute of a ship, and close up it towered above the *Safire*, which was barely a third of its height. But, Luka reminded himself, it had been a massive ship last time they'd taken it too. Its very size was its weakness. It made a plenty big target.

Silke's own caliver men, along with archers and ratings with swivel guns, opened fire with a rippling salvo that sounded like canvas tearing. The shots sent Guido's men in behind their pavis boards. On the *Safire*'s rolling deck, much lower down, Casaudor and some of the men-at-arms started heaving lit grenades up at the barque's side. Some blasts blew out sections of the pavis, and dead or dying men tumbled down between the two mashing ships. But Casaudor had another target in mind. He lobbed his next smoking bomb up through the nearest gun-hatch, ten feet above him.

The grenade exploded inside the barque and blew the hatch faring off. A moment later, a much greater blast tore out. The flames of the bomb had touched off the powder in the gun bay. An entire section of the massive oak hull, around the gunport blew outwards in a blizzard of fire and splinters. With it came the huge culverin itself, propelled by the blast, its carriage burning. It flew out into the air, as if it had taken flight, and crashed down onto the *Safire*'s mid-deck with huge force, rolling and coming to rest, smouldering. Some of Silke's men ran forward with pails to douse it.

A great, gaping rent now showed in the side of the *Demi-urge* at gun-deck height.

'To it. To it!' Luka yelled, as the men-at-arms ran forward, through the clotting smoke, and hurled grapples and lines. There was no longer any need to brave the solid pavis and the defenders at the rail above. A much better access point had been created.

The *Safire*'s men-at-arms, with Luka at their head, swung across the gap and clambered in through the grossly damaged section. The air was black with smoke and soot, and the dim gundeck was littered with debris, some of it human meat. The deck gang above fired down at the crossing party, and dropped some away dead with their shots, but Silke's calivers replied, smacking their bullets into the targette boards.

Luka was in now. The air was hot and filthy. The nearest gun-bays had been abandoned, presumably after the powder blast. Luka saw streaked puddles of blood on the deck where men, injured by shrapnel, had been dragged away.

He made his way forward. In a few heartbeats, he encountered the first of the resistance. Gunners, most dressed in little but calico trousers and scarves, rushed the boarding gang. They had armed themselves with cut-lesses and ramming rods. Luka, and all the men-at-arms with him, were weighed down with several firearms apiece, each one primed and strung on a lanyard ribbon for ease of use. Luka raised a snaphance pistol in each hand and crackled off the shots. Two gunners collapsed and died. The men-at-arms with him fired as well, and the narrow companionway filled with acrid white smoke.

Luka dropped the snaphances on their ribbon-cords, so they swung down at his hips, and snatched up the next two. Casaudor pushed past him, a matchlock in one hand and a boarding axe in the other. He shot one of Guido's bastards

as the man came running forward and, as the fellow fell,
finished him with a back-chop of the heavy axe.

Behind him, Luka could hear shots and cries as the next
wave of boarders came in through the hole.

He found steps, a narrow wooden flight that led up to the
mid-deck. The Reiver beside him lurched backwards, blown
open as the blast of a musketoon punched through him.
Luka glanced up and saw the man with the musketoon on
the steps, trying to reload. He fired both pistols, and
brought the man's body bumping and cracking down the
step-well.

As he stormed up the steps, Luka felt the *Demiurge* shake
hard as another pounding from Tusk's guns ripped into its
starboard side. He heard a whickering, chopping sound
from the deck above – the unmistakable, wicked sound of
chain shot in the air – and winced at the terrible screams
that followed. Fresh blood poured down the hatch-top at
the stairhead, drooling over the edges, like run off in a
heavy sea.

He reached the deck with the first of his men-at-arms. The
place was a mess of smoke and broken wood, bodies and
blood. At once they found themselves in a ferocious running battle with the *Demiurge*'s crew. Pistols barked, blades
flashed and chimed. Luka fired the last of his loaded guns,
then drew his shamshir. He hacked its edge through the
throat of a man armed with a sabre, and used the butt of the
spent snaphance in his left hand as a club against another.

This was the worst phase of any sea-fight, and Luka knew
it. Close quarters, the hand-to-hand. Cannon-action was a
thunderous thing, and often settled any fight before it
became this personal, this dirty. But when it came down to
the level of face to face killing, it was all about brute
strength, terror and the savage temper of the pirate. Whole
engagements could be won or lost in a close brawl like this.
If Guido's men drove off or slaughtered the boarding party,
he might yet cut free and win the day, despite the bloody
beating he had taken thus far.

It was hard to see more than a few feet in any direction,
such was the thickness of the smoke. White coils, lifting
from gunfire, mixed with the boiling black clouds, laden
with sparks and glowing ash, that rose from the sections of

the *Demiurge* that were on fire. The *Lightning Tree*'s guns had fallen silent. Tusk had spied that Luka's men were now aboard the enemy, and did not wish to do them harm. Instead, calivers were cracking, as Tusk's marksmen got up into the yards and began an assault. The *Lightning Tree* closed in. Bullets thumped into the deck, or into flesh. Men fled. Arrows and pellets from slings and bullet crossbows lashed down too. The deck was littered with dead.

'For Manann, for King Death, and for the Reivers!' Luka yelled, raising his shamshir, and his men cheered as they layed in. Turning, Luka performed a radical trepanning on the Lightfinger who tried to close with him, then pulled his wet blade free. A rapier flashed at him, and sliced him across the left arm. Gasping in pain, Luka re-presented, blocked the next strike, and found himself sparring with Alberto Long.

'You picked the wrong side,' Luka growled, and threw himself forward.

NEARBY, CASAUDOR AND a gang of four men-at-arms reached the binnacle and engaged with a mob of Guido's crew. Few men had the strength of arm to wield a cut-less like Casaudor, and he spattered the deck with blood as he ploughed in. Handsome Onofre, howling his master's name, confronted the *Rumour*'s master mate, and tagged him across the cheek with the tip of his Arabyan nimcha. It was a deep and gruesome wound that would scar Casaudor's face for the rest of his life.

Casaudor hit back, striking at Handsome Onofre with his cut-less and forcing him into retreat. Onofre fought to return, raging and feral, and actually wounded one of his own men close by in his fury to gut Casaudor.

Their blades tangled and wedged, Onofre grunting as he tried to force the advantage of his longer edge across the guard of Casaudor's cut-less. But Casaudor knew that the only way to defeat treacherous dogs like Guido's mob was to outdo them in treachery.

He kicked Onofre squarely between the legs. As the man shrilled and staggered, quite folded up in agony, Casaudor swung his cut-less and cut more, smashing it side-on into Onofre's face.

As he fell, dead, onto the deck, Handsome Onofre no longer deserved the epithet.

BLINDLY, HIS EARDRUMS ringing from the awful bombardment, Sesto moved through the smoke. He'd recovered a dadao from a dead Lightfinger he'd found sprawled on the afterdeck. The sword, a heavy, two-handed cleaver from Cathay, felt awkward and unwieldy in his grip, accustomed as he was to lighter, more refined blades like the sabre or the rapier.

But he held it tight. It was a sword, at least. Belissi's chisel was tucked into his belt.

He was closing on the poop deck stairs. Quite nearby, but utterly invisible in the thick smoke-wash, he could hear a tremendous fight raging across the port side of the mid-deck. He glimpsed figures toiling and dancing in the gloom.

The deck shook as another blast detonated deep below. A grenade? A powder keg firing? If the flames reached the mail-screened magazine deep below, there would be no deck left at all to shake, no *Demiurge*.

A pikeman ran at Sesto, his face bloody from a scalp wound. Sesto side-stepped the stabbing pole, and put both arms into his sword-stroke. The dadao, heavy but razor-sharp along its single, curved edge, cut the end off the pike, and Sesto was suddenly glad he had taken it up.

The pikeman dropped his severed pole in fear and backed away.

For the life of him, Sesto couldn't bring himself to hack at an unarmed man.

'Run,' he suggested.

The pikeman did as he was told.

Gripping the dadao in both hands, Sesto climbed the short flight of steps onto the poop deck.

Through the streaming vapour, he caught sight of Guido, near the wheel alongside Kazuriband, fighting to turn the tiller and rip away from the *Safire*. The lee helmsman, decapitated by chain shot, lay dead at their feet. Curcozo was at the port rail, firing a caliver down at the *Safire's* deck.

'Guido!' Sesto yelled, coming forward, hoping his entry was dramatic enough to stay the renegade in his tracks.

It seemed to be, for Guido stared at the young man of Luccini in horrified disbelief.

Then something interposed itself between Sesto and his target. Vinegar Bruno, gleefully banging his tambour against his thigh, rushed out at Sesto with a sabre.

Sesto tried to ward off the attack, but the cumbersome dadao was too slow and heavy to swing it like he wanted to. He merely succeeded in blocking Bruno's blade, catching it across the old sword's hooked quillons. For a moment, they struggled, neither wanting to break and offer advantage. Then Sesto wrenched hard, twisting his sword around. He meant only to throw his opponent off. Almost by accident, he poked the tip of the curved blade in under the corner of Vinegar Bruno's jaw.

Blood, hot and bright, jetted out into Sesto's face. Dropping his sabre and his tambour, Vinegar Bruno backed away. He clutched at his throat, gazing at Sesto in disbelief.

Sesto was so amazed, he actually said, 'I'm sorry.'

Vinegar Bruno fell onto his back, a prodigious quantity of blood pooling around him, and went into his death throes. His body shook and vibrated, his feet and the heels of his hands drumming the deck more vigorously than he had ever beaten his tambour.

Sesto gazed, frozen, at Bruno. He was utterly unprepared for Curcozo.

The Lightfinger's master mate threw aside his spent caliver and charged across the deck, drawing a dirk. He slammed into Sesto and crushed him against the rail. Sesto gasped and dropped his sword. Curcozo punched Sesto in the face and then drew his dagger up to spear him through the left eye.

AN EXPRESSION OF dismay and disappointment crossed Alberto Long's face. He dropped his rapier with a clatter and embraced Luka Silvaro. Luka felt the man's hot breath against his cheek.

'Feel that?' he asked.

'I do,' Alberto Long gasped.

Luka's shamshir was buried up to the hilt in Alberto Long's midriff. Luka broke the embrace and wrenched the blade out. Most of Alberto Long's entrails burst free from the newly-formed exit.

Yelping in stifled agony, Alberto Long fell down on his knees.

'Like I said, you picked the wrong side.'

'For the love of Manaan,' Long replied, blood bubbling at his lips. 'Make it quick.'

Swinging his shamshir like a scythe, Luka Silvaro obliged.

CURCOZO'S DIRK STABBED down, but suddenly he reeled away. Something had smashed into the side of his head and removed his left ear. Released, Sesto fell. Curcozo staggered away, blood streaming down his thick neck, and found himself facing the boucaner Ymgrawl.

'I left you for dead!' Curcozo cried.

'Not as dead as thee might have liked,' Ymgrawl said, and hacked at Curcozo with his cut-less. The bleeding master mate blocked frantically with his dirk.

There was a crack, and a pistol ball missed Ymgrawl's head by a tiny fraction. Ymgrawl turned, and, with his left hand, hurled his tanning knife. It impaled Guido through the right shoulder. Guido Lightfinger screamed and fell, dropping the wheel-lock pistol he had just discharged.

Kazuriband left the wheel and ran at Ymgrawl, sweeping with a double-fullered, Kang dynasty dao that had been his father's before him. Ymgrawl ducked and leapt back, avoiding the next stroke, and clashed his little cut-less against the edge of the big Cathayan sword. He stroked low, then high again, and menaced Kazuriband's loose left quarter guard, forcing the helmsman to tighten his arms and parry short.

Then Ymgrawl feinted cleverly, drew his blade tight in, and delivered a thrust that punched the cut-less through Kazuriband's neck. Ymgrawl yanked the blade free and the helmsman fell on his face.

A big fist hit Ymgrawl on the side of the head and knocked him onto the deck. Two more savage punches followed, forcing him to curl up into a protective ball. Curcozo kicked the cut-less away and wrapped his meaty fingers around the boucaner's throat, throttling the life out of him.

Ymgrawl fought and kicked, but the bigger man was all over him, impossible to dislodge. Curcozo's fingers tightened, and Ymgrawl began to feel the cords of his neck buckle and collapse.

There was a solid impact, metal forced into meat and bone. Curcozo's grip suddenly slackened, and he toppled away from Ymgrawl. The boucaner sat up, wheezing and coughing, and saw the chisel sticking out of the back of Curcozo's skull.

Ymgrawl looked up at Sesto.

'I'm the one supposed to be protecting thee,' he gurgled.

'Well, consider that an act of gratitude,' Sesto smiled.

BLADE IN HAND, Luka reached the poop deck, just as Casaudor led the charge up the opposite stair. But the fight was done and over. The bodies of Kazuriband, Curcozo, Vinegar Bruno and the lee helmsman were draped across the bloody deck. Sesto was pulling Ymgrawl to his feet.

Luka crossed to them and shook Sesto by the shoulders.

'Gods of the deep, but I'm glad to see you!'

Sesto smiled. A lesser man might have thought Luka only interested in reserving his reward, but there was a look in his eye, a genuine happiness that Sesto was still alive.

'I knew you'd come,' Sesto grinned.

Luka laughed, and got up onto the rail, waving his arms at the *Lightning Tree*. 'Cease fire! Cease fire and hold!' he yelled.

On the high stern deck of the *Lightning Tree*, Luka saw Jeremiah Tusk wave back, and give orders to his men.

'May I kill him,' Casaudor asked, 'or do you want that honour yourself?'

Luka looked around, and saw that Casaudor had his blade edge against Guido's throat. The master of the Lightfingers was on his back, a long knife stuck through his right shoulder. There was a look of abject fear in Guido's face.

'That's mine,' Ymgrawl said, and wrenched the tanning knife out of Guido's shoulder. Guido wailed in agony.

'Don't kill him,' Luka said quietly.

'By all the daemons of the sea, you're not going to give him yet another chance, are you?' Casaudor cried.

'No,' said Luka. 'He's used them all up. But he got the sea to lie for him, and before he dies, I'll know how he did it.'

XXVI

Burning, the Demiurge was cut free. Sobbing clouds of black smoke from its hull, it drifted away from its conquerors, and listed into the swelling waves. Already, it was low in the water, the sea having flooded in through its ruptured hull. Unguided, it bellied away for half an hour, its starboard side tipping slowly towards the sea line. It tipped again, and the black smoke gushing from it suddenly extinguished itself, and was replaced by a rapid rush of vapour, as sea water met fire, and created steam.

Rolling away across the heaving grey sea, the barque slumped further, its masts leaning out, draping the water with torn canvas and dragging ropes. A huge litter of debris washed out behind it, falling and rising on the waves: pieces of wood, scraps of kindling, clothes, the private possessions of the dead crew, bodies and Vinegar Bruno's tambour.

Just before evening set in, the hull finally gave way. A melancholy splintering sound echoed across the waves, and the *Demiurge* folded up, timbers collapsing under stress. It took less than three minutes for the mighty barque to sink

beneath the waves, leaving nothing except a seething blot of
air bubbles bursting where it had been.

'WELL, GUIDO,' LUKA said. 'You cheated me or you cheated
the sea. One or other. I want to know how you did it.'

Pale, weak from loss of blood, Guido simply shook his
head.

They were on the foredeck of the *Lightning Tree*. The sun
was setting, the seas had eased greatly, and there was little in
the way of chop. The *Safire* lay off their port quarter.

'We'll test him again,' Luka said. He glanced over his
shoulder at Jeremiah Tusk, Casaudor, Sesto and Ymgrawl.

'If you must,' Tusk replied and clapped his hands for the
work to be set.

'There's no need,' Sesto said. 'I know how he did it. I've
been thinking about it, and I'm sure I know.'

'So tell me,' Luka said.

TUSK'S MEN HAD secured the board to the side rail of the
Lightning Tree. There was no need to summon the eaters this
evening. The blood and the bodies in the water from the
brutal fight had brought them in, in their hundreds. Looking over the rail in the fading daylight, Sesto watched them
churn and fight in their frenzy.

'Are you sure?' Luka asked him.

'No, but can you think of a better explanation? The sea
itself would never cheat you, Silvaro. It must have been
Guido's handiwork.'

'We're ready!' Honduro cried.

'Bring him forward,' Luka said. Guido was manhandled to
the rail and set up on the end of the board.

'What?' he cried defiantly. 'Will you not bind my arms?
Mask me?'

'Not this time,' Luka said. 'You'll simply walk the test, eyes
open. You can do that, surely?'

Guido glanced down at the threshing, moonlit waters,
waters that churned with eater-fish.

'Go on, now,' Luka said.

Guido began to edge his way along the plank, his arms
splayed out to keep his balance. His footsteps became tim-
orous and careful.

'Hard, isn't it?' Luka called. 'I mean, without Vinegar Bruno's beat to keep you informed.'

'What?' Guido gasped, wavering.

'That's how you did it, isn't it? Bruno and his drum. His rowdy-dow-dow. The beat of it told you where you were. How much board there was left. That's how you cheated me.'

'In the name of holiness, Luka, I don't know what you mean!'

'Oh, I think you do, Guido.'

'Please, brother! For you are my brother when all other things are aside! Show me mercy! Show me mercy now!'

Luka looked at Tusk and Casaudor. Then he turned back to stare at Guido halfway along the plank. 'Mercy. It is the name Honduro has given to this fine axe.'

'What?'

Luka stepped forward and raised the huge, curved Arabyan axe Tusks master mate had leant him. With one hefty blow, he severed the plank at the rail end.

The rest of the board, and Guido, dropped into the black water.

Guido screamed. He went under and then surfaced, and screamed again. The eater-fish closed around him, scything in, their fins cutting the water.

One of them took him down. Dark blood frothed the surface.

'And that's an end of it,' Luka said, handing the axe back to Honduro.

Guido suddenly surfaced again, screaming and flailing. The water around him was black with blood. Eater-fish swung in, taking chunks out of him.

'He hangs on to life, that one,' Tusk remarked.

'Get me a pistol,' Luka said.

'Wait… oh gods,' Sesto exclaimed, clutching Luka's arm. 'Look!'

The water all about Guido was suddenly frothing and swirling. Like a whirlpool, like a maelstrom, it was twisting and lapping so fiercely the *Lightning Tree* rocked.

'Oh dear Manann…' Sesto gasped.

Open jaws burst up through the whirlpool, thrashing the waves back. They were huge, as massive as the bow of the

Demiurge. Scaly, brown, wide open, they displayed teeth the size of cut-lesses. Rising out of the monumental foam, the jaws spread wide, swallowing Guido and several of the eater fish into its maw. The last any of them saw of Guido Lightfinger was his body bursting apart as the massive jaws closed.

'Mother mine!' Belissi wailed. 'Mother, mother mine!'

For so it was.

THE GIGANTIC BEAST slumped back into the sea, like the face of a glacier sliding into the polar flow. The impact of its colossal snout kicked up a great whitewater impact that rolled both the *Lightning Tree* and the *Safire* violently to port. Men tumbled and pitched across the decks, for most had been so stunned by the monstrous vision that they had not been braced to hold on. Belissi was screaming and cowering, but his voice was just one of many rising in fear and frantic prayer. Panic had seized almost every soul, even the hardest and the most robust.

The beast raised its snout again, jaws wide and chomping at the frothing water. Then it slipped low. At the rail, Silvaro gazed at its great bulk, a scaled, brown shadow in the churning, sunset sea. It was like a crocodile in form, but giant flippers drove it forward in place of legs. It was at least the length of the *Lightning Tree* itself.

''ware!' Luka bellowed. 'It's going under us!'

The deck vibrated with a dreadful impact, and they could hear the grind and scrape of the beast's horn-plated back against the *Lightning Tree*'s bottom.

'Get cannon!' Luka yelled. 'Train guns upon it as it surfaces!'

'Against that?' Honduro screamed back. 'Our biggest culverin would not even make a mark!'

'Then what? What?' Luka shouted. Except for the wildest stories, he had no idea that any creature so large dwelt upon the face of the world.

Mother mine, curse that fond name, rose again between the *Lightning Tree* and the *Safire*. The tumult of its surfacing threw spray across both decks, washing men off their feet with such pressure, they clawed at lines to hold on. The poor *Safire*, dwarfed by the creature's mass, broached wildly, dipping her masts down towards the sea and all but capsizing. Luka saw men tumble off into the waves.

He ran across the pitching deck and began to struggle to reload the nearest swivel gun on the port rail. It was hopeless, but he was damned if he was just going to stand by while the beast devoured them.

Ignoring the beleaguered *Safire*, the monster swung back towards the *Lightning Tree*, as if it knew somehow that poor Belissi was hidden upon that vessel. The snout struck against the ship's side like a battering ram, and there was an angry crackle of timber. The whole ship lurched to starboard, its tonnage knocked against the grip of the sea by the massive blow.

Holding onto a ratline, soaked through, Sesto saw Belissi. The old carpenter, struggling to keep upright, was hobbling towards the port rail.

'What are you doing?' Sesto shouted.

'I must offer myself,' Belissi cried back. 'Give myself to Mother mine so that she might spare the rest of you!'

'Don't be a fool!' Sesto answered, but from the look on the faces of the desperate crewmen around, this was an idea they were heartily in favour of.

'Belissi!'

The carpenter was almost at the rail, but the beast struck again, shivering the hull with another titanic strike, and Belissi lost his footing and fell. He got up, clawing to grip at the rail and pull himself over.

'No!' Sesto yelled, and lunged at him. They grappled.

'Let me go!' Belissi shouted. 'I must do this!'

'No, I say!' Sesto replied. Belissi wrestled and shoved at Sesto, trying to break his grip. 'I won't let you do this!'

'Please! I must!'

Belissi managed to wrench himself free from Sesto's grip. Frantically, Sesto threw a punch. He had no wish to injure the old man, but it was all he could think of. His fist caught Belissi's chin and cracked him down onto the deck. Sesto grabbed his unconscious form and began to drag it back across the soaking planks, volumes of spray crashing down upon them both.

Sesto looked up at the rail as he struggled, and saw the vast maw of the beast opening wide as it rose up to rip a chunk out of the *Lightning Tree*'s side, and them with it.

'Luka! Stop that nonsense and help me!'

Luka turned from the swivel gun and saw Tusk struggling across the deck. The old pirate lord was clutching a large golden box in his arms.

'Luka, help me stay upright!'

Tusk was facing the rail, and the immensity of the rising beast. Luka grabbed him and steadied him as he let go of his walking stick and opened the box. Tusk let the box fall, and held up its contents in both hands.

It was a tooth. One, single tooth, but it was huge. It matched in size any of the long fangs in Mother mine's grin, but where they were the long, dagger-shaped teeth of a reptile, this was flat and triangular in shape. Ancient, grey, pitted and worn, it was precisely like the saw-edged tooth of an eater-fish. But what scale of eater-fish had ever filled its jaws with teeth like that?

Gold wire had been wound around the tooth, and strange runes etched onto its surfaces. It was as wide as a man's chest and as long, at the tip, as a man's forearm and hand. Tusk had to hold it with both hands, like a shield or a salver, his bone-hook notched around one corner. He raised it high and brandished it at the great beast. Luka fought to keep them both on their feet.

For long seconds, striking the sea into great troughs with its giant paddles, Mother mine raised its head and neck above the water to threaten the near-swamped *Lightning Tree*.

Then it closed its baleful yellow eyes and slipped back, like an avalanche, into the sea, sliding down out of sight.

Slowly, the tormented waves began to calm.

Tusk lowered his arms, and with Luka's help, leant against the nearest firm cordage for support. He was exhausted. Luka took the heavy tooth from him.

'Place it back in the casket,' Tusk said. 'Please, with care and due reverence.'

'What is it?' Luka asked, marvelling at the thing in his hands.

'The Bite of Daagon, it is called,' Tusk replied. 'An amulet. I won it from a corsair in an action off Copher. A potent talisman against the devils of the water, as you see. Even a beast like that likes not to glimpse the teeth of that which would menace it.'

'I would not like to see the manner of monster that other monsters fear,' Luka said.

'None may live any more, not even in the deepest places. The Bite is very old. But the other devils remember its like. It wards well against evil.'

Luka placed the tooth inside the casket and, with a shudder, closed the lid.

THE TUMULT SLOWLY calmed away, though the open sea was still brisk and heavy. By the time full night had fallen, the men cast over the gunwales in the incident had been recovered from the ocean. Miraculously whole from the swell they came, for the arrival of Mother mine had driven all the eater-fish from that stretch of brine.

As Honduro and Casaudor attempted to light the deck lamps and rally some semblance of order amongst the *Lightning Tree*'s rattled crew, Sesto helped Luka conduct Jeremiah Tusk down to his cabin. The old man was pale and breathing hard, as if greatly exercised by the grim events.

His cabin was in more disarray than usual, for many objects and pieces had been tumbled onto the deck by the violent shaking of the ship. Sesto placed the golden box on a bench, and hurried to trim the lamp-wicks, looking around in quiet wonderment as he did so. Silvaro helped Tusk to a seat, then poured him a reviving shot of rum.

'I'd prefer tea,' Tusk said, 'but there's no time for boiling water now. Rum will do.' His hands were shaking as they took the heavy lead glass. 'I am most fatigued. See, Luka? I told you the fire had gone. I'm getting too old for this game.'

'I'll not hear such talk,' Luka said.

The pair sat in the yellow lamplight and conversed for a time, while Sesto quietly inspected the marvels of the room. Slowly, Tusk's vitality seemed to return a little.

'So, where are you for now, Luka?' he asked.

'Back to Aguilas, to see what shape my poor *Rumour* is in.'

Tusk nodded. 'You told me about Guido's treachery, but not about what business had taken you to Aguilas in the first place. Hardly a port friendly to men of our stripe.'

'Friendly enough,' Luka said, 'to a man who bears letters of marque and reprisal.'

Tusk stared at Luka for a moment, and then burst out into such a fit of wheezing laughter that both Luka and Sesto feared for his continued respiration.

At last, the splutters subsided. Tusk wiped his eyes. 'So the Hawk himself has taken letters? A privateer! Surely, this is a world turned upside down!'

'Why should that be so funny?' Luka asked. 'You yourself have taken letters in your time, from different lords, when the enterprise suited you.'

'Luka, Luka,' Tusk replied, leaning forward and warmly pressing his good hand around one of Luka's massive, scabbed fists. 'I have done many things in my life, many things, that I would never expect you to do. I am capricious and ill-humoured, and I ply one course on one day, and on the next, another. But you, Luka, you are a single-minded pirate prince, free, impetuous, phlegmatic, and owned by no man or master. That's what I've always admired about you. I cannot think of a cause so great, even with riches attached, that would bend your will to the service of another m...'

His voice trailed off. He swallowed and fixed Luka with a terrible gaze. 'Unless... Oh, Luka, say it is not so! Say you have not undertaken the task of which I am thinking.'

Luka smiled. 'I have sworn to rid the seas of the Butcher Ship, old friend, or die in the attempt.'

'Why? Why would you do such a thing?'

'Because someone must, for the good of every soul upon the water,' Luka replied. He was rather pleased with the drama of his answer. It had a better ring to it than 'because

the Prince of Luccini gave me little other option than a gibbet tree on Execution Dock.'

Tusk shook his head sadly. 'And what manner of king has
made you such an offer of letters that you could not refuse?'

Luka was about to repl, when Sesto answered. 'My father,
sir. The Prince of Luccini.'

'Indeed!' Tusk glanced around. 'Making you…?'

'Giordano Paolo, sixth and youngest son of his majesty
the prince.'

Tusk was too tired to rise, but he bowed his head low in genuine reverence. 'My young lord, I had no idea whose presence
I was in, nor what noble blood was guest upon my poor brig.'

'There's no need for bowing, sir,' Sesto said quickly. 'The
honour is mine to be here.'

'Are you, as the Estalians have it, rescate for the comple-
tion of the deal?' Tusk asked him.

'Sesto joins us of his own free will,' Luka said. 'No ransom
is involved. No rescatadores, we, I assure you. Sesto has
come to observe the dealings, and make report back to his
father on our success.'

'Of your own free will,' Tusk mused, impressed, 'you gave
up the handsome life of court to join a pirate company, a
company, moreover, engaged upon such a suicidal quest?
Young sir, may I say there is more fire in the royal blood of
Luccini than I ever suspected.'

Sesto coloured a little.

'And what of your fire, Jeremiah?' Luka asked. 'Kindled a
little after this action? Losing the *Demiurge*, though we had
little choice thanks to Guido, was a setback. She was meant
to be the backbone of my force against the *Kymera*.'

Tusk sighed. 'Oh, Luka, not another favour. Please. I
broke my oath to my men in supporting you here against
your wicked kin. That was for old times, and it has left me
spent. My fire is gone, and I am sailing to my cross, and that
will be the end of it. Do not ask me to sail with you against
the Butcher.'

Luka nodded. Then very quietly, he said, 'There is still the
matter of three times.'

Jeremiah Tusk chuckled. 'You are ever the knave, Luka. I
would say we're square. I have fought with you against the
Demiurge, as you asked…'

'That's one,' said Luka.

'...and I have driven off the sea-dragon where none else might have.'

'And that's two,' Luka said.

'I think you should be more generous,' Tusk said. 'That dragon alone was worth three, or four, or five, or however many times you might have saved my life.'

Luka smiled and nodded. 'I know. I know, my old friend. But I had to ask.'

Tusk smiled back. 'Of course you did. And in the spirit of fairness and the ancient code of our brotherhood...' He picked up the golden casket from the bench beside him and slid it across the table to Luka.

'There's three,' Tusk said. 'If the Butcher Ship is half the daemon they say it is, you'll have more need of the Bite of Daagon than I will. Take it. Take it with my blessing. Now get on your way! I hate goodbyes, especially final ones, so I won't say it. Get off my ship and begone.'

Luka stood, picked up the golden box and looked one last time at the old pirate lord hunched in his seat.

'May you find your cross, Jeremiah Tusk, and let it be where you left it.'

'And may you find your Butcher Ship, Luka Silvaro, and let King Death be at your side when you do.'

THEY TOOK THE longboat back to the *Safire*, Casaudor and Belissi stroking the long oars, Sesto and Silvaro in the stern. Belissi seemed calmer and more bright-eyed than Sesto had ever known him, as if he was looking forward to a whole new lease of life.

'What does it mean,' Sesto asked Luka, 'to be sailing to your cross? What did Tusk mean?'

'No pirate worth his salt carries his riches with him,' Luka replied. 'He simply carries a private chart, often writ in code or other devices so that it may be read only by those privy to the making of it. On that chart is a cross, an X, which marks the location of his secret, buried trove. The cross, you see, marks the spot. And when a pirate reaches the end of his career on the waves, he makes an oath to his loyal crew, and they sail for that cross, under the captain's direction. So, at that cross, when it is found, they uncover the riches and

share them out, a portion to every man as befits his service
and duty and rank. And that is the end of it.'

'But what of the ship and the men?' Sesto asked.

'Some of the crew may inherit the vessel. Honduro, perhaps, will take command and become the new master of the
Lightning Tree.'

'And what of the pirate lord?'

Luka shrugged. 'I cannot say. In truth, Sesto, I have never
known any captain who has lived long enough to sail to his
cross and retire.'

THEY CLAMBERED UP the side of the waiting *Safire*, the sloop
lit up with lanterns in the night. In the blanketing darkness,
by the vague moons-light, they saw the great shape of the
Lightning Tree draw up sail against the westerly wind and
swing away into the rising flood.

The *Lightning Tree* cracked off one last, fiery salute, then
pulled in its guns, closed its ports, and vanished into the
night.

XXVIII

'COME HARD ABOUT off the wind!' Roque commanded. 'Lose a little from the tops there!'

'Hard about off!' Benuto repeated, bawling at the men. 'Tops away, you laggards!'

'How does she feel?' asked Captain Hernan.

'Considering the time the wrights of Aguilas have had to work upon her, almost perfect,' Roque replied with a smile.

It was midday on the seventh day following Luka's departure aboard the *Safire* in pursuit of Guido and the *Demiurge*. Under Roque's command, the *Rumour* was making her first sea trials out of Aguilas Bay, testing the repairs to the hull. They were running up the coast northwards, skirting the shoals and reefs, tracing a course along the wooded foreshore. The sun was bright, the wind running, and the sea crystal blue in their wake.

'She's a fine ship,' Hernan said, standing beside Tende and Saybee at the wheel. 'A little too small and light for my tastes, but I was schooled on the voluptuous galleons of the Estalian Navy. Still, I can appreciate her fleet stride and fast turns. A sprightly señorita, there's no mistake.'

Seniors of the crew came up to the poop to report to Roque. Vento, tugging the tails of his white coat out of his waistband, described how some of the new cordage was over-stretching. It was still damp, which affected the efficiency of the handling, especially on more subtle corrections of trim. Largo said the fresh canvas was good, but bellying well, due to its newness. They'd get more speed and fatness off the wind for a week or two, which was fair enough, so long as they knew it was coming. Clean sheeted, the *Rumour* would pull faster than usual for a while, and that would make her headstrong, and as hard to handle as an unbroken horse, unless they were wary.

Sheerglas, who refrained from coming to the deck and the sunlight, sent one of his head gunners, and the man reported splitting and seeping from the sections of the repaired hull below the quarter deck. Patches had been wedged and caulked in, but the wood was yet to settle.

'That's something to watch,' Hernan said studiously. 'The hull repair is good, as good as we could do in the time, but it'll be weak until it sets and binds. Turn too hard into a force of water, and it will pop, and that will be your end. And, whatever you do, don't present that side to an enemy's batteries. They'll find that vulnerability in a second.'

Roque nodded. 'I'll mark that and pass it on to the captain when he returns.'

'If he returns,' Hernan muttered dubiously.

Roque ignored the jibe and rolled out a waggoner. 'I say we chase for that atoll, and pass around it, before returning home.'

Hernan nodded. 'Let's run her out as we're here.'

They were turning when they heard a cry from the top-castle. 'Sail! Sail yonder!'

Roque picked up his scope and directed it where the look-out had pointed. Close in to land, in the next bay, a small boat was drifting, tugged along by the wind in its lone sail.

It was a ketch, single-masted, and it seemed adrift. There was no sign of any crew, and tangled lines trailed out in the water behind it.

'Let me look,' Hernan requested, and took the scope from Roque.

'What do you think?' the Estalian master-at-arms asked.

'A vessel in trouble… or so far past trouble that it's dead. Master Roque, as sea captain of Aguilas, I am required to assist and inspect such traffic. Can we, if you don't mind?'

'Of course,' Roque said.

Losing more sheet, the *Rumour* close-reached and swung into the wide bay. In less than twenty minutes, it had drawn within rowing distance of the drifting ketch, ratings at the forecastle lead-lining to make sure they did not run into any sandbar or hindrance. Roque ordered the tide-anchor rattled out and yards bare. A boat was lowered, and Captain Hernan descended with six of his marine guards.

'Benuto, the watch is yours,' Roque said, and hurried to join them.

'The watch is mine, aye sir, so tell.'

The strong arms of the marine guardsmen rowed them across the bay. Sunlight glinted off the guards' breastplates and comb morion helmets, and glittered off the clear, green water. They were close enough to shore now to hear the hiss of the surf on the beach, and smell the walnuts, olives and dates thriving in the shoreline forest. Roque could even hear parrots and the thump of deepwater turtles. Looking over the bow, he saw the sea was like a clear glass, filled with racing, darting shoals of coloured fish, the swishing, silver shapes of barracuda and the slow-rippling, mottled wings of rays.

The sun was hot. Thicket insects itched from the shore. The oarsmen splashed and stroked, splashed and stroked.

The ketch hove in close. It had the taint of death about it. Roque made a charm-touch to his iron belt buckle and drew his sword. Hernan took off his helmet and pulled out his sabre.

They edged in, the front two marines reaching out to manage the meeting of the boats, pulling them round against the ketch's side.

Two more of the marine guards stowed their oars and stood up, priming their muskets.

Hernan clambered onto the ketch, followed by Roque.

'Stand ready,' Hernan called to his waiting men.

Roque and Hernan searched the vessel. It was alarmingly empty, as if it had been abandoned in a hurry. Ropes lay untied; a half-drunk glass of rum sat beside the unmanned wheel. A tricorn hat lay on the floor of the mid deck.

'This is blood here,' Roque called. 'There was a lot of it, but the lap has washed it away. See how it stains the wood?'

Hernan nodded.

'Who'd sail a little boat like this out into waters this dangerous?' Roque sighed.

'A fool,' said Hernan. 'A naturalist, I think. An explorer. His samples are all laid out below.' Hernan had already inspected the lower cabins.

'Samples?' Roque asked.

'You know the sort of thing. Wooden boxes for plants and other specimens–'

Hernan frowned as Roque suddenly pushed past him and went below.

'What is it, sir?' he asked, following Roque down the wooden stairs.

'Oh, gods, look,' Roque said, as he sorted through the little pine crates stacked on shelves in the master's cabin. 'These are plant boxes! And the names… the names are writ on the lids in Tilean!'

'Plant boxes?' Hernan echoed. 'What does that matter?'

'She wasn't lying after all!'

'Excuse me, who wasn't?'

'The witch!'

'The… what?'

'Look here, Hernan. On the label here, Salvadore Laturni, botanist. It's written in his very hand!'

'Master Roque, I don't know what you're–'

'This was predicted, Hernan! Predicted to me! By Sigmar, this might tell us where the Butcher Ship is!'

Hernan shrugged. 'How in the world- ?'

'Look for an orchid, man! An orchid!'

Hernan, puzzled, started to sort through the boxes. Roque was all but tossing them aside to search. Wooden crates hit the deck and broke open, spilling out dark loam and precious bulbs and shoots.

'The Midnight Silhouette?'

'No! Keep looking!'

'The Crown of Tobaro?'

'Not that! Gods, it's got to be here somewhere!'

'What about this? The Flame of Estal.'

Roque looked around. Hernan broke open the box. The tiny orchid inside was the colour of flame.

'Oh, so bright!' Roque cried. 'So very bright!'

As EVENING FELL, the *Rumour* came in out of the sound and sailed into Aguilas Bay. The city's lights had begun to glow. A vessel stood at the harbour side.

It was the *Safire*.

THE COMPANY OF the Reivers, and just about everyone else in the harbour town, had set to celebration on the *Safire's* return. Fireworks were bursting and fizzling in the town squares, and festivities had broken out all along the harbour taverns.

'Luka! Luka!' Roque shouldered through the press of drunken ratings, clutching a stack of plant boxes. Hernan followed him, similarly laden. Whooping Reivers swept off Hernan's hat and sported it amongst themselves.

'Bastardos!' Hernan cried, struggling to keep hold of his boxes.

'Roque!' Luka cried, cup in hand, dancing with the crowd on the quay to a fife reel. 'We've returned from–'

'Not now, Luka. You have to see this.'

THEY WENT ABOARD the *Safire*, into the master's cabin, and plonked the boxes down on the table. Up on deck, Silke and his cronies were drinking and laughing as a jig played on whistle and guitarra.

'This had better be good to draw me away from such a party,' Luka said, taking a swig of rum.

'It is,' Roque said. 'Put that glass down and listen. The Flame of Estal.'

'Which is what?'

'It's an orchid. A precious orchid. Here, look at it. Lovely, isn't it?' Roque pulled open the top of one of the plant boxes.

'Why, yes, indeed.'

'It was collected by a Tilean gentleman, a botanist, named Salvadore Laturni. For his trouble, he was voyaging up the Estalian coast, collecting rare specimens.'

'So?'

'Listen to Roque, sir,' Hernan said.

'He was killed. Murdered, I believe, by the Butcher Ship. Don't ask me how I know that part. The important thing is, our poor friend Salvadore met with the *Kymera*.'

'So why is this flower significant?'

Roque smiled wolfishly at Luka and took out a leather-bound log book. He laid it open and flipped through the water-damaged pages. 'Because, according to the last entry in Salvadore's log, he had just sampled and recorded the Flame of Estal. His fate must have befallen him shortly after that. The entry was a week ago.'

'And the Flame of Estal grows only in one specific place,' Captain Hernan added.

'So you see,' Roque said. 'We know where the Butcher Ship is.'

XXVIX

THE FLAME OF Estal, that rare and precious flower, grew only in a wide bay called the Golfo Naranja, which lay up the mainland coast, north of Aguilas, beyond Porto Espejo. It was four or five days' sail away, no more than three, if a ship pressed on through the nights.

At noon the next day, the Reivers left Aguilas. The *Safire* led the way, the *Rumour* chasing her wake. It was a bright, hot midday, with a thin wind, but the threat of storms grumbled out on the horizon. It reminded Sesto, unhappily, of the storm that had menaced them at Isla Verde, before that particular night of horror.

That seemed so long ago now, on the other side of the summer. In truth, the season was changing. Autumn was setting in, and behind that came the gales and heavy weather of the winter. This was their last chance. If the *Kymera* could not be hunted out within the next few days at most, the turning weather would force them to suspend their mission, perhaps until the spring. Though the day was warm, Sesto could see how the colour of the sea was changing, and the feel of the wind too. It was autumn, the time for careening and respite, not desperate expeditions.

A third ship, flying the ensigns of Aguilas and Estalia, accompanied the Reivers' vessels. The *Fuega*, commanded by Captain Hernan, carried a detachment of marine guards and considerable munitions. His excellency the marquis had originally refused to allow the galleon to leave Aguilas vulnerable, fearing that while the *Fuega* was out looking for the Butcher Ship, the Butcher Ship might come looking for Aguilas. But now the whereabouts of the menace were better determined, he saw the sense in adding the *Fuega*'s considerable muscle to the fight. It was by far the largest of the three ships, and the most potent, though the *Rumour* and the *Safire* had to trim their speeds to allow her to keep pace with them.

On the *Rumour*'s quarter deck, Roque drilled the men-at-arms at their battle quarters, while Casaudor checked the state and readiness of every firearm and the sharpness of every blade. Silvaro himself went below and inspected the gun-decks. He explained to Sheerglas that, when battle came, he would favour the *Rumour*'s starboard side, so as to protect the weaker, repaired port. Sheerglas ordered three of the port-side guns to be remounted on the starboard, so the *Rumour*'s battery potential would not be squandered. Aguilas had provided good quality powder, as Sheerglass had requested, and also canister and faggot shot to be used against rigging and personnel. The canister shot had been blessed by the cardinal of Aguilas himself.

'A nice touch,' Silvaro said. 'It may help us.'

'Aye,' Sheerglas nodded. 'Just don't expect me to handle the stuff.'

SESTO FELT IDLE amid all the toil and industry. Every member of the crew was engaged in sailing the ship or preparing for the task ahead, and more than ever, he felt like a passenger. He told this to Ymgrawl.

'I'd rather stand and watch others work,' the boucaner laughed, 'but if it's labour thee wants…'

At Ymgrawl's invitation, Sesto joined one of the rope-gangs, and put his back into the hard work. Saint Bones was in charge of that particular gang, and when orders came via Benuto, the man started singing his infernal hymns as a rhythm for the men to time their pulls against. The gang took sport in singing with gusto, trying to drown out the ribald chanteys of the other rope-gangs with their saintly hymns. Sesto raised his voice as loud as any of them.

THEY SAILED NORTH up the Estalian coast, staying no more than a mile or two from land. Distantly, on the eastern horizon, they could spy the nearest of the islands and atolls in the archipelago. By day's end, they had long passed the lonely bay where Roque had found Salvadore Laturni's ketch.

Night fell, and they sailed on into the darkness. The night was heavy and humid, and lightning flashed out in the south, over the open sea, but the storm failed to draw in, and remained a distant rumble and spark all night.

Once, Sesto heard Roque cry out in his sleep.

THE SECOND DAY was damp and cold, like a forest after rain. There was a drizzle in the air, and banks of mist covered the shoreline until well after noon. In the latter part of the day, the wind got up, and the sea darkened as it lashed and rolled. Heavy rain came out of the east and drenched everyone bone-cold.

The rain let up after dark, and the night was fair, though still cold. Long past the middle of the night, with blackness still across the world, Casaudor called Luka to the deck.

Away to the north-west, a vast pink glow, trembling slightly, lit up the sky.

'What is that?' Luka said.

'My guess,' said Casaudor, 'is it's Porto Espejo.'

THE GLOW OF the terrible fires remained in view all through the night, and before dawn they were even able to smell smoke on the air. As dawn came up on a thin, drab day, they saw the great, dark pall rising from beyond the northern headlands, bruising the sky in a wide brown stripe that drifted west and became fainter and yellower as it faded into the distance.

The smell of burning grew stronger.

Silvaro ordered ready quarters, and signalled this to the other ships.

By mid-morning they had come around the Espejo headland. Though the town was not yet in sight, there was no doubting that the fire had been seated there. The ships were passing under the trailing smoke, into the gloom, as the overhead smoke-bank starved the light. The scent was pungent and harsh, and scads of ash fell out of the air, like snow upon the decks.

The steady thump of drums began, echoing across the water from the regal *Fuega*, as the marine guards assembled.

Just before noon, they rounded the spit and got a sight of the town.

Porto Espejo was a small place, just a trading stop, with a fair natural harbour, popular with fishing boats. Not a scrap of it remained intact. The shoreline and quays showed the signs of furious bombardment, as if they had been systematically pulverised from the sea. The town itself had been torched and razed. Only the black shells and smouldering rafters of the buildings remained. The temple tower was half-fallen. From this burning ruin, the column of smoke rose into the wan sky.

The flames from the town's destruction had spread and, through his spyglass, Silvaro could see where the woodlands and plantations on the neighbouring hills were now on fire in great swathes. There had been boats in the harbour, but all had been destroyed. Luka saw shattered, half-sunk hulls, and twisted masts poking up from the waterline.

The water of the harbour itself was littered with debris that lapped and rocked against the quayside walls. Then Luka realised it wasn't debris. It was the corpses of the townsfolk, hundreds of them, washing together on the slow tide. Gulls circled above the water, dropping to feed on the pitiful bodies.

'HERNAN SIGNALS HE wishes to put ashore,' Roque said.

'For what purpose? There's no one left to save, and we know damn well what wrought that havoc. Signal him no. And bring us about. I want to quit this place and press on. I want to find that butcher.'

* * *

SILVARO WENT BELOW in a black mood. Sesto found him in his cabin. Silvaro had opened his personal weapons chest and was laying every device out on the table. Dirks, daggers, boot knives, two shamshirs, a dadao, three assorted cutlesses, swept hilt rapiers, sabres, a hooked tulwar, a hand-and-a-half greatsword from Carroburg, two axes, one beak-backed, the other round-bladed, a pole-arm...

Sesto marvelled at the collection. Luka was sorting through the weapons, flexing blades, testing sharpness, assessing feel.

'You're angry,' Sesto said.

'Damn right.'

'Because we arrived too late to save Porto Espejo?'

Luka flexed the blade of his favourite shamshir between both hands, and then soughed a practice chop through the air. 'No,' he said bluntly. 'Oh, it's a miserable scene, and I'd wish no ill on those people. But it's the waste of it.'

'What do you mean?' Sesto asked.

Luka began stroking a whetstone gently along the shamshir's edge. 'Sesto, I've seen plenty in my life. I've seen horrors at least the match of what we just witnessed. I've seen atrocity, massacre, slaughterous ruin, all of it committed by pirates. In fact, I've done a share myself. But every last crime, every life taken, was in the name of gold and riches. For gain, Sesto. For the love of wealth.'

'So it's all right to slaughter when there's money at the end of it?'

Luka laughed. 'Not in your eyes, I know. But by my code, yes. What the Butcher Ship did here, and what it has done throughout this bleak year, is kill for killing's sake. Those poor wretches back there did not even get to pay for their lives with gold. They were simply murdered. That sickens me. That is not part of my life, or any code.'

Sesto sat down and picked up a curved gold and ivory dagger with beautiful inlay. 'I've come to know you, Luka. But sometimes, I don't think I understand you at all. You have a skewed moral philosophy.'

'I have the only one that works out here,' Luka replied. He had evidently settled on the cutting weapons he wanted: the shamshir, a long dagger, a dirk, a cut-less and the round-bladed

boarding axe. He placed them aside on the bench and began
to return the others to his sea chest.

'Anything you want?' he asked Sesto.

'No, sir. Thank you.'

'Take the dagger. The gold makes it true and the ivory
makes it lucky. It's from Araby.'

'My thanks, Luka, but I'm fine with what I've got,' Sesto
said, putting the dagger back in the chest. 'I have enough
weapons.'

'You can't have enough,' Luka replied, 'not where we're
going. Please take the dagger, as my gift to you. The luck in
the ivory–'

'Really, no.'

Luka shrugged, placed the last of the blades in the chest,
and closed the lid. 'Then help me with this,' he said. He
opened another heavy long box and began to take out his
firing pieces. Sesto lent a hand. There were dozens of pistols:
snaphance, wheel-lock and several heavy flintlocks. Some
were matched pairs, some single pieces of exquisite inlay,
some long and heavy, some small and fat. A small teak cof-
fer contained a presentation pistol, a brass-mounted
sea-service flintlock that had once been the pride of a Tilean
admiral. Almost every piece was strung to a lanyard of ribbon or silk-cord. Under the pistols in the chest were the
larger guns: matchlocks, muskets, calivers. Sesto took out an
Arabyan miquelet-lock rifle, its triangular maplewood stock
decorated with coral and gold. Luka lifted out a musketoon
and a marksman's long musket, and weighed them both.

'All too big,' he said. 'Just pistols, I think.' They put the
long guns back in the chest, and then Luka sorted through
the pistols, choosing a pair of small snaphance guns, three
wheel-locks of various design, and the heavy presentation
piece.

They laid the six pistols out on a cloth and began to clean
and load them. Silvaro had the finest quality powder and
lock-oil, and well-cast shot that Sheerglas had made for
him. The snaphance and wheel-locks he intended for single
use, but the flintlock, with its power and smooth action, he
required reloads for. As Luka oiled the guns, Sesto sorted fifteen of the best lead balls into a drawstring purse, and then
prepared two dozen cartridges, carefully weighing out each

powder charge on a small brass set of scales, and winding it tight in twists of paper as Roque had taught him.

They worked in silence for some time. Eventually, Luka said, 'Do you fear me, Sesto?'

'Fear you?'

'After all we've been through, I had fancied that there was some comradeship between us, but then you speak of my skewed philosophy, and it reminds me of our differences. You are a prince, and I am a rogue and a murderer. I see myself through your eyes, and it troubles me. You must fear me.'

'I think… you dismay me, sometimes. I would count you as a friend, Luka, but then no friend I've ever had could take a list of atrocities, and sort them into those that are evil and those that are acceptable. Back home, all men of moral standing would simply dismiss such a list wholesale. To them a murderer is a murderer, with no degrees.'

Luka sighed.

'But that was back home. I was a prince, remember. I wanted for nothing, lacked no luxury or finery. My father killed his enemies, but he did so using his army and his fleet, and the killing happened far away and was called war, and no one ever considered him a murderer. I never had to fight for my life, never had to wonder where the next meal was coming from and who I might have to kill to get it. I never had to brave the sea and stand at the front of a boarding raid just to put a shirt on my back and boots on my feet. I have five brothers, and not one of them would ever betray me. I think, when all's said and done, I have been educated in the real world, sir, thanks to you. And I am reassured that even killers live by a code of conduct, however harsh, and that they are not so heartless and inured to violence that they will allow anarchy.'

'Well, there's a blessing,' Luka smiled. 'At least your time with us has not been entirely fruitless.'

Sesto smiled. 'In answer to your question, no. I do not fear you.'

Luka Silvaro tutted. 'I must be losing my touch.'

He rose, the work finished, and began to arm himself. The dirk went into his boot-top, and he buckled the dagger, cutless and fine shamshir around his waist. The three wheel-locks and the presentation pistol he looped around his torso on their lanyards, and he tucked the snaphance pistols into his sash. The purse of shot and the cartridges Sesto had prepared went into a satchel at his hip. He picked up the boarding axe and clutched it in his hands.

'Well, am I ready?'

'Now I'm scared of you,' Sesto said.

Luka laughed. 'Go ready yourself, Sesto. Arm up and prepare.'

'Is there any need?' Sesto asked. 'You seem set to face an entire army all by yourself.'

IN THE LATE afternoon, the three ships rounded the spithead of the Golfo Naranja. It had become hot and close again, the sun burning through sweltering clouds, and thunderheads threatened in the darkening western sky. The wind had dropped, and was gusting fitfully. The sea had become as heavy as oil.

The Golfo Naranja was a wide basin, eight miles across, with a long, lean spithead at the southern end and a bluff headland to the north. According to the chart, the bottom of the basin was beyond measure, and the bay deep right up to the steep beach. The shoreline was thick with verdant rainforest and thickets of spiny gorse. Somewhere in that green forest, and only there, bloomed the precious Flame of Estal.

Largo, at the topcastle, bellowed, 'Sail,' but they all had seen it from the moment they had rounded the spit.

There, at anchor in the inner waters of the Golfo Naranja, as the witch had foretold, as Roque had calculated, and as poor, dead Salvadore Laturni had attested, sat a great crimson barque. It was two hundred and twenty paces long, and mounted forty guns. A hazy, uncanny mist seemed to roil off it.

It was the *Kymera*, the craft of Red Henri the Breton. The Butcher Ship.

'Strike our mark,' Luka Silvaro said to Benuto, 'and raise the jolie rouge.'

THUNDER ROLLED OUT across the mouth of the bay. The sky, in the sliding light, had become orange, swirled by thick, violet cloud. There was an electric charge upon the humid air, a tension that waited to snap under the weight of the gathering storm. A tension hung upon the Reivers too. As the *Rumour* came about, Roque brought the fighting men to quarters. The pavis raised with a clatter, and the guns ran out. The caliver men and the marksmen took their places in the rigging.

The odd quality to the air brought on by the storm did nothing to quieten the nerves of the men. They stared at the Butcher Ship ahead, sweating, pale, terrified of what it might do. Drums began thumping from the *Fuega*, and that added to the strain.

'Keep her steady,' Luka growled. Casaudor instructed Tende at the wheel, and Benuto relayed the commands to the yard-gangs.

'Battle quarters,' Roque's runner reported to Luka.

'Signal the others,' Luka said to Casaudor.

The flags ran up. The *Fuega* acknowledged, turning wide to meet the Butcher Ship at its port side as the *Rumour* swung round to her starboard. The *Safire* ran out, lateen bulging, at the *Rumour*'s port flank.

'She's just sitting there...' Tende said.

Thunder rolled again. The *Kymera* was still at anchor, as if asleep. No, thought Luka, asleep is the wrong word. Dormant. Like a volcano.

They closed to two miles, well inside the crescent of the Golfo Naranja. The unearthly mist continued to sob from the Butcher Ship.

The sky became very black suddenly. A crosswind picked up, and Vento's riggers had to fight to correct the trim. Sesto, at Silvaro's side, heard Saint Bones singing out one of his Sigmarite hymns as his men drew hard.

The light was stained brown with the overcast. Lightning flashed at their heels, drawing in from the open sea. The heavy air tingled with static.

'Why isn't she moving?' Casaudor said.

'Close in, now,' Luka ordered. 'Lose some sheets and let the *Fuega* ride ahead.'

'Lose the royals!' Benuto cried.

The drumming from the Estalian galleon continued as it purred in across the Butcher's port flank. A mile and half now.

'Two points to port,' Luka said.

'Two points, aye!' Tende replied, and wound on the king spoke.

Canvas cracked and flapped above them. The wind was turning, and turning fast. The first spots of rain fell on the dry deck, dark as blood. A huge boom of thunder crashed behind them, and the sea began to white-head. Lightning flickered in the gathering gloom.

'Steady,' Luka said.

'Range in four minutes,' Casaudor reported.

'Keep steady. Keep turning out,' Luka said.

'Steady as she goes!' Benuto bawled. 'Keep turning out to port, so tell!'

'The *Fuega* is deploying!' Casaudor said.

Luka raised his spyglass, and saw four, long launches leaving the *Fuega*'s port side, twelve-oar longboats, filled with marine guards. At the prow of each sat a guard, manning a swivel gun. Between the oarsmen, an inner rank of guards raised shields to protect the men. Stirring like water-skaters, the longboats sped towards the Butcher Ship. Luka knew that Captain Duero was in command of the lead boat.

The gathering storm continued to flash and crackle above them.

'Corposanto!' a rigger yelled.

Luka looked up and saw the fizzling, white-hot brushes of light burning along the *Rumour*'s topgallants. Saint's Fire was a bad omen to any mariner, and everyone on board touched iron and wished for it to dissipate. A flock of cormorants was also wheeling around the *Rumour*, cawing in the slow rain.

'How many more ill omens can we take?' Luka murmured. 'Sesto? Go fetch Tusk's gift from my cabin.'

Sesto nodded, and went below.

'Sheerglas reports we have range,' Casaudor reported to Silvaro. 'And so the daemon ship must have too. The *Fuega* is easily inside its shot now.'

'Why isn't the bastard loosing then?' Benuto asked.

'Which bastard?' Luka asked. 'The Butcher or our comrade Hernan?'

'Hernan, of course,' Benuto said.

'Because Captain Hernan is a wise and crafty seaman,' said Luka, 'and he will wait until the very last, so his guns do the most damage.'

Vicious thunder exploded above them again, masking the first shots of the *Fuega*'s guns. Hernan had begun his combat, coming within a half mile of the Butcher Ship. The *Fuega* cracked out a massive broadside, covering the sea beside her with smoke, and then let loose another. Luka watched the galleon's side flash and boom.

The cannonfire should have destroyed any ship, but the *Kymera* seemed unmarked. The *Fuega* cut loose a third and a fourth time. Now the bay was fogging with white powder-vapour, and the *Rumour* was running into it.

'That's right,' Luka murmured. 'Give it to the bastardo, Hernan.'

The *Fuega* fired two more salvoes as it closed, its launches rowing in behind it.

The *Rumour* and the *Safire* had come around through the inshore waters, circling the Butcher Ship at its starboard.

The thunder storm broke in, covering the Golfo Naranja in churning, sooty clouds and spears of lightning.

The *Fuega* fired yet again, another full side.

At last, the Butcher Ship woke up. Venting mist, it ran forwards, sheets swelling, ignoring any pull of anchor or direction of wind. Its sails, crimson red, were suddenly – impossibly – full and bulging with wind.

There was a terrible, overlapping series of cracks as the *Kymera* fired its first broadside, gunning at the *Fuega*.

Struck hard, the *Fuega* lurched away. Luka saw a mast fall and rigging strip away.

Then there was a flash. A burst of light brighter than any lightning. The *Fuega* vanished in a cone of fire. Luka heard a whistling shriek as an entire mast flew overhead and impaled itself, tip-down, into the headland three miles behind him.

The *Kymera*'s opening shots had hit the *Fuega*'s handling chamber and magazine, touching off a calamitous blast. The mighty Estalian galleon, and Captain Hernan, and all his crew, had been annihilated in a blast of shocking force that lit up the entire bay. The *Rumour* and the *Safire* fought to control their courses in the shock waves that followed such a catastrophic demise.

And then they were on their own.

THE BUTCHER SHIP was closing on the *Rumour*. It seemed to radiate foul red light, not only from its heavy iron lanterns, but from the bloodstained hull and crimson sheets. The Reivers could taste the pestilential evil in the air. The Butcher cut through the chopping water, somehow unencumbered by the swell or the storm, as if the lashing rain and lightning suited it as sailing weather, just as a bright, fresh day would suit an ordinary vessel. Silvaro could almost believe that the storm was no coincidence. The gale, the thunder and the pitch-black sky attended the Butcher Ship like consorts.

They could see figures upon the deck, silhouettes backlit by the ruddy fog. They were grim and still, blades in their hands, as if waiting for the moment to strike.

'Hold the line!' Roque yelled, sensing that fear was beginning to spoil the firm wall of pavis and pike. A pulse was beating in his head, and he felt sick to his gut. His shoulder itched.

'She's trying to come around on our port!' Luka cried. 'Steer wide! Steer wide! By the gods, it's like she knows which side we're vulnerable!'

Tende raised his eyebrows. 'Either side of us is vulnerable to that devil,' he spat.

'Have a care!' Casaudor roared.

The *Kymera* had begun to fire on the *Rumour*. There was a fierce, rolling crackle of guns, and cannonballs whistled at them. Some splashed the rough water beside them, others shrieked overhead, punching through the luff of the mainsail.

The *Kymera* fired again. Every man on the *Rumour*'s deck dropped, for this time the enemy had range. The ship quivered as if stricken, as blasts tore into hull and rail. Wood splintered, thrown high into the air, and men died. One shot hit the gilded breastwork of the *Rumour*'s stern, two more shredded through the quarter deck.

But the damage had only just begun. Alarmed, Luka saw that these were not regular shots they had taken. Fire sprang up at each site of impact, foul red flames that did not belong on earth. It was as if the fell sorcery of the *Kymera* had spread like an infection into the *Rumour*'s wounds.

'Douse it! Douse it there!' Benuto yelled, but no amount of water could quell the creeping red flames.

Another salvo tore in at them, doing miserable harm and killing over a dozen more men. One shot, from a small saker, hit the rail near Silvaro, bounced off, and rolled across the deck, misfired. Silvaro stared at it. The black iron ball, the size of a grapefruit, was still smoking. Its surface was studded with metal spikes, like the head of a mace. It was a foul thing, an evil star thrown out of heaven.

'Get that off my deck!' Luka cried, and Saybee hooked it up with a marlinespike to sling it over the rail. Instantly, the lee-helmsman cried out in utter disbelief. Spikes were sprouting out of the black iron sphere, like squat fingers or tendrils, and it clung to the end of his marlinespike as if it intended to crawl down it like some ghastly beetle.

Saybee flung the thing, marlinespike and all, over the side.

That was enough. 'Give 'em hell!' Luka yelled.

Down in the hot darkness of the gundeck, Sheerglas heard the order and signalled with his linstock.

The *Rumour* returned fire. With satisfaction, Luka saw the heavy shots blast into the *Kymera*, though they seemed to deliver far less damage than he had expected. He suddenly had the dreadful notion that the Butcher Ship might be proofed against mortal damage by some charm or ensorcelment.

'Fire again! Again! At will!' Luka shouted, and the *Rumour*'s batteries answered him. The *Safire*, which had been shadowing the *Rumour*'s turn, now pulled clear and began an assault of her own. The guns of both Reiver ships blazed at the crimson monster.

The *Kymera* showed no sign of being troubled in the least. It came on through the storm, now clearly bent on grappling with the *Rumour*. The vile red fires on board the *Rumour* were spreading with terrible fury, and despite all efforts to beat them out or drench them, they could not be quenched.

XXXI

SESTO REAPPEARED ON deck, carrying the golden box. He was sweating and dirty from smoke, having tried to assist the beating out of the fires below.

Luka grabbed the box, opened it, and took out the Bite of Daagon. At once, the red flames eating at the *Rumour's* structure sputtered and went out, leaving just smouldering, black charring behind.

'That's more like it,' Luka smiled. 'A charm against a charm.'

Sheerglas fired the guns again, and now, where they struck the *Kymera's* red hull, there were blasts and savage splintering. They had at last bloodied the Butcher Ship's nose.

'Again!' Luka roared. 'Put canister and faggot shot into their rigging!'

The blessed canister shot scorched out and caused wild flurries of white fire to cascade along the *Kymera's* deck. Rigging tore and twanged away, and some of the shadowy figures fell. But up until the moment they fell, none had yet moved.

A volley of faggot shot went off next. These shots were metal cylinders cunningly fashioned to come apart in whizzing geometric sections. They struck the *Kymera* with devastating effect.

The Reivers began to cheer. 'Hold the line! Hold it fast!' Roque yelled at his men-at-arms. His left shoulder was aching miserably now, and his throat was parched. He took a swig of water, but it did little to soothe the terrible dryness.

The Butcher Ship began to turn, and fired its guns once more. The *Rumour* took more hits, but more went wide and struck the *Safire* for the first time. Silke's craft was not warded by the Bite of Daagon like the *Rumour*, and crackling red fire took hold of her bows.

Luka handed the Bite to Sesto. 'Hold that up and keep it high,' he ordered. 'It's the only luck we've got in this fight.'

The *Kymera* had closed with them enough for the swivel guns and calivers to start their fusillade. Roque gave the order, and the muskets and long guns started to bark and fizz.

'Gods, but the *Safire*'s really in trouble,' Casaudor growled. Silvaro turned to look, and saw that the baleful red fire had spread savagely along the *Safire*'s starboard side. Two of Silke's men, ablaze from head to foot, threw themselves over the sloop's side, but the sea did not put out the flames. Swirling pink light remained visible beneath the waves as the bodies sank, still burning.

Silke was at the wheel of the *Safire*, and seemed hell-bent on bringing her around at the *Kymera*, despite the inferno sweeping across his deck. The few operational guns the *Safire* had left blasted at the Butcher Ship in defiance.

'Can we not help her?' Sesto asked, appalled by what he was seeing.

'How?' Silvaro replied. 'We're locked into this with the *Kymera* now. We can't break off to go to Silke's aid. And even if we could, what could we hope to do?'

'Then they must abandon her before they all burn alive,' Sesto cried. Tende, Saybee and Benuto all shuddered at the words. The dimensions of a pirate's life were determined by water, but fire was, ironically, his nemesis. The greatest fear of any pirate was to burn alive.

Silke must have already given that order. Crewmen were leaping off the *Safire*'s stern into the sea. Two boats had been dropped, and some of the floundering bodies were managing to struggle into them. The *Safire* continued to power forward, fire leaping up at the masts and rigging, consuming the wide lateen sail like paper. They could still see Silke, alone on the burning poop, standing firm at the wheel, his long, expensive robe on fire.

'Sweet gods,' Silvaro said. 'Silke, what are you doing?'

The doomed *Safire*, struggling, it seemed, not to die too soon, swept on across the *Rumour*'s bow. It looked nothing more than a fire-ship, entirely ablaze above the waterline, the raging flames lifting sparks and ash into the air in a huge stream behind it like the glittering train of a noblewoman's gown. Silvaro now understood Silke's last, valiant act as a Reiver.

The *Safire* smashed into the *Kymera*'s port bow, fracturing wood and exploding boards. It locked against the Butcher Ship's side for a moment, burning furiously, and then crumpled away, its back broken. There was a fierce gush of steam and sucking water, and it went down, stern first. The broken bow-end rose up out of the waves like the beak of a whale, and then slithered away rapidly as if it was rolling backwards down a launch ramp. A veil of steam and smoke rose up out of the whirling vortex of whitewater, and there came the sound of timbers cracking and decks compressing. Still burning from the unquenchable eldritch flame, the *Safire*, like its crewmen before it, sank away, still visible under the water as a ruddy, pulsating glow that slowly, slowly disappeared into the deep.

Sesto was astonished. Silke had always seemed one of the more slippery, less reliable men in the company, with affections as much for Guido as for Luka. But he had gone to his end in such a display of tenacious courage and loyalty to the company that Sesto suddenly wished he had known the man better. All pirates wear disguises and mask their true selves, for better or for ill. Sailing with the Reivers had taught Sesto that at least. But Silke's crafty, distanced exterior had clearly concealed a most excellent and intrepid heart.

In truth though, and this was galling to see, Silke's sacrifice had won little or no advantage. Though blackened and torn, the *Kymera*'s bows were still sound. It had withstood the ramming action.

As if exhilarated by the overthrow of a second adversary, the Butcher Ship renewed its attack on the *Rumour*, doubling its fury. Its guns howled and boomed across the storm-driven spray, and piteous injury was taken by the brigantine. Though warded against the infection of the red flame, the *Rumour* was still vulnerable to the force of the whizzing cannon balls. Gunwales exploded in blizzards of fine wood-shards. Men exploded in mists of gore. Chunks of the main wale burst like the skin of a fruit. Three metres of the jib boom tore off at the jack staff. Shrouds and tackle stripped away from the mainmast like spiderweb in a typhoon. There was a terrible cracking and rending of hull timbers.

Two of the *Kymera*'s shots had impacted just above the waist and ripped into the gundeck. By some lucky chance, no powder was touched, but two positions – the second culverin and the third cannon – were obliterated. The terrible impacts destroyed the weapons, shattering solid wood carriages and fracturing the iron of muzzles. The gun-teams manning each weapon were either struck dead by the concussion of the hits, or slaughtered in the welter of fragments and shrapnel that immediately followed. Two powder boys died too, and men in adjacent teams were wounded. Smoke, thick and hot, filled the gundeck.

Sheerglas got to his feet. He had been knocked down by the blast. He winced, and looked down to see a splinter of gun carriage wood, the length of a man's forearm, impaled through his belly. Sheerglas grimaced and slowly dragged it out of him. No blood came with it. It had missed his heart by a finger length.

'Better luck next time, Henri,' he growled, and tossed the splinter away.

'On your feet! On your feet!' he started to yell. 'Resume firing! Fire at will, as ready! Move, you dogs, or I'll sup upon you! Come on, now!'

The pale gun-teams scrambled to their master's bidding.

'Clear this tangle away!' Sheerglas demanded, indicating the wreckage and the broken bodies. 'You men on the port! Do it! Bring two cannon across in rapid fashion! No, three! There's hole enough for three now!'

The gunners hurried forward, shovelling the debris clear and showing no care for the mutilated bodies they swept

aside. If there was time for service later, so be it. Hauling on
the drag ropes, they heaved three of the port-side weapons
over and lashed them in place, their muzzles running out
through the scar in the *Rumour*'s side where two gun ports
had previously stood.

'Charge them!' Sheerglas yelled, as the other guns started
to boom and roar again. He felt weak, giddy.

'To me, boy!' he called to the nearest powder monkey, a
lad of fourteen years. Knowing what was expected, the boy
hurried over and turned his head to the left. Sheerglas
leaned over and bit deep, taking his measure from the
youth's neck.

'Good lad,' he said, wiping his mouth. 'Now back to your
duties quick smart.'

Sheerglas felt better at once, lifted, vitalised. 'Quicker with
the rods, you bastards! Quicker and quicker still! Let's
pound this monster down to devil Manann's locker!'

THE THUNDER OF the *Rumour*'s guns renewed, and Luka was
glad. But still the *Kymera* was punishing them fiercely. Sim-
ple logic dictated that they would eventually lose this
frenzied brawl. The Butcher Ship was bigger, and outgunned
them.

'We have to close!' Roque yelled, running up onto the
poop. 'Let us bring this down to sword and pistol and try it
that way, for this cannon fight can only end in our deaths!'

Roque seemed almost wild in his countenance. His shirt
was ripped open, and where every other man on the *Rumour*
was sweating like a hog, his skin was dry and tight. Sesto
could see that he was agitated. There were marks upon his
exposed left shoulder, around the fresh scar there. Splinter
wounds, most would believe. But Sesto realised they were
the marks of feverish scratching.

'Are you all right?' he said.

'Yes!' Roque snapped at him. 'This is not the time for–'

'I think it is,' Sesto said.

'Shut your mouth!' Roque turned back to Luka. 'For
damnation's sake, let's close now, while I still have men left
in the pavis line to put aboard!'

'If we come in, we'll be right at their mercy for the last few
yards,' Luka said.

'We're at their mercy now!' Roque cried.

'You know how this works, Roque. The closer we bring ourselves, the more they will strike us, and the harder. Attempting to close and board under this assault could finish us.'

'I think we're finished anyway,' Casaudor said quietly. 'Let's do as Roque says and come in. We've nothing left to lose.'

A fresh noise came in, across the rush of the storm and the fury of the bombardment: the crump of distant guns. Plumes of water burst up from the roiling sea around the Butcher Ship.

Silvaro and the others ran to the port-side rail and gazed out into the rain and the tempest darkness. Red flashes again, another round of guns, out in the distance, in the outer limits of the bay.

And then they saw her.

Full sheeted, coming in at them like a monster of the deep, square-rigged and glorious under the ink-black sky.

The *Lightning Tree*.

'The old rogue has not forgotten us after all,' Silvaro murmured. 'Gods bless him for his loyalty.'

Regal and splendid, and every bit a match for the *Kymera* in size and guns, the *Lightning Tree* bore down, firing as she came. She left an immense, fuming wake of white gunsmoke trailing off behind her on the wind.

'Now we close!' Luka cried. 'Now we damn well close!'

Tende hauled on the wheel, Saybee adding his muscle to the effort. Roque leapt down off the poop and ordered his men-at-arms up to ready. The shields clattered together, and the pikes ran out through them. The caliver men began firing at the *Kymera*'s port side as it rushed close in.

The *Lightning Tree* ran around the sterns of the two ships in such a wide turn her sails were momentarily taken aback. She gybed hard, and bit into the wind again, riding up along the Butcher Ship's starboard quarter and unleashing firepower from her yawning gun ports.

Vento's men threw out fenders as the *Rumour* came in against the crimson monster's port beam. The calivers and swivel guns set off a fizzling tumult as the two ships came together, and bowmen in the ratlines stuck the enemy deck with arrows and bolts.

In the misty, glowing redness of the *Kymera*'s decks, the Reivers could see the figures of its crew, silent and unnaturally still, waiting for the assault.

The ships thumped and scraped together with a violent judder. The Reivers hurled out lines and hooks, catching at the rail and gunwales and hauling the vessels tight against one another. Musket and caliver fire rang out from the *Kymera*'s sheets, and men in Roque's line dropped or lurched backwards. Some of the shots had actually punched through the targettes and raised shields.

'On them. On them!' Roque yelled, leading the boarding charge. He had never been so thirsty in his life. He wished only to wash the dryness from his gullet. Blood would do it.

The first wave of men went across into the red glow suffusing the Butcher Ship's deck. Luka clambered over the rail of the poop and swung across, his boarding axe in his hand. Casaudor followed.

Ymgrawl looked at Sesto. 'Don't thee even think on it,' he said, and leapt across onto the *Kymera* in one pantherbound.

'Yes,' Sesto smiled after the boucaner. 'Right.'

LUKA LANDED ON the stern deck, feet first. He had entered a world of red luminescence. A dry world too. The deck seemed parched and baked, the boards shrunk, and the air griddle-hot. Three metres away, on the *Rumour*'s poop, the air was cold and dark and filled with rain. Here, it was like a hot autumn night during a drought. There was the oddest scent of resin on the wind. On the far side of the ship, he could hear the *Lightning Tree* firing as it closed, and now also the ferocious reply of the *Kymera*'s starboard guns.

Luka started to hack away the sheets and cordage with his sharp boarding axe, cutting painters and ratlines and thick hawsers, intent on crippling the *Kymera*'s aft running gear. Casaudor and Ymgrawl boarded behind him and started doing the same, Casaudor with an axe, and Ymgrawl with his cut-less. Other Reivers followed them, Tende and Saybee, Fanciman and Laughing George, a dozen more. From the mid-deck came a furious clamour of fighting as Roque's men-at-arms stormed aboard and tore into Henri's main complement. The red-lit air fumed with powder smoke.

Luka pushed on, hacking and chopping at gear and blocks. A figure loomed in the ruddy glow ahead of him. One of Henri's men at last, face to face. Luka didn't break stride. He swung the axe and sank it deep into the man's collarbone.

The man kept moving. He didn't even flinch. He plucked the axe out of his shoulder with his good hand and threw it aside. Luka saw him properly now. Eyes blank and sunken, skin taut and dry, the structure of his bones sticking out starkly from his wizened flesh.

A deathless thing, dressed in the rotting clothes of a pirate.

Luka baulked in horror. The zombie swung at him stiffly with a cut-less. Casaudor's musketoon boomed and the ghoul flew backwards across the deck, its head torn off.

'My thanks,' Luka whispered.

More lurching figures appeared, menacing with blades and cudgels. Casaudor tossed his musketoon aside and slammed his boarding axe down through the skull of the first. It tottered and fell, but continued to writhe upon the deck.

Luka snatched up two of the wheel-locks dangling on their lanyards around his torso, and fired them at the next lumbering devil. The shots blew it backwards, shredding off both its arms at the shoulders in billows of dry, dusty scraps. Luka dropped the wheel-locks so that they swung at his hip, and raised the third, firing it almost point-blank into the forehead of the next zombie. Its skull exploded with a hollow, sooty cough, like a flawed pot bursting in the heat of a kiln. It toppled over.

Ymgrawl had hacked another undead thing down with his cut-less. 'What is this?' he cried. 'What manner of curse hath taken this ship down?'

The fighting quickly became desperate and hand-to-hand. The ghastly crew members of the Butcher Ship, plodding and emaciated, came in from all sides. Luka took off a head with his shamshir, and exploded another skull with his powerful presentation piece. Casaudor hacked about with his axe, removing arms and hands. Tende laid in with his Ebonian blade, and nearby Saybee was whirling a two-handed sword that ripped through dried fibres and warped bones.

Jan Casson shrieked as a zombie ran him through with a rusty lance. Laughing George was pulled limb from limb by clawing, undead hands, and his torment was so excruciating, several other Reivers were stunned in their tracks, and fell prey to zombie fury themselves.

Fanciman ran out of pistols – even though he'd brought nine, and felled as many zombies – and drew his rapier. The blade broke across the rotting breastplate and shrivelled ribcage of his next attacker. Fanciman plunged the broken blade end in again and again, and his body continued to repeat that action for several seconds after the zombie's scimitar had taken off his head. Spurting blood like a geyser from its severed neck, Fanciman's body fell.

Many of the husk-zombies dropped to their knees and began to suck up the blood spilt over the deck-boards from the fallen Reivers. Luka and Casaudor hacked some of them apart while they were thus occupied. The dry, severed hands and arms of despatched zombies clenched and grabbed at the Reivers' feet.

Luka pressed ahead, scything and striking. He could see the *Lightning Tree* over the rail. It was hurt, and billowing red flame. Then a figure interposed itself between Luka and his view.

It was Henri the Breton, Red Henri himself.

A massive man, built like an ox, Henri was clad in black velvet and black half-armour. He had always ruled his crew with the power of his arm and the fury of his nature. Luka had admired him, and had counted him a friend.

Not one spark of that person remained, except for a vague physical semblance. Henri's face, cased inside the comb morion helm, was devoid of life or intellect. The flesh was swollen and white, as if bloated up. He looked like a drowned soul plucked lately from the flood, swelled up by decomposition.

'Henri?' Luka gasped. 'Is it you?'

In reply, Red Henri the Breton swung his sabre at Luka Silvaro.

ON THE BUTCHER Ship's quarter deck, Roque and the force of men-at-arms were caught in a pitched battle against the greater part of the Butcher Ship's crew. There was a dreadful din of clashing blades and discharging shot, but all the cries and oaths and screams of pain came from the Reivers. The ghouls of the *Kymera* fought on in stiff, flat-eyed silence.

In the midst of the carnage, Roque could see that the starboard guns of the Butcher Ship were still pounding the *Lightning Tree*, doing it grave harm and preventing it from closing to board. He tried to fight through the press, hoping to lead an armed party below and silence the guns. But the numbers of the vile enemy were too great. Although they could be stopped by hacking or blasting them apart into dusty scraps, it often took three or four of the sort of blows that would have clean-killed an ordinary mortal man to finish one of these. Reivers were beginning to die as they were overwhelmed by the lurching foe.

A sudden throaty cheer went up. Hacking a sword away from his face, Roque turned and saw armoured men boarding the *Kymera* over the bow-rail, coming up from below. Two of the *Fuega*'s launches had survived the devastating demise of their mothership, and their furious, determined rowing had finally brought them against the Butcher Ship. Captain Duero led his men over the rail, all firing with muskets and pistols.

Their arrival was enough to swing the flow of the battle. The focus of the fighting became the foredecks. Able to break free from the melee, Roque headed for the nearest deck hatch. Three of his men-at-arms – Tall Willm, Sabatini and Rafael Guzman – followed him.

'Reload your guns!' Roque said, quickly charging his heavy flintlock. Tall Willm and Guzman had musketoons and Sabatini a good caliver.

'Any grenades?' Roque asked.

'I've one,' Tall Willm replied.

'Two here,' Guzman said.

'Let's go! Let's spike that gun-deck for good and all!'

The Estalian master-at-arms led the way. The thirst upon him, the dryness in his throat, was now so great it had half-driven him mad. He ached only to kill and destroy, and that desire he turned upon the *Kymera*'s ghouls.

The upper starboard gundeck was so thick with smoke and poorly lit, it was hard to see at first. But the flashes of the guns lit the scene in brief flickers. Roque saw more of the deathless ghouls manning the cannons, loading and firing, their actions stiff and mechanical, like marionettes or clockwork automata.

Roque and his three men came in down the deck, firing at the gun crews, blasting the desiccated creatures into shreds. The heavy musketoons did the most damage. Some of the ghouls turned and snatched up weapons to fend off the attackers, but Guzman tossed one of his grenades.

'Get back!' Roque cried, and the four of them just managed to cower in behind the heavy oak bulkheads before the scorching fireball blistered along the deck, incinerating the rag-and-bones ghouls and blasting some of the guns out through the ship's side into the sea.

Roque and his men reloaded their weapons quickly while the smoke boiled through the darkness around them.

'Willm!' Roque said. 'Take your grenade and see what you can do to cripple the portside decks. Sabatini, go with him. Guzman, follow me.'

The *Kymera*'s lower gundeck on the starboard side was still firing sustained salvoes. Roque and Guzman plunged down the narrow stairs into the hot gloom, but barely got into the lower gundeck before the wretched ghouls fell on them. Guzman fired his musketoon, but almost immediately was pinned to the bulkhead by a cut-less that went through his chest. The last grenade fell from his twitching hand and rolled away before it could be lit or thrown.

Hacking with his sabre, Roque tried to fight clear. He saw two kegs of powder that had been brought up from the magazine to furnish the guns. The lid of one had just been prised off when he and Guzman had burst in.

Hurling himself backwards towards the doorway, Roque threw his cocked and loaded pistol at the kegs. The weapon struck the deck right beside the kegs, and did so with enough force to jar the mechanism so that the lock snapped shut and struck the flint.

The gun discharged, and the blurt of flame from its muzzle touched off the powder kegs.

A monstrous blast tore through the side of the *Kymera*, annihilating guns and ripping sections of the hull out. The force of the blast lifted Roque and threw him down a companionway and clear through a wooden coping into the hold. He landed amongst rotting sacks and the shrivelled bodies of dead rats.

Slowly, Roque got to his feet. His ears were ringing, and he was covered in cuts and contusions, but he ignored all that, and the dire thirst that was still upon him.

There was a curious light down there in the hold, and a curious smell. He picked up his sabre and clambered towards the light. It was red, but pale, like a lamp. And the smell was that of turpentine, bitumen and a tang of hot resin. Where had he smelled that before? What did the odour remind him of?

Then he remembered. It was the dryness of sand and ancient dust, the odour of embalming wax and natron, as from an old tomb entirely buried in the desert. It was the smell of his nightmares.

Roque approached the light. There, by the glow of it, he saw wonderful things.

XXXIII

Luka ducked down hard, and Henri's sabre scythed over his head. The Butcher fought with none of the skill and finesse he had owned as a man, merely slashing and striking about with sword blows of astonishing power. He did not even raise a proper guard. It took Luka every scrap of his agility to stay clear of the merciless strokes. Luka thrust in with his shamshir and landed several deep hits, but nothing seemed to slow Henri down. He did not raise a proper guard because no sword could injure him. Both Casaudor and Ymgrawl set in to support Luka as the deck-brawl allowed, but for the most part they were occupied in fending off the other murderous ghouls.

'What became of you, Henri?' Luka panted. 'What did this to you? What foul sorcery has you in its thrall?'

There was no answer, except in the language of the sword, and Luka expected none. Like his crew and his ship, Henri the Breton was dead, transformed into a mindless, implacable instrument of destruction. Soon enough, Luka's mortal frame would tire and slow, and then Henri would cut him down.

Henri hacked out a blow of huge force that caught Luka across the guard of his sword and tore it out of his hand. Luka dived headlong, partly to recover his weapon, and partly to avoid the next whistling blow from Henri's sabre. It was a valiant attempt, but Luka fell short, the shamshir just beyond the reach of his clawing hand. He rolled, and Henri's soughing blade bit into the dry deck where Luka had just been lying.

Seeing his captain in grave danger, Tende hurled himself forward, knocking two stiff ghouls aside, and buried the tip of his Ebonian axe deep into Henri's left shoulder. The Butcher rocked slightly, and, without even looking round at his new adversary, struck out with his left fist and sent Tende flying the length of the poop deck.

Luka had managed to grab his sword, and came up fighting. But Henri brushed aside the first two strikes Silvaro made, and then sliced his sabre into Luka's left side.

Luka cried out in pain, feeling the cold agony of the wound and the hot drenching blood spilling from it. The sabre would have chopped clean through his torso, had it not been partially stopped by one of the spent wheel-locks dangling at his side on its lanyard. Even so, it was a crippling blow.

In desperation, more out of instinct than anything else, Luka punched with his shamshir to break away from the massive Butcher. The blade severed Henri's right wrist, and his hand and his sabre fell upon the deck. Luka staggered back, believing that by disarming his foe he had at least bought himself a moment's respite.

But Henri's left hand lunged out and caught Luka by the throat.

The Butcher's grip tightened, and he lifted the choking Luka off the deck. Blacking out, Luka lost his sword, and clawed at the arm holding him with his bare hands. He could smell the sweet putrefaction of Henri's desiccated flesh. He could feel the bones of his neck grind and his windpipe close.

He could feel his death overtaking him.

There was a loud crunch, a violent lurch, and the grip released. Luka fell back onto the deck. He opened his eyes and saw Henri staggering backwards. The Bite of Daagon had been plunged tip-first into his chest.

'Sesto?'

'Get up, Luka,' Sesto urged, hauling at his arms.

'You did that?'

They stared as Henri took another step or two backwards. Where the Bite had opened his chest, thousands of white grubs and maggots were spilling out, as if it had been the pressure of them inside Henri that had bloated his flesh so.

Henri fell upon his back and before their eyes, he rotted away, his flesh collapsing and blackening, his bulk evaporating into dust, until he was just a jumbled skeleton upon the deck with the Bite of Daagon lodged through its breastbone.

'The Butcher's dead,' Luka breathed, leaning on Sesto for support. The wound in his side hurt like a bastard and he was streaming blood.

'But his men are not,' Sesto said. Around them, and down across the forward decks, the ghouls fought on with single-minded fury. The *Lightning Tree* had now managed to close with the *Kymera*, and had grappled itself to the starboard side so that Tusk's crew could join the savage action hand-to-hand. But the fight to close had cost the *Lightning Tree* dear. Its decks were a place of ruin and broken bodies, and its masts and rigging were shattered and torn. The great ship was listing badly, and the infernal red fire seethed across its sheets and stern.

'The sorcery still remains,' Luka said. 'Henri was a part of it, not the root. We must find the true source of the magic and destroy it, or even now we will not be the victors this day.'

'You're hurt!' Sesto cried.

'I can find time to be hurt later,' Luka snarled, picking up his shamshir and sheathing it so he could reload his presentation piece. 'Come on!'

'Where to?'

'To wherever on this damned ship the magic is hidden!'

THEY STUMBLED BELOW, fighting off grisly foes that loomed out of the smoke and fog. The lower decks, choked with vapour and powder-fumes, were lit up by the cold, red light. It seemed to glow from the timbers themselves. Above and around them, through the decks, they could hear the constant clangour of feral war.

'Down here!' Luka cried out. He limped down the wooden steps that led into the afterhold. The glow was brighter. There was a strong smell of turpentine and wax. The air was so robbed of moisture, their tongues dried in their mouths.

Luka sat down on the lowest step. 'Give me a moment,' he gasped, fighting the pain.

'Rest here,' Sesto told him. 'I'll check ahead.' Raising his sabre, Sesto edged down the cavernous hold, past shadowy stacks of rotten barrels and ballast, towards the light.

'Great gods!' he exclaimed.

'So you see it too,' Roque said. 'Good, I thought I might be dreaming.'

The hind space of the *Kymera*'s great afterhold glimmered like a treasure cave. Great caskets of gold were stacked around, and with them statues and figurines all gilded and set with jewels. Some of the caskets were open, revealing the piles of coins and precious stones within, and also scrolls of fine parchment and antique weapons enamelled with cloisonné.

Roque Santiago Della Fortuna stood in the midst of it all. The lupine Estalian looked sick and ill. His face was haggard, his skin drawn and blotchy, and his breath came in short, rasping gulps. He was leaning for support against a vast golden sarcophagus that lay in the centre of the hold space, the treasures piled around it. The casket was shaped in the form of a supine figure, arms crossed over its chest. Gemstones, enamels and bright paint gave a sort of life to the moulded visage on the casket lid. An emperor, perhaps, a king, a regal lord, with gold about his brow, and staring eyes lined with kohl.

'Behold, Henri's treasure and his doom,' Roque said.

Sesto gazed about in wonder. 'I've never seen its like,' he said. There was a style and quality to the treasures, to the weapons and the designs, that Sesto had not seen before. Strange pictograms were etched into the casket cartouches, showing slaves and river boats and oxen and long-billed birds. Everything was gold, enhanced by bars of white and pure blue, and occasional red. The golden statues, which seemed to stand guard over the great sarcophagus, were human figures with the heads of falcons, cats and rams. Two wore the faces of long-eared hounds or desert dogs.

'Aye,' said Roque, 'you've not seen its like in the Old World, my friend. This is loot from the sands of Khemri, plundered from some dust-dry tomb. It's ancient. Older even than the cities where you and I were born.'

'Khemri…' Sesto murmured.

'This is Henri's curse, Sesto. The fell cargo that he took from a damned treasure ship and, in so doing, damned himself and his men. The cursed grave goods of an ancient tomb king, his solace in the afterlife.' Roque stroked a hand across the carved face on the sarcophagus lid. 'You, old one, old king, this is your doing.'

'How can you know this?' Sesto asked, stepping forward.

'Can't you feel the malice radiating from this lustrous horde?' Roque said. 'Evil and magic, summoned by a dead thing who did not like how his eternal sleep had been disturbed. It's the dry dust of the tomb, Sesto, the trickle of sand. It has been calling to me in my dreams.'

Roque touched the scar on his shoulder, raw now from constant scratching.

'Your dreams?' Sesto said.

'My dreams. My dry, ghastly nightmares. Contact with this unholy treasure made Reyno a daemon, and I've been connected to it ever since he marked me with his talon.'

'What do we do?' Sesto asked.

'We break it. We destroy it. This gold, this matchless treasure, makes no man rich in anything except death. Help me.'

Roque had picked up a golden-handled adze from the mounds of treasure nearby, and began to employ it as a crowbar to prise off the lid of the sarcophagus.

'Are you sure we–'

'Help me, Sesto!' Roque cried, struggling.

Sesto grabbed another adze and set in beside the master-at-arms. Together, they heaved and wrestled, splintering the gilded wood of the lid, breaking ancient seals of wax and resin.

Slowly, slowly, the lid raised up. Foul dust billowed out from the dark cavity within, reeking of natron and embalming salts.

The lid slumped over onto the hold floor with a terrible shudder of wood.

The tomb king lay within, hands across his breast. Sesto had expected to see some hideously shrivelled corpse, or dry, dusty mummifer, but the body that lay within seemed shockingly fresh. A boy, just a boy, no older than Gello. He was swaddled in linen wrappings that were as fresh and white as a summer cloud, and gold jewellery plated his forearms, chest and forehead. His skin, where it was exposed on his beringed hands and face, was pink and vital. His face was beautiful, dusted in gold, with extravagant lines of black around his sleeping eyes.

Sleeping, Sesto shuddered. That was it. This long-dead thing seemed only to be sleeping.

Roque reached out his hand and hesitantly picked up the amulet the tomb king wore across his chest, just above his folded hands. It was a heavy thing, fashioned in the shape of a winged beetle, the thick gold set with turquoise and ruby. The long, weighty gold chain dangled behind it as Roque pulled it free.

Roque made a sweet, low moan. 'This is it, Sesto. This is the talisman, the seat of power. Oh, it sings to me! I have heard it oft times in my dreams, fragile voices singing in a tongue I do not know, though I understand every word. This is the very essence of the curse.'

Sesto nodded. 'Then that is what we must destroy.'

'Yes, yes,' Roque said. He remained gazing at the amulet in his hands.

'Roque? Sir?'

The Estalian turned away. A sudden, dreadful alarm filled Sesto. He reached for his dagger, drew it out, but could not bring himself to plunge it into Roque's back, even though every instinct told him he should.

'Oh, Sesto,' Roque said sadly. He turned back. The amulet was in his left hand. The dirk in his right had plunged deep into Sesto's ribs.

Sesto gasped. A vice of white pain clamped his mind. He fell back, the dirk still embedded in him.

'Oh, Sesto,' Roque repeated. He looked aghast, and if there had been any water left in him, he would have been weeping. 'You failed me. If you see me wavering, I said.

Wavering or hesitating. I begged of you, to make your strike sure and clean.'

Sesto fell sideways against the sarcophagus and slid to the deck. Blood soaked his shirt around the dirk's grip and ran out onto the boards. Against nature, the beads of blood began to stream counter to gravity, up the sides of the golden casket, and down within. The sleeping boy-daemon in the sarcophagus sighed gently.

'What have you done?' Luka Silvaro said, limping forward, his shamshir raised. 'Roque, what in the name of the devil have you done here?'

'Just what I am bid, Luka,' Roque replied. Clutching the amulet in his left hand, he drew his fine sabre of watered Estalian steel.

'No closer, old friend,' he said.

'Gods,' Luka looked down at Sesto. 'Gods, I offered you ivory for luck, Sesto…'

Luka glanced back up at Roque and shook his head. 'Friends, Roque? Friends. Comrades. That's what this fell cargo feeds upon. That's what it delights in undoing and damning. Henri, Reyno, you and I. The fine bonds of the code and good company, cut asunder by this madness that pits brother and ally against one another.'

'Friends?' Roque smiled. 'Friendship? You think it cares about that? The tomb king desires nothing except blood and gold. Friendship is something that gets in the way of that appetite.'

'Then I'm another obstacle,' Luka said. 'Toss away your sabre and set aside that abominable trinket. Or come through me to leave this hold alive.'

Roque slowly looped the golden chain of the amulet around his neck, scooping out his long hair to let it fall clear. The golden talisman now hung at his chest.

'I can't do that, Luka,' he said. Already, Luka could see how Roque's eyes were beginning to glaze, as if ice was forming across their surface to dull the colour of the pupils. His skin was beginning to stretch and wizen.

Luka lunged forward, ignoring the lancing pain in his side. Their blades struck together and rang out, blow following blow, feint and riposte, lunge and parry. Sparks flew off from the razor-sharp edges.

Luka Silvaro prided himself on his swordsmanship. He'd
won every duel he'd ever found himself in, including some
where he'd pretended to be a swordsman of lesser skill in
order to goad an opponent into overconfidence. That had
certainly been his tactic with poor Captain Hernan. Luka
had wanted to make a point there, not slice the man to ribbons. But now he was sorely hindered by his awful wound.

And there was one swordsman in the entire breadth of the
sparkling Tilean Sea that Luka acknowledged to be his better with the sword. They had fought many times, and Luka
had always lost, though only ever in practice sparring.

Until now.

Roque Santiago Della Fortuna was the most gifted
swordsman Luka had ever met. The dance and feint of
swordplay came naturally to him. He knew moves and parries that sword masters the length of Tilea and Estalia both
would have gladly sold up their schools to learn. And his
watered steel was the finest of weapons, far sounder, truer
and sharper than Luka's precious shamshir.

Right from the start, Luka knew he was outmatched. But
still he fought, putting every erg of effort and every iota of
finesse into his furious rallies. He was determined that he
would not lose, could not lose. He thought of Hernan,
bested in swordplay, but still staunch and heroic to the bit-
ter end, sailing his ship into the face of doom. Likewise
Silke, and Tusk, Sesto, and even Reyno, most like.

There came a time when skill itself was no longer enough.
There came a time when a man had to learn from others
about sheer courage and win out that way.

What mattered most was not a man's talent, or his hand-
iness with the steel. What mattered most was his heart, and
the fibre of his soul. Only that measure could truly win the
day.

Except here.

Luka sallied forward, riding a low parry into a half-thrust,
and almost speared Roque through the throat. But the Estalian slid aside, executed a long lunge that pinned Luka's
shamshir against the side of the sarcophagus, and snapped
it below the hilt with a flick of his wrist.

Luka stumbled back, trying to ward himself with the
feeble broken sword, and Roque lunged furiously, driving

the entire length of his sabre through Luka's left shoulder.

'Gods!' Luka grunted.

Roque ripped the sabre out, and Luka fell against the sarcophagus and sagged down.

Roque hovered the tip of his bloody sabre at Luka's left eye. 'I'll make it quick, old friend,' he hissed.

Luka spat at him.

Roque pulled back his arm to strike. The golden amulet on his chest suddenly rose up, as if lifted into the air by some dark magic. Roque shuddered. His mouth gagged open, and white grubs spilled out.

The amulet fell to the deck, its golden chain broken. What had lifted it off his breast was a full hand's span of blade from a tanning knife.

Ymgrawl dragged his long dagger out of Roque's back, and the cursed Estalian fell over on his face.

Luka looked up at Ymgrawl.

'Too late for the pup,' Ymgrawl said, glancing at Sesto's body. 'But not too late for thee, I trust?'

'Help me up,' Luka said. Ymgrawl heaved Silvaro to his feet. Luka was shaking, unsteady.

He moved forward and picked up the fallen amulet.

'Now we break this. Hammer it apart,' he said. His voice trailed off.

Luka could hear distant chanting, frail singing echoing in the air. A scent of musk and spices, the slow wash of funeral dhows upon a tranquil river. Priests and oxen, pipes, heavy drums, the odour of fresh basalt tombs, open for the last time. The setting sun. The racing stars. A huge pyramid, rising above the bend of the river. A thousand voices.

The dry, dry grit of the piling sand.

He felt thirsty. Parched.

Blood, that's what Roque had said. Blood. The tomb king was thirsty for blood. That was the curse it had put upon the *Kymera*, to kill, and kill, and kill again across the waters of the sea to find enough blood to slake its eternal thirst.

And make it live once more.

It was so close now, so close. Luka gazed at the boy in the casket, saw the rude health in his complexion. Just another

few measures of blood to drink, and he would live again.
And unleash his woe upon the Old World.

Just another few measures. Ymgrawl, he would furnish
plenty. And Casaudor and Benuto. Blood was blood. There
was almost enough of it now. Gods, but it was hungrier than
Sheerglas on a bad night. It wanted to drink up the world.

'Luka?' Ymgrawl said, staring at Silvaro, his bloody knife
still raised. 'Not thee too,' he sighed.

'Enough blood,' Luka mumbled. 'Enough blood. There
must be enough blood, or it won't awake from its endless
sleep.'

'Luka!' Ymgrawl yelled.

Clutching the amulet, Luka Silvaro staggered away up the
hold steps, clambering up through the smoky bowels of the
Butcher Ship to the deck. There, men and ghouls still fought
in the swirl of the storm and the vile fog. As Luka stumbled
across the corpse-littered deck, fresh blood flew up from the
timbers and was sucked up into the golden amulet he
clutched.

In the hold, the boy-king's eyes flickered open.

Luka fell to his knees and struggled to the broken stern
rail. He looked down at the amulet in his hands. It
belonged to him. It needed him like he needed it, like an
addiction, like a true love. The yearning was unbearable.

'Thirsty?' Luka said to it. 'Are you thirsty?'

Yes, hissed the fragile voices. Down in the hold, the boy-
king's mouth moved and echoed the word.

'Drink this,' said Luka Silvaro, and hurled the amulet out,
away from the stern rail, into the fathomless water of the
Golfo Naranja.

XXXIV

WITH A TERRIBLE wailing, as if the distant, fragile voices in Luka's head were now projecting out of each and every dry mouth, the ghouls collapsed. The red light faded away, like a mist curling off at dawn, and the *Kymera* became a rotting black shell.

The bodies of the fallen ghouls, clutching their cut-lesses and pikes, shrivelled away, like the last ash from a fire at cold daybreak. Just a blackened, soaked and worm-riddled ark now, the *Kymera* began to founder. Its decayed masts fell, its rotten lines snapped and shredded.

'Luka?' Casaudor said, coming to his side.

'The curse is lifted,' Luka wheezed. 'The Butcher is dead.'

'You men! Help the captain up here!' Casaudor yelled. Tende stumbled forward, and Saint Bones and Benuto.

'I'm fine!' Luka said, rising. 'Get to the *Rumour*. Cut her free before this bastard sinks away.'

The Reivers ran to the port side, hacking away the lines and grapples, and leaping across the *Rumour*'s gunwales.

Luka turned and saw Ymgrawl behind him. The boucaner was holding Sesto's body in his arms.

'Does he live?' Luka asked.

'Aye,' Ymgrawl nodded.

'Can we save him?'

Ymgrawl closed his eyes and shook his head.

'Take him! Take Sesto here!' Luka yelled. 'Get him aboard the *Rumour* and get Fahd to see to him.' The Arabyan cook was all that passed for a surgeon on the Reivers' ship.

Men ran forward and took Sesto's limp body from Ymgrawl.

'Where are thee going?' the boucaner asked.

'To slice the *Lightning Tree* free,' Luka said. 'She does not deserve to be dragged down with this accursed hulk.'

Luka limped away across the pitted, smoking deck. The boards under his feet were wet-black and decaying, and he stepped over mutilated corpses and damp scatters of bones and rusted armour.

Luka yanked a boarding axe out of the deck and started to hack away the grapple lines and stays that bound the *Lightning Tree* to the *Kymera*. He ignored the shooting pains in his side and his shoulder.

Water, cold and fast, began to bubble up through the *Kymera*'s hatches. The deck dipped. Luka cut away the last lines and leapt across onto the *Lightning Tree*. He looked back and watched as the *Kymera* sank straight down into the tide, water filling its guts and weighting it, dragging it into the measureless sound.

From far below, there came a scream, choked off, as from a tyrant boy-king, who had woken from eternity to find himself drowning in the deepest pit of the ocean.

The scream died away. The dark water frothed and churned.

Luka limped across the *Lightning Tree*'s perilously slanted deck. Smoke streamed through the air, and the heavy rain doused the last of the fires. There were bodies all about, tangled on the deck, cut to ribbons in the terrible fight.

Luka saw Honduro, dead with a cut-less through his heart. A score more at least. The carrion birds were closing in.

He found Tusk.

The old man had taken a pike though his gut, and he'd bled out on the quarter deck.

He was still alive, just.

'Luka?'

'Jeremiah, you old dog. You came back for me.'

'I was concerned. A matter of three times, and I was worried I had not matched them.' Tusk's voice was tiny and distant.

'You've matched them all, and over again. I could ask no more of you.'

'Well, that's good, then,' Tusk said. 'I've no bloody more to give.'

Luka bowed his head.

'Did you get him?'

'Who?'

'The Butcher, Luka. Did you get him?'

'We got him, Jeremiah.'

Tusk slid back. He reached into his bloodied coat with his good hand.

'One thing, Luka, for you, now all I have is gone and done. Take it.'

Luka took the blood-wet fold of parchment.

'Do what I could not,' Tusk sighed. 'Get out of this business.'

Luka was about to reply, but Tusk's head rolled sideways. He was gone.

Tucking the parchment into his sash, Luka ran for the side. The *Lightning Tree*, as if sensing its master's demise, was shaking and jolting. Planks burst and timbers tore away. In a terrible death-rattle of sundering wood, the *Lightning Tree*, scourge of the Tilean Sea for so many years, sank away into the flood.

Luka Silvaro dived headlong from the rail.

XXXV

It was a bright, hot day, with a free wind, the last they would probably have before the winter. Luka Silvaro limped onto the poop deck of the *Rumour*, trying not to test the stitches Largo had sewn into his wounds.

Tende was at the wheel, with Benuto at his side. Casaudor smiled as he saw the master approach.

'To Aguilas?' Luka asked.

'In this chop, just a day,' Casaudor said.

Luka nodded. 'Stay on, friend. I'll be below.'

'Sir,' Casaudor said. 'What of us now?'

'Trust me,' Luka replied. 'I'll never see the Reivers wrong.'

Luka thumped into his cabin, limped across the deck, and all but fell down in his seat. His wounds ached monstrously. Blood seeped out between Largo's fine stitchwork.

'Oh, Sesto,' he sighed to himself. 'What are we to do? We've pulled the stroke your father wanted from us, and set the seas free from the Butcher's ire. And all for what? A promise of an amnesty? A reward? It seems so hollow now the seas are open. Such a desperate effort, and for what?'

The cabin remained silent.

'I said, for what?' Luka repeated.

'Sorry,' said Sesto, hauling himself up on his cot with a stifled groan. 'I didn't realise you were speaking to me.'

'I wasn't,' said Luka. 'Just thinking aloud.'

'Will you sail us homeward now, to Luccini? To collect your price?' Sesto asked, wincing at the pain from his slowly healing wound.

'If you want to go home, of course,' Luka said.

Sesto smiled. 'Don't you want your amnesty?'

Luka shrugged. 'I wonder, my friend, when all's said and done, if I'll not have trouble being respectable.'

Sesto smiled. 'I can see how that would be a problem. Well, Silvaro, I'm just along for the ride. Did you have something else in mind?'

Luka tugged the parchment fold from his coat and opened it out on the table. 'Jeremiah willed me his cross. I think I might sail to it. I could then reward the Reivers better than any Prince of Luccini.' He looked at Sesto. 'What say you?'

'I say my father would probably have you hanged no matter what my word. I say I am bored of my life at court and hunger for high adventure.'

Sesto smiled at Luka Silvaro. 'Sail on and find that treasure. Sail on, and take me with you.'

'So tell,' Luka nodded, and began to shout his orders aloft.

ABOUT THE AUTHOR

Dan Abnett lives and works in Maidstone, Kent, in England. Well known for his comic work, he has written everything from the *Mr Men* to the *X-Men* in the last decade, and received particular acclaim for his five year run on *The Legion* for DC Comics. He is currently writing *Majestic* for Wildstorm, and *Sinister Dexter* and *The VCs* for 2000 AD.

His work for the Black Library includes the popular strips *Lone Wolves*, *Titan* and *Darkblade*, the best-selling Gaunt's Ghosts novels, and the acclaimed Inquisitor Eisenhorn trilogy.

CRUEL, TREACHEROUS, EVIL (AND HE'S THE HER

Join the meanest dark elf in the Old World as he battles for his soul in this epic new fantasy series.

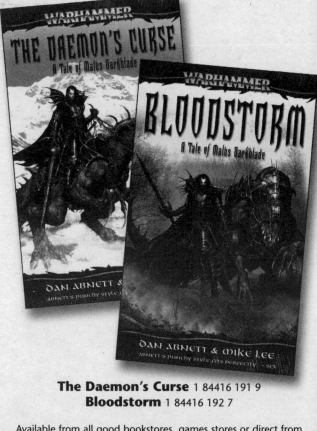

The Daemon's Curse 1 84416 191 9
Bloodstorm 1 84416 192 7

Available from all good bookstores, games stores or direct from
www.blacklibrary.com

READ TILL YOU BLE